A

(Honest Rustlers)

Thanks,
Virgil R. Cooper

BY
Virgil R. Cooper

An original A-Bar-V Publishing edition,
published for the first time anywhere.

A NEW THREAT

COPYRIGHT © 1996
By
Virgil R. Cooper

First printing March 2000

ISBN: 0-9668804-2-0

Printed in the United States of America

A-Bar-V Publishing
614 W. Cherry
Drumright, Oklahoma 74030

"Why he's just a kid. He can't face them jaspers. It won't be fair."

"How old was David when he went up against Goliath?"

He had a varied reputation. He was a carbon copy of Geronimo some said. Others compared him to Huckleberry Finn or Tom Sawyer while a third opinion was Billy the Kid.

"He's all of them rolled into one." One fellow opined.

Maw just called her youngest, Virg.

"Let the old man go." Virg spoke as he stepped into the street. He didn't have his pistol out because he was afraid that would have set the guns to blazing and resulted in the death of the old man "He hasn't done anything to you."

Bart stood with a cocked pistol to the farmer's head . He glanced around but the pistol stayed where it was.

Mitch, whirled around to face Virg. His hand brushed the handle of his weapon.

"Let 'em go, Bart. This half breed's the one we want." Mitch had a grin on his face as he moved back down the street toward his horse. He kept a close watch on Virg as he eased away from the building where the judge and marshal were. "We'll get down here where our backs won't catch a slug when we show this breed how to draw."

"Okay but let me have an even chance at him. First one gets a slug in him wins the pot." Bart holstered his iron.

Virg was hoping to settle this without gunfire but it looked like they were determined to make a fight of it.

The two gunslingers turned to face him.

"Hey mex, you've been braggin about this breed." Mitch snarled. "I'll show you how a real hand works with an iron."

"My gosh!" Virg exclaimed under his breath when he caught sight of someone moving toward the space between the two buildings to his left. "That's maw. She'll be out here and right in the line of fire in no time."

Turning his attention back to Bart and Mitch, Virg snapped a sharp question. "What'll it be, Gotchear?"

Stung to the quick, Mitch reached for his weapon. It looked like Bart was ahead of him. No doubt about it, they were fast.

ACKNOWLEDGEMENTS:

First I want to express my thanks and love to my wife, Ann. Without her help and patience I could never have made it. Second in my thoughts are my three children and 6 grandchildren. They have always served as an inspiration for me. My mother would have to be included in any expression of appreciation. She has been the guiding hand on me throughout my life. Her side of my family still holds a firm grip on my heart. Several friends have read some of my material and encouraged me to go forward with my writing. They will never know the full effect they had when I often thought of tossing it all aside and would have if it hadn't been for their support.

A special note of thanks is reserved for a man I just had the pleasure of being in contact with.

MR. BARNABAS GRAYSON

Of

Eufaula, Oklahoma

He did my cover art.

Thank you Mr. Thompson, Eufaula History Teacher, for getting us together.

The man in the shaded area near the top of the ridge sat quietly watching the layout below him. From time to time he got up and walked to the top of the ridge and cast a look toward a small bunch of cattle down below, on the back side.

Two men were with the cattle but didn't appear to be trying to move them. They just sat in the shade and watched them crop at the lush grass. They moved quietly every so often to keep the group together.

The man returned to his position. It was still fairly early in the morning and he had been there since daylight.

"I hope he gets gone soon. He's taken off for their place every day so far." He said impatiently. "Be just our luck to have him stay here today."

He made another trip to the top of the knoll then returned to his spot.

"Ah. There he is now." He watched as a man walked to the barn and soon came out leading a horse.

Mounting up the man rode at a trot down a lane between two fields before disappearing.

The watcher hurried back to the top of the knoll. Removing his hat he waved it back and forth several times then he walked along the top of the ridge to where he found a tethered horse. He mounted it and rode away. His job was done.

"Things will pop now." He chuckled. "This is pretty slick."

Dad Hale looked at his son, Joe. He had a frown on his face.

"Now let's see if I have this right, Joe. You want to go off down in Texas to help a man down there round up a herd of cattle and make a trail drive all the way to Colorado."

"That's right, Dad, I can maybe make enough on the deal to get my own place." Joe explained. "I would like to stay here and help you but now that Lanny is about grown, we all kind of get in each others way."

"Joe, you know that there will never be to many Hales around here to suit your mother and me. I guess it's just hard for me to let any of my boys go." Dad Hale had a serious look on his face. He turned and stared off into the distance.

When he turned back toward Joe there appeared to be a bit of moisture in his eyes.

"Dad, I know it's been hard for you and mom since Zeb was shot. It's been hard for all of us boys too." Joe blinked his eyes. "But we have to go on with things anyway."

"I know that, son, so I won't ask you not to go. Every man has to live his own life. How long do you think it'll be before you leave?"

"I won't go for a few days yet. And, Dad, I want to thank you for saying that and what you and mom have taught all of us boys."

"We've just done our best to get all you boys to grow up to be men who we could be proud of. To be honest and stand up for what's right. We haven't seen anything to make us have regrets so far."

"Thanks, Dad, some of us have been pretty rowdy at times but we've tried to stay honest. Speaking of that, here comes Mr. Honesty himself now." Joe waved his thumb toward an approaching rider.

"He's right on time." Dad Hale smiled as he watched the young man ride in. "Dan is more than likely the most honest man I ever met, even if he is my own son."

"Maybe he'll stay over tonight if we work him hard enough." Joe offered. "He sure likes that place of his though."

"I doubt it. He'll want to quit in time to make it to his place by dark. Maybe we can pull a fast one on him and keep him here for some of Mom's home cooking."

The rider pulled his horse to a halt and smiled at his father and brother.

"Get down, Dan. The work's waiting."

"Okay. Let's get to it so I can get back home."

"Dan, this is home. You are just staying over at that place of yours." Dad Hale admonished him.

2

Dan just smiled and nodded as he slid off his horse. He was soon headed for the field with Joe.

Dad Hale watched proudly as they walked away. "Fine boys if I do say so."

Alex Averill leaned back in his chair and blew a cloud of smoke at the ceiling. He was pondering he needed to do about a problem facing him.

"I think the time is about right for me to go in and lay down the law to that marshal in Paden." He smiled as he blew another puff of smoke. It formed a perfect ring as it drifted toward the ceiling.

"That's a good sign so I better hop to it. We can't afford to lose any more cattle to these thieves or we'll be broke and I may be out of a job."

Getting to his feet he walked out the door and headed for the barn to saddle his horse. From time to time one of the hands offered to do this for him but he declined the offer. His horse was a one man horse and he planned to keep it that way.

He paused by the rail fence where one of his men was occupied with a horse.

"Gomez, how's the critter doing?" He called out. "I want him ready pretty soon."

"Si, senor. He's doing very good. He'll be ready before the time is up." Gomez informed him. "You want me to ride with you today?"

"No. I'm just riding in to talk to the marshal at Paden. If anyone asks, I'll be back later. You know what you're supposed to be doing so keep after it."

"I will be busy, senor. I try to remember some more things to tell you about the people around here."

Averill continued on to the barn and saddled his horse then took off at a lope toward Paden.

"That Gomez doesn't know how valuable the information he's furnishing me is." Averill smiled as he recalled the explanation he had given.

"I just want to know about my neighbors." He had told Gomez. "He never told me they were a bunch of rustlers."

3

Gomez had thought it made sense because Averill and almost his entire crew were new to the area. They had taken over the operation when the former rancher, Hance Gannon, had run into difficulties.

Difficulties like flying lead from one of the local settlers.

The marshal was taking his ease in his office. He could look out through the door and see a good deal of the main part of the town of Paden.

There wasn't much to worry about in the way of excitement since Hance Gannon's crew had been practically wiped out.

"I'm glad I didn't get in the middle of that little deal." He said to himself as he recalled how suddenly it erupted and ended. "A fellow would have had to be mighty quick to buy into it though. It was over almost as soon as it started. It's been mighty peaceful around here since then."

He saw Molly and Newt walking down the other side of the street together. They made a nice looking couple.

"I can't figure out why he doesn't marry the girl and get it over with. He'd better before some other guy does." He pondered this for a moment. "That kid, Virg, is real friendly with her but he doesn't try to side track Newt at all. Can't hardly understand these young folks."

He heard the sound of hoofbeats coming into town. He leisurely got to his feet and stepped to the door to see who it was. Who ever it was didn't appear to be in any great hurry so he saw no reason to be at all concerned. He just liked to keep an eye on the coming and goings of folks.

"I believe it's the new man from that cattle outfit north of here. He took over Gannon's operation. I need to find out what kind of fellow he is. Maybe he won't be as difficult as Gannon was where the settlers are concerned."

He watched to see where Averill stopped. He decided to walk over there and introduce himself.

"He's coming on down this way. Maybe I can get him to stop here and visit a minute." The marshal said in a low voice. "Danged if it don't look like he's already decided to do that."

Alex Averill rode up to the hitch rail and stopped. He

4

sat his saddle for a moment studying the man that represented the law in Paden.

"If my information is correct, you're Marshal Earl Simmons." He stated. "They tell me that if we need the law inforced, without fear or favor, you're the one to see about it."

Marshal Simmons received this good news with pleasure. Not to many folks appreciated the job that a marshal had to do.

"I try to do what's right." He responded. "Get down and come in if you have time to visit a minute?"

"I have the time. In fact I rode in to talk to you about a problem we've been having out our way."

It's about missing cattle." Averill kept his voice even. "We've been losing one every now and then since I got here but lately bunches at a time are disappearing."

By now they were seated facing each other.

"That could get serious pretty quick if you're at all like the other cattlemen I've run across." Marshal Simmons said. "You never said anything about losing any earlier and I've seen you ride through a time or two."

"I just figured as long as it was a single one now and then, it was some hungry nester with a bunch of kids to feed and I could well afford it." Averill pursed his mouth as if to figure out how to word his next statement. "I come from a country where they ride out and hang cow thieves."

"You can't--" Simmons started to reply but stopped when Averill held up his hand.

"I started to finish by saying that I know the problem here with the line running through the country. It being Indian Territory over here, I can't just take the law into my own hands. That's why I came in to see you." Averill stopped.

"That was a wise move on your part. You could get into deep water in a hurry if you came over here and messed with any of the Indians." Simmons warned. "I don't do much riding around the country looking for cow thieves but I can see it from your point of view."

"What can I do then? I'm not about to set still and see all of them run off. You mean you can't do anything?"

5

"I'll arrest anyone that a complaint is filed against but my job is mainly here in town. I go out if someone has a reason for me to. I just don't have time to go out trailing stray cattle. Besides I'm not much of a tracker."

"How are things like that handled then? I want to go by the law, what ever I do, if it's possible. But I don't plan to sit around and see every head swiped."

"If you locate some stolen cattle, get some witnesses, then file a complaint. I'll do the rest."

"Sounds like a funny way to do things. We do our own detective work and you do the arresting. Well thanks, marshal. If we locate any I'll let you know."

Averill walked outside with an odd look on his face. So he had to do his own tracking did he. This was an interesting development. His odd look had turned to a thoughtful one.

Marshal Simmons followed Averill outside and watched him ride off.

"I believe I can work with him. He seems reasonable enough to me. At least he wants to let the law handle things."

"Dan, it's to late to ride all the way back to your place. Stay here for the night and you can go back early in the morning." Dad Hale urged. "I still want to remind you that this is home."

"Yeah, Dan, I might even ride over there with you in the morning." Joe added. "You won't get much of a jump on things by going back tonight."

"It's tempting but I want to go on back. I just like the idea that something is mine." Dan explained. "When I lay down in my own place to go to sleep it just gives me a good feeling."

"You can't argue with that." Mrs. Hale spoke up. "That's a feeling that most everybody has. Do you remember why we came out here?"

Dan chuckled as he watched his father and brother try to figure out some reply.

"You fellows have anything to say?" He asked. "If not, I guess I'll be on my way. Thanks, mom, I can always count on you."

"Maybe I better get started on finding a place." Joe said. "I could use some of this good feeling."

"Mother, you're going to be the cause of all our boys leaving home." Dad Hale complained. "Soon we won't have any of them left."

"That's kind of the nature of things." Mrs. Hale said before she returned to the house. She had a big smile on her face.

Dan was laughing as he rode away from the home place. It would be late before he arrived at his place but already the good feeling was beginning to expand in his chest.

"Boy, I'm sure tired. It'll be good to hit the hay. I may sleep a little late in the morning."

Alex Averill waited for his two men to come to the house. He didn't want to take a chance on them misunderstanding their instructions.

"I believe Trig and Dode can handle this all right. They're pretty fair trackers. Let them take a couple of the other hands with them." He turned to Mitch. "Be sure that you lay it out for them. I'm getting tired of losing cattle. I'm riding over west to see that Slater fellow."

Bart and Mitch nodded in agreement. They were seldom very far from Averill. Some even thought they were bodyguards.

"Which one of us do you want to trail along?" Mitch asked.

"Bart will take this trip with me then we'll all meet In Paden tomorrow. I'm leaving it to you, Mitch, to give Dode and Trig their orders. We've lost enough cattle"

"Don't worry about that, boss. I'll handle it." Mitch smiled.

Dode and Trig walked through the door.

"Did you want to see us, boss?"

"I sent for you because word was brought to me that they had located some of our stolen cattle. Mitch will tell you all about it." Averill told them. "He will lay out the proper proceedure you're to follow. Bart's going along with me."

7

Averill and Bart headed for the corral to get their horses.

"You mean to go through Paden and get that pair and take them with us?" Dode asked. "They may get in the way and besides they're probably friendly to the thieves." He cast a disturbed look at Mitch.

"That's the way he wants it. Bring the guy in. You can talk tough about what to do with him but he's to be brought in for the law to handle. Do you understand me?" Mitch stared straight at Dode and Trip. He let his hand brush the butt of his pistol.

"It sounds odd to me but you're the boss on this deal according to Mr. Averill." Dode answered. "Trip and me just follow orders. Ain't that right, Trip?"

"You called the turn on that. We sure wouldn't have done it that way out west but I wasn't hired for my ability to think I guess."

"You called the turn on that." Mitch repeated Trip's phrase. "Leave the thinking to us."

Dan Hale rolled over in the bed. He thought he had heard someone ride up but wasn't sure. He had been enjoying his sleep to much.

"You, in the house, come out here." A loud voice sounded. "Don't be all day about it either."

Dan got out of bed and pulled on a pair of trouser, walked to the door and opened it then stepped out.

Five men sat their saddles in his front yard. They didn't look overly friendly. He thought he recognised two of them. One was the marshal from Paden.

"Get down and I'll boil some coffee. Don't have much else but you're welcome to what I have." Dan made the offer in a friendly voice.

"We don't plan to spend time being sociable, Hale." The same voice that had yelled before sounded. "The marshal here is arresting you for stealing cattle."

"Are you crazy? I never stole anything in my life."

"I'm sorry, Dan Hale, but you're under arrest. These men claim some of their cattle are in your small pasture back here." Marshal Simmons announced. "One of you men saddle his horse for him. I'll go in with him while he gets

8

ready to head for town."

Dan Hale was to stunned to say anything further.

Chap 2

"Buck, old boy, it'll be good to see all the sights in Paden again. You might even get a chance to try your luck in a race."

The horse flicked his ears and tossed his head in response.

"Virg, you talk like that sawed-off thing you call a horse could understand you. He may be able to at that. As much time as you spend in the woods stalking and messing with varmints you may have learned to speak their language." Jim Cooper was seated on the seat of the wagon beside his young wife, Mary, as they moved toward town. They had been to visit his parents. "He's not big enough to run with real horses."

His brother was sitting with his feet dangling out the back of the wagon bed. He had decided to accompany them. His small horse, Buck, trailed along behind.

It was easy to tell that the two brothers were part Indian by their black hair and facial features.

"He's enough horse for me. He has shown some of those fancy nags a thing or two when it comes time to get the job done."

"I guess he about fits you. You're both kind of runty at that. As much as you eat it looks like you would add a little to your size. Does he eat like you do?"

"He likes to eat all right. I might grow a bit if all of you didn't work me so hard before you'll let me eat anything."

"You could never do enough work to pay for the amount you eat. Feeding you for the work you get done is a losing proposition."

"I'm worn to a frazzle before I get to eat. That way the food just helps me recover instead of grow."

Mary had been chuckling as she quietly listened to the exchange between the brothers. They carried on like this

9

most of the time. A person would be mighty wrong if they thought the boys were not fond of each other.

Jim and his older brother Jace were over six feet tall. Jim was a bit on the slender side but sturdy enough. Jace was a big fellow going around two hundred pounds. He was as strong as a bull.

Virg indeed was the runt of the family. He stood five feet seven and weighed about one hundred thirty some pounds soaking wet. He still had some time to grow though as he was only seventeen.

"Well, I'll fix up something when we get to the house." Mary informed the squabbling brothers. "Maybe that will hold you until we get to town."

"What do I have to do before I get to eat?" Virg wanted to know. "Jim would faint if I ate without working for it. He'll think of something. I'll bet on it."

"I didn't plan to do anything until we got back from Paden but if you insist on some work I'll try to find something." Jim grinned at Mary.

She returned his smile as they drove into the yard. "You two figure out your plans. I'll run down to the hen house and get some eggs to scramble. We have some biscuits and ham left. We can make out on that."

"While she is doing that you can help me haul some wood up here from the creek. I would put it off but I know how guilty you feel about eating our food and not doing something to show your gratitude." Jim chuckled as he clucked at the team.

"I knew it. I knew it. Gotta work before you eat. Show my gratitude. Ha, Ha. Do a days work for one meal of left overs. Well, let's get it over with."

They were soon busy tossing pieces of wood into the wagon. They had continued the banter.

"Yeeek! Help! Jiimm!" The sound came from the direction of the house.

"What was that?" Jim jerked to attention. "That was Mary yelling." He took off for the house at a dead run.

Virg threw the piece of wood he held into the wagon, jumped aboard and whipped the team into a fast gallop. He checked his pistol as he neared the house.

10

Mary stood in the middle of the yard pointing toward the chicken pen. She was clearly shaken.

"It's right in there." She told Jim as he came out of the house with a shotgun. "Brrr! That thing was right under my feet. I'll probably never be able to gather eggs again."

"What's up, Jim?" Virg asked.

"Snake." Jim answered. "I'll take care of it."

"What kind?" Virg wanted to know. "Let's take a look."

"You get in there and kill that thing. It almost scared me to death. I am still shaking. Brrr." Mary shuddered as she talked.

"I'll shoot it and then take a look." Jim said. "That's the way to deal with snakes."

"Wait, let me see what it is." Virg admonished him. "You don't want to get rid of the good ones."

"Good ones." Mary shuddered again. "Are you crazy?"

"Well okay. Take a look but we have to get rid of it one way or another." Jim turned to Mary. "Don't worry. It'll be gone for good."

Virg moved to where he could look into the hen house. "There he is. We better look around. They usually travel in pairs. Looks mean but it's only a big old Bull Snake. He probably wanted a mess of eggs."

"What are you going to do?" Mary asked. "I won't have that thing around here."

"I'll give him a ride down the road a ways."

"I'm not cooking a bite until that thing is gone."

Virg picked up a long stick and easing into position pinned the snakes head down and then grabbed it behind the head and carried it out.

"He was as scared as you were, Mary."

"I doubt that."

"Here, put it in this." Jim came up with a sack.

Virg took the sack, dropped the snake in, then mounted Buck and headed down the trail. He soon had the snake's mate in the sack with it and headed toward home.

"I wish I had time to take these critters on home to our barn so they could clean up the mice there." He said as he

11

reached a point about a mile from Jim's place. "This looks like a good spot. Maybe I can find them later."

Releasing the reptiles he returned in time to set down to a good meal.

Mitch walked into the room above the saloon where he found Bart and Alex Averill seated at a table with a bottle and glasses available.

"We brought you a glass, Mitch. Don't worry it's clean." Bart greeted him.

Averill took the extra glass and poured a generous shot of liquor and handed it to Mitch.

"How are things at the ranch?" Averill asked. "Did everything go all right. How about the stolen cattle? Any luck in finding them?"

Mitch took the drink and sniffed at it before taking a small sip of the liquid. He made a wry face after swallowing the drink. He then set the glass on the table.

"They found them right where they were reported. The thief is in the jail across the street and there are plenty of witnesses."

"That's good. I'm glad you two didn't take the law into your own hands. I better look the marshal up and sign the legal complaint. He said that was the proper way to handle it and I agree."

"We used to hang cow thieves." Bart gave a reply with a slight tone of disgust. "It didn't take very long either."

"That's why I'm running things and you're one of the hired hands." Averill reminded him. "You're here to follow orders. I hope you understand that." He looked directly at Bart.

Bart dropped his eyes and seemed to be interested in the toes of his boots.

"I get your drift."

"Good. Now I'll go hunt for the marshal."

Mitch watched Averill walk out the door then turned to Bart. "Let him think he's the big wheel. It's better that way."

"I see what you mean." Bart grinned at his sidekick. "We really know who's running things."

12

"Now Joe, you forget that stuff about finding a place of your own. There's enough around here to keep us busy and it's all part yours." Dad Hale was admonishing his son as the worked to repair the lot fence. "Some day all of it'll belong to you boys."

"When we divide it up between the seven of us, the slices will be pretty thin." Joe responded. "I'm perfectly happy here but some day I'll need enough to support a family of my own."

"You're right, Joe but I would like to keep you boys as close as possible. We need to check on getting some of the land next to ours. That way you boys could have places of your own and we would all still be together." Dad Hale thought he had come up with a right good idea. "That'll solve all of our problems in one deal."

"That is a good idea. I think I'll ride into Paden and do some checking about that as soon as we finish this job."

Dad Hale had a pleased look on his face when he watched Joe ride toward Paden a short time later. Maybe he could keep them close.

Joe felt good about the discussion with his father. He had no desire to move away from home and the suggestion of getting some adjacent land was something he looked forward to. He might have to go off somewhere to work for short periods of time but his permanent base would be with the family.

"I'm going to do everything in my power to hold the family together." Joe said to himself as he neared Paden. "Dan is not very far off and the others are almost within shouting distance. That's the way it should be with families like us."

He rode by some people shortly before he reached town. They seemed a little restrained in returning his greeting.

"I wonder what Jed has been up to this time." Joe muttered. "That brother of mine is going to cause us grief if he doesn't quit pulling his pranks on people."

He smiled as he thought of some of the things that had happened and the fights that sometimes occured as a result.

13

"One thing about us Hales is that we're known to be honest even if we are poor." Joe laughed. "Some might think we're a bit too full of fun though."

As he rode into Paden he noticed some strange looks being directed his way.

He rode up to the rail at the general store and swung down.

"Hey Joe, I need to talk to you." It was Newt Smith. He sounded nervous. "Let's go over to my place."

"Don't look so serious, Newt. Things will work out between you and Molly." Joe chided his friend.

"You ought to make it to town without passing out." Jim said as they moved toward Paden. "I'd say you ate about a dozen eggs and half a hog. I still think you eat so much it wears you out to carry it around. That's what keeps you from growing to full size."

"I wore myself out loading all that wood and then hauling that snake off. I had to have something to revive me." Virg patted his full stomach. "Hope Aunt Marge is there with some of her good cooking."

Mary just shook her head and sighed.

"That snake kept us from getting anything at all out of you." Jim shrugged his shoulders in resignation.

"Looks like we are about to have company." Mary interrupted the discussion. "Some riders off yonder."

"We'll find out soon enough who it is." Jim spoke up. "Wonder if they will have any news?"

"It's Tom and Tod Ames and they have something exciting to tell us." Virg informed them.

"How the devil do you know that?" Mary asked. "You charm snakes and now this."

"Recognised the horses. Everybody has a way of riding that is kinda different. I have Indian eyes you know."

"Some more of the things the Cherokees taught him I guess." Jim added. "He keeps practicing that stuff."

"You two might have picked up some information if you had had eyes for anything but each other." Virg grinned at them.

"How do you know what they have to say is exciting?"

14

"Watch how eager they are to beat each other to meet us." Virg pointed out. "You can tell a lot by the way people act."

Mary just looked at Virg and shook her head.

The two horsemen rode up at a gallop.

"Guess you are going in for the hanging?" Tod Ames called out before they came to a stop. "They're going to hang Dan Hale. He stole a bunch of cattle from that new rancher-"

Tom Ames held up his hand. "Hold it Tod. I'll give them the straight of it."

"Well if you insist." Tod was not very pleased to be interrupted but gave way to his older brother.

"What do you mean, hang Dan Hale? The Hales are not known as thieves. Must be some kind of mistake." Jim was plainly puzzled.

"They found these cattle in Hale's pasture. They belonged to this new owner of the herd west of here. He had Hale arrested and brought in for trial. This new owner hates thieves I guess, so he says he is going to see that stealing is stopped before it gets out of hand." Tom was preparing to go on. "They'll get a judge to come in and-"

"Just a minute, Tom. You say they found them in Dan Hale's pasture. Are they sure he put them there?" Jim asked. "You have to be on pretty firm ground before you hang a man. Where are you going, Virg?"

"I'm going to hustle on into town and see what's going on. Dan Hale is no thief." He had dropped out of the wagon and mounted. "I'll see you in town." He set out in a steady lope.

"Don't do anything foolish." Mary called after him. "Mrs. Rankin says he always gets involved in other peoples problems." She turned back to hear the rest of Tom Ames story.

Paden was busy. Several horses were tied in front of the saloon. Their owners were inside drinking toasts and betting on the outcome of the coming trial.

A group of men had gathered across from the jail. A lively discussion was taking place when Virg rode up.

15

"I tell you, Dan Hale wouldn't steal anything, much less a bunch of cattle." Newt Smith was saying emphatically.

"The cows were there and some of us here saw them." A man answered.

"There were horse tracks from where they were driven into the pasture that led right up to his barn." Another fellow spoke up. "I would doubt it myself if I hadn't seen the evidence. Sure looks bad for Dan."

"Well he's not convicted yet." Newt reminded them. "I'm going to do all I can to help. Hi Virg, maybe we could get you to go out there and take a look. You're a pretty good tracker. At least John Billy says you are."

"Hi Newt. I'm willing to try but would like to talk to Dan Hale if I could."

"Can't do it. The only ones they let in is Joe Hale and a lawyer if he has one."

"I better see Joe then. I'm sure not a lawyer even if my Grandpa Smith says that I ask more questions than one."

"Dan had come over to our place and spent the whole day. He left to go home after dark so had gone in, put up his horse and gone to bed. When he woke up the next morning there they were, ready to hang him. Lucky for him, I guess, that some of the settlers were along so they took him to jail."

"Joe, does your dad know about this yet?" Virg asked. "He must have been in jail here for a day or two."

"Not unless someone else has taken him the word. I didn't because I was afraid he would rush up here and tear this place apart. I wanted to be sure of everything before I told him."

"What about Dan? Would he do anything like that?" Virg looked closely at Joe.

"I tell you that Dan, of all the Hales, wouldn't steal anything. He's so honest he makes the rest of us almost ashamed of ourselves at times." Joe answered.

"I guess that's clear enough, Joe." Newt chimed in. "I figured that's what you'd say."

"They're not going to hang him you can bet your boots

on that." Joe was almost pleading but looked like that he would be ready to go the outlaw route if it took that. "I'll help dad bust him out if need be. They're not going to hang any of us Hales."

"Joe, Newt and I are going to ride out there and look around. We might discover something. Why would anyone want to frame Dan?" Virg was thinking out loud now. "He never bothers anyone and the only thing he has is his place and it will probably wind up in his brother's hands. I wonder. Hmm, We'll wait and see. This could be a new threat to all of us."

"What are you looking so puzzled about?" Newt wanted to know. "And you keep mumbling about a new threat."

"Nothing much. Just a wild idea. Joe tell Dan not to give up. Maw says there's always hope. She's a pretty smart lady. She's kept me around all these years. Of course some folks wonder if that was all that smart."

"Virg and I are going out there now and look the place over. Hold off on any wild moves, Joe." Newt warned him. "We don't want to outlaw anybody if we can help it."

"That would be a new threat."

"What's this new threat business?"

"Making outlaws out of people."

"Boss, Newt Smith and a kid are going out there to look around." Bart was reporting to the man in the office above the saloon. "Kid's a tracker I guess."

The man leaned back in his chair and blew a cloud of smoke at the ceiling. He then took a slow drink from the glass on the table. "I've heard this kid is quite a tracker and sign reader. Are you sure that everything is okay? You might take Mitch and mosey out that way and keep an eye on them just in case."

"We could take care of them if you want. That would make sure."

"No, not unless you have to. Things are going pretty good. No use stirring up suspicions." He waved his man on his way.

"We have company, Newt. Don't look around any more than you have been or you'll tip them off." Virg and Newt had been examining the Dan Hale place for about an hour. There had been so many horses coming and going that no worthwhile sign could be discovered.

"Could you just give me a hint as to where our company is?"

"They are on that ridge just to the west. I think they're only watching us. Could some one be worried about what we'll find? Let's take off in the direction from where the cattle came from. Maybe we can figure out where they were before they came here."

"I know where they came from, Averill's place."

"Sure thing, but what if some clear horse tracks pop up along with the cattle on their way here?"

"Oh! I see what you are driving at. Somebody sure drove them here. They didn't come wandering in here by themselves."

"Newt, you keep on and you'll be a right clever fellow. Let's see if our friends come along."

They started off in the direction of the Averill place, casting back and forth for the sign made by the cattle on the way to Dan's pasture.

"Our friends are trailing along."

"Virg, I can't believe this. I haven't spotted a thing and I've been watching everywhere and you don't act like you have ever looked anywhere but at the ground. If you have seen anything, it was tracks."

"Newt, I'll explain about the animals and the birds one of these days. Those guys have spooked several rabbits and even a deer back a ways. Several birds have had a change in plans about flying into places. Indians watch for these signs in order to stay alive. Don't doubt it, they're there."

"What are we going to do about it?"

"Maybe we should ask them if we can help them find what they're looking for. When we go into this next bunch of trees I'll drop off and you take Buck and go on a ways and then stop in the best cover you can find. Stay perfectly still and don't let your horse give you away."

They rode on a short distance with Newt leading Buck.

18

When he glanced back Virg was gone. "Now I know what they are talking about when they poke fun at him about being like a ghost in the woods."

Chap 3

When Virg dropped out of the saddle he had quickly stepped into the woods and made himself almost invisable . The clothing he wore blended with his surroundings.

"That pair are over on the other side of this patch of woods." He said to himself. "They must be pretty sure that we don't know about them. I'll just see how close to them I can get. They don't act like they're all that used to the woods."

"Lucky for that pair the boss didn't give us the go ahead to stop their snooping for good. The way they move around a person could slip up and knock them on the head." Bart boasted to Mitch as they eased through the woods parallel to where Virg and Newt traveled.

"You're sure right about that. They don't know anyone's in a mile of 'em. Gomez says that some kid around here is real good with a six-shooter. This could be the one. He probably never met a real hand. I don't usually shoot kids but might make an exception of him if the need arises. He tries me and it'll be his last try." Mitch growled.

"I've seen you in action and even though some say I'm as good as they come I'd sure hate to face off with you." Bart was thinking in his mind that he was a shade faster than Mitch but followed the usual practice of boosting the other fellows ego.

"I spent some time in New Mexico and there were some real quick hands there. A few called me and I'm still around." Mitch talked as if he were discussing the weather. "That's why Averill brought me back here with him."

"Well all we need to do now is keep an eye on this pair unless it looks like they're about to find something we don't want them to."

"Wonder where they are now? I haven't seen them for a few minutes." Mitch glanced around.

"They went right through there. I can see their tracks." Bart pointed.

"You fellows looking for someone?" The question almost caused Bart and Mitch to fall out of their saddles. They didn't see anything but heard a voice.

When Virg dropped out of the saddle and faded into the brush before Newt had looked back, he began using the stalking skills learned from the Cherokee boys. He had spent the last few minutes traveling along listening to the conversation between the two self proclaimed gun fighters. So they didn't think he was aware of the things surrounding him.

The two horsemen had been startled but the speed with which they palmed their pistols indicated that they had not been just blowing hot air. They were instantly ready to shoot. The problem was, there was nothing to shoot at, at least they didn't see anything.

"Where the devil are you?" Bart growled.

Pow! Mitch did not hesitate but fired at the first movement. His slug took some fur off the tail of a rabbit that had spooked.

Virg held his silence. He was using the same skill that the Cherokee lad Squirrel had perfected by keeping a tree trunk between himself and the gunmen. The shot had not even been in his direction.

"Hold your fire Mitch. We aren't hunting rabbits."

"You better watch your mouth. Say, you! Step out here and show yourself."

There was a rustle in the brush as the rabbit hit a bush in it's rush to leave the area. Bart and Mitch glanced that direction. Virg used this opportunity to change his location.

"You fellows are a little to nervous with your guns for me to step out and be a target."

They whirled to face his way again. Again they faced blank space.

"Why don't you put your guns up. I could have shot both of you by now if I was a mind to. I just asked you if

20

you were looking for someone." They still hadn't seen Virg even though now they knew his approximate location.

Bart and Mitch put their pistols up. They were both confident that if they desired they would have no trouble drawing and plugging whoever this happened to be.

Virg stepped out in the open just a few yards from them.

"We were on our way to Paden." Bart offered. "You could get shot by suddenly jumping people."

Mitch was still puzzled by the fact that they hadn't been able to spot him. "Are you a danged Indian or something? Sneaking through the woods like a heathen. I ought to plug you on general principals."

"I don't think I would recommend that. If you remember I was with someone. He might just be eyeing you over a rifle sight right now."

There came a rustle in a tree behind them. They both whirled to look that direction. A bird flew off. When they turned back Virg was gone.

Mitch jerked his pistol out and spurred his horse in the direction where Virg had been standing.

Bart followed him for a short distance and then called out. "Hold it, Mitch. Lets get on into town and report to the boss."

Mitch was ready to agree. This chasing a shadow through the woods was about to unnerve him. He had come from the wide open spaces.

"Okay but I better not spot that sneak again or I'll put enough lead in him to hold him still."

Virg returned to the trail left by Newt and the horses. He soon joined them.

"Well, tell me what transpired. I heard a shot."

"That one jasper was a might jumpy. I guess he thought that a rabbit was going to do him in. He took a shot at it. Almost hit it too. I don't think they'll be on our trail any more though."

"Why? What did you do to get rid of them?" Newt asked. "Come on Virg, tell me what happened."

"Okay. I just asked them if they were looking for someone. They seemed a little nervous about not being able

21

to keep track of me so I think they headed for town where they could see the ones nearby."

"From the stories I hear, you could make anybody nervous about keeping track of you in the woods."

They went on about the business of trying to find any clear sign of tracks along where the cattle had been moved. At the end of a couple of hours they had to give up and head back toward Paden with nothing to show for their efforts.

"I tell you that kid is like a shadow in the woods. He was there then he was gone. Before that he spoke to us and I didn't see anything. Did you, Mitch?" Bart was filling the boss in on the events of the day.

"No but when I do see him I think I'll teach him not to try to make a fool out of me." Mitch was still steamed about not being able to find Virg after having him right in front of him.

"That kid is part Indian and you won't make much headway with him in the woods from what I hear." The man informed them. "I don't see how it's going to scare these folks much if you best a kid though."

"I'll bet this is the one Gomez has been talking about. When I see him I plan to run him out of town." Mitch stalked out of the room.

"We better go along and see that he doesn't make a mess of things for all of us." The boss said as they followed Mitch.

Virg and Newt rode into town and pulled up at the hitch-rack when Mitch came striding out of the saloon with Bart on his heels.

Earll Averill stopped in a doorway and watched when he saw Mitch. He noticed a well dressed man standing just inside the saloon.

"Hey you, Injun, I've got you where I can see you now. Get down off that pony and see if you can dodge a bullet." Mitch took a stance in the middle of the street. "You won't disappear out here in the open."

"You talking to me?" Virg asked.

"Yes I'm talking to you. You half-breed."

22

"Why don't you just go back in and have another drink." Virg responded. "Besides I'm not a half-breed. I'm about a quarter Cherokee, more or less."

"Well I'll just shoot--"

"Hold it! Both of you." Marshall Simmons stood to the side and behind Mitch. He had a double barrel ten guage in his hands. "We'll have no gun fights here."

"Then I'll slap him around some."

"Thanks, Marshall Simmons." Virg told him. "You don't have to worry about me starting anything." He slid off his horse. "Hold still, Buck."

He saw Mitch start in his direction.

"We may have to use one of the tricks we learned, boy." Virg spoke in a low voice to his horse.

"I'll just slap him around a bit and teach him some manners." Mitch said as he strode forward and reached for Virg.

Virg stood still as if he was scared stiff

"I'll-" Thud, Whooof. The sound of a blow being struck was followed by the explosion of air leaving lungs.

"Gosh amighty. Did you see that?" A surprised onlooker gasped.

"It was mighty quick, I'll say that." Another answered him. "Poor devil."

"Guess that ends the fight for now so you folks be on your way." Marshall Simmons urged the people that had come up. He moved over to the prostrate figure on the ground who was still gasping for breath. Both hands were grasping his middle.

Several chuckles drifted back as the people move off down the street.

Mitch was folded up holding his middle and trying to get some air back in his system.

"Sorry mister, but Buck doesn't like for folks to mess with me. We're kind of buddies you might say." When Mitch reached for him, Virg had given a short whistle. He knew he was no match for Mitch in such close quarters. "Hope you're not hurt much."

This signal had been enough for Buck, who planted one of his heels in Mitch's middle ending the contest before it

23

got started. It had taken a lot of work training him to do that. Lots of horses kicked but Buck had better than average aim with his efforts.

"Maw might not fuss so much about all the time I spent on the training if she could see how useful it can be." Virg said as he watched Mitch gasping for breath

"Virg, you and Newt move on down the street. I think Joe Hale wants to see you. He's over at Newt's place."

They found Joe sitting on the front porch of Newt's place.

"What did you fellows find out?" Joe asked as they walked up.

"Now don't get to upset when we tell you, Joe." Newt urged. "It's been some time since the cattle were driven out there and all the movement back and forth made it difficult."

"That's right. We tried to follow the trail back to where it came from but it was pretty well mixed up." Virg added. "There's one thing though. Evidently there was some concern about it as we had a couple of fellows keeping track of us."

"There has to be something some where because we all know that Dan is not a thief." Joe was getting worked up. "He's not going to hang. I can tell you that right now."

"I agree with you, Joe about Dan not being a thief but if you go around making war talk it will alert the ones that would try to stop you." Virg counciled. "Don't jump off the deep end until you have to. We will keep trying to find out what this is all about."

"Virg is right." Newt offered. "They would have to bring in a judge from Okmulgee as this is still Indian Territory. That will take some time. Let's keep the talk down about taking things into your own hands. Don't want to turn the honest folks against you."

"That's good advice. I'm not usually one to fly off the handle but Dan never bothered a soul in his life. The rest of us are pretty rowdy but not him." Joe shook his head in puzzlement. "I better check with the rest of the family."

"We'll be seeing what we can find out in the meantime." Newt assured him. "Don't give up."

"Maw says there is always hope as long as you don't

quit." Virg added. "We'll be busy."

Chap 4

"Mitch sure handled that business with the kid in fine shape." Averill sneered as he stood glowering at Bart. "I hire you guys for doing what I tell you, not to go out and make fools of yourselves."

"It would have been a different story if that horse hadn't kicked me." Mitch chimed in. "My turn will come, and when it does I plan to make him sorry he ever saw me."

"Yeah, I don't like the way he sneaks through the woods like a wild Indian." Bart added.

"I have you here to provide a tough image in case it's needed. Jumping a kid and coming off second best is not a very good way to go about it." Averill growled. "You're not to go off on your own."

"The people around here think he's something special." Bart replied. "Maybe it would help if he was knocked down a notch or two."

"Just make sure you do it right. It won't look very good if two or three of you jump one scrawny kid even if you win." Averill told them. He shook his head in disbelief. "Keep it out of town. I can't believe I'm discussing how to handle a kid with grown men. Now get out of here."

When they started on he called after them.

"Say if you see that new lawyer, Nelson, send him over here. Looked like you were with him before you tackled that kid. Take Slater out to the ranch with you when you go."

Bart and Mitch walked outside where they saw Virg and Newt returning from their visit with Joe Hale. They were surprised when they got a smile and a wave from Virg.

They had expected a dirty look at least. The smile only served to infuriate them.

"I'll get him." Mitch growled. "He has to go home. Wonder what Averill thought about us being in Nelson's office."

"Hope he doesn't get suspicious. There Slater is now.

I think they call him Toad." Bart said. "He may know the country around here."

"Jim, I think I'll ride over and see Zach Vaughn. You and Mary tell the folks I'll be there sometime tomorrow if you see them. Tell Maw I may have a solution to the mouse problem." Virg met them as they were preparing to drive out of town. "Mandy may have something special cooked up. I'll stop at the store and take the kids a little something too."

"You better watch out for that fellow Buck kicked. He didn't act like he was to happy about it."

"I doubt if I would've been either." Virg gave his brother a big grin as he drove off.

"It's good to see you, Virg. We thought you had forgotten where we lived." Zach had a big smile as he reached out to shake hands. His pearly white teeth fairly sparkled against the background of his black skin. "Mandy will have something to eat in a while. All we have to do is sit over here in the shade and visit until she calls."

"I have a surprise for Jerimy and Nell if they aren't to bashful to come see what it is." He looked at the two youngsters and reached into his saddlebag and pulled out a sack.

"We're not bashful, are we, Nell? You know that we talk when we have something to say. Some folks just don't listen when we do." Jerimy came forward. Nell was right behind him.

"What kind of surprise is it this time?" Nell asked. "The last time it was a frog. Almost scared me to death when it jumped out of the sack."

Jerimy burst out laughing at the reminder. "Go on, Nell grab that sack and look in it."

"You look yourself. I don't trust Virg. It's probably something to scare me so you can all have a good laugh."

"Here, Jerimy. I guess she doesn't want any of this." Virg handed the boy the sack of candy. He wasn't worried about it being shared. For a nine year old boy, Jerimy exhibited unusual consideration for his sister who was

26

two years younger.

Jerimy pulled some of the candy out and looked at it. "A whole sackfull just for me. Thank you, Virg. I'm sorry, Nell, that you don't want any, but I can handle it all by myself."

Nell was not to be drawn into begging even though it was obvious that she wanted to share the candy. "I guess I'll just go hungry and you'll probably get the belly ache."

Zach smiled as the two youngsters moved into the house to show their mother the special treet. He had no concern about them sharing it with each other and he knew that they would insist that their parents also have a bite. They didn't get many luxuries.

"I noticed one of your neighbors seemed to be gone." Virg said as he joined Zach. "What happened to him.? The one just south and east of here."

"He's gone for good I guess. He wasn't very friendly with us but we got along. The fellow that had the place on past him came by here on his way out and told me a story. I didn't know whether to believe him or not."

There was a period of silence.

"If you want to tell me okay, If not okay, Zach. We have a strange situation in town. They have Dan Hale in jail charged with stealing cattle from that new man, Alex Averill."

"I better tell you then. That fellow told me that he found some cows in his pasture. Some cowboys rode up and said they were going for the law. He tried to explain but they wouldn't listen. Finally one of them said if he would sign over his place and leave the country they would forget it. He signed."

"They couldn't get away with that. The new rules for changing land titles would stop them." Virg looked at Zach. "Didn't he know that?"

"Yeah, but he had something in his past that he was afraid would come out if he was tried in court so he signed and left. He told me that the same thing happened to the one you found missing. I bet they don't work that on Dan Hale. He's an honest man."

"They have witnesses though. Reliable men at that. I

wonder if--hmmm. Thanks for the information Zach. I'll keep it out of general circulation. Don't want to cause you any trouble if I can help it. This could be a new threat to us though."

"Come and get it before I throw it out." Mandy called. She gave them a big smile as they took seats at the table.

They enjoyed a good meal. Virg had a good time joshing the two children of the Vaughns. This was a happy family.

"I better head on home." Virg informed them. "I have a chore on the way. We need a mouser and I think two of them are available at a certain place."

"Good thing I kept this sack with me. Mary said she wouldn't have it in the house after what we put in it. I wonder if my two friends are still in the neighborhood?" Virg was muttering to himself as he circled the spot where he had dropped the two snakes.

Tying Buck up he moved about on foot. He had left them in an area where some rocks were. To leave it they would be forced to travel across open space that was pretty bare. They might do this at night but probably not in daylight.

"There you are. Where's your better half? I just want to take you to a place where you can fatten up on big juicy mice." He soon had the snake in the sack. The other one was soon located and joined it's mate. They settled down after threshing about a bit.

"Now to hit for home. You fellows will like it there. Just lay around and eat. That one looks like he has already been at it. More than likely full of eggs. What a life."

Chap 5

"You're sure he'll come this way?" Bart asked.

Mitch eyed the burly Slater. "We just want to slap him around some. Teach him to keep his smart mouth shut, the danged half breed."

"I have a score to settle with him too. He shot one of

28

my brothers and hit me up side the head with his pistol."
Toad Slater rubbed his head when he thought of the
incident. "This is the way to their place. If we play it right
we can have our fun."

"Here is how we'll work it." Bart explained. "This
works every time." He went on to lay out a plan.

Virg was riding along giving some thought to the
problem of stolen cattle and the settlers that had been
accused. "Wonder if any others have had this problem? I
think I'll go back in tomorrow and talk with Newt and Joe
about this."

As he rounded a turn he spotted a man lying face down
in the middle of the trail. The figure didn't move as he rode
up to him. "Say mister, are you hurt?"

"No but you're gonna to be if you make a false move."
Toad rolled over with a gun in his hand. "Come on out
men. I've got him."

Bart and Mitch eased their horses out from behind the
trees.

Virg was disgusted with himself as well as with Buck.
They had walked into this like two rank greenhorns. Let it
be peaceful for a spell and you get careless. He guessed he'd
just have to pay the price.

"Let's move off here a ways so we won't be disturbed
and we'll teach this half-breed some good manners." Mitch
told them. "Let him keep his iron. I hope he tries to pull
it. Give me a chance to show him what a real hand can do
with one."

Toad mounted and they motioned Virg to move off the
trail.

Virg knew he was in deep trouble. He could in no way
match the three of them in a brawl and if he tried to pull his
pistol they wouldn't hesitate to shoot him. He might drop
one or two but they were spread out to much for him to have
a chance to get away in one piece.

He would just have to watch for any chance that might
come his way. Didn't look very encouraging for Maw's
youngest. However she always said, 'Don't give up hope,
the Lord looks after fools and drunks.'

"Hmm, I'm not drunk, so wonder where that leaves me? I better concentrate on watching for some opportunity to get out of this mess."

"Cut out the mumbling. Okay this is far enough." Bart called out. "This looks like a good spot."

They were in a small flat opening surrounded on three sides by trees. They were well hidden from the trail so anyone passing by wouldn't spot them.

Virg studied his surroundings. If he could only get into the trees. He had no worry about Buck's ability to outrun the three horses but he would be shot out of the saddle before reaching cover. He had to make a move soon or take the beating they were sure to give him. That might be better than being shot though.

"What you got in that sack?" Toad demanded. "Give it here."

"Just a--", Virg started to tell him then an idea hit him. "Just something for my Maw."

"Let me see it."

Virg held it behind him.

"I told you to give it to me."

"Now Mr. Slater, you wouldn't mess up something I got for my Maw would you?" Virg held the sack back from Toad's reaching hand. "It has to be handled easy. You notice I'm carrying it along real gentle like."

Mitch and Bart eased a couple of steps closer. They craned their necks to see what was going on.

"Please don't bother this. I have to handle it carefully or it'll mess it up." Virg put a whine into his voice. "It's for Maw."

Toad leaned forward in the saddle and grabbed the sack and jerked it out of Virg's hand. He shook it vigorously, then looking Virg straight in the eye, stuck out his chin in a belligerent manner, shoved his hand down into the sack. "Don't you tell me what to do."

Mr. Bullsnake was getting a might put out about being caught and sacked. Then to add insult to injury his mate had suffered the same fate. They had been jostled along for some time and now this latest indignity of being shaken around like a sack of rocks.

30

He wasn't planning to stand for it any longer. He would just take so much then he would attempt to fight back no matter what the consequences.

When the hand descended into the sack he decided it was time for action. He'd show these human things not to mess with him.

This thing shoved down into the sack had a bunch of different prongs. One of the smaller extensions on that hand was about the right size to fit his mouth so he clamped down on it.

This produced some unusual results. The biting Mr. Bullsnake wasn't quite prepared for what happened but he held on with all his might.

Toad jerked his hand out of the sack in a hurry.

Mr. Bullsnake was not about to turn loose when he had his tormentor on the run. He held on.

"Gosh all mighty!" Toad yelled as his eyes bugged out when he saw the snake on his hand. He gave a heave of his arm in a whirling motion to rid himself of what he was convinced was a full grown rattler.

His slinging motion accomplished the task of ridding Toad of the snake. It's mouth slid off of the appendage it had a hold on.

Mitch started to laugh at Toad when he saw what he had attached to his hand. He cast a glance at Bart so wasn't prepared for what happened.

The snake flew through the air, swapping ends in the whirling motion and landed with a whipping action around Mitch's neck. The two ends passed each other as the middle smacked into Mitch's adams apple. They came on around and passed each other again.

Mitch saw the snake coming when he turned his attention back toward Toad but had no time to duck. He forgot all about his gun and grabbed for the snake with both hands and jerked to free it. This failed to improve the situation however as it was wrapped completely around his neck.

When he grabbed it, he got a good hold and started to pull with both hands. This only tightened the coil around his neck. The more he pulled the tighter it got. Looked

31

like he might be the only man in history who strangled himself with a bullsnake. His eyes began to bug out.

Mr. Bullsnake was really getting mad now. He reacted to the pull on his torso by grabbing a mouthful of one of the flaps growing on the side of Mitch's head. He tried to bite a hunk out of it. Maybe they'd let go of him if he succeeded in inflicting some pain. Besides he was getting fighting mad.

Mitch was pulling with all his might. He had a deathly fear of snakes and had gone completely berserk. All he could think to do was pull until the thing was gone. He didn't know that he might wind up looking like an earmarked maverick. All he wanted to do was pull this horrible creature off of him. He kept pulling.

Meanwhile Mrs. Bullsnake decided it was time to escape. The sack had landed in Toad's lap and had been kept from falling by the tree of the saddle. She began to slither out of the sack with some difficulty because of the close quarters. Her head went up over the tree of the saddle and it looked like freedom was hers as soon as she cleared the sack. Drop to the ground and be off. She didn't quite make it.

Bart sat stunned for an instant when the first snake came out. He didn't like snakes. When you saw one you shot it. At least that had always been his way of thinking. He jerked his pistol up ready to fire at the first target. He stopped just in time. Couldn't shoot or he might hit Mitch.

Shoot the kid, that's it. Turning he spotted the snake headed across Toad's saddle. He opened fire.

'POW'! Pseeer. The ricochet sounded loud in the sudden silence.

Mrs. Snake, jerked her head back toward the sack. It didn't appear to be safe out there after all.

"What you trying to do, you fool?" Toad screamed. "You almost gut-shot me." He looked in horror where the bullet had glanced off of his saddle horn. Then seeing the second snake he threw it and the sack away. He didn't think he wanted any more snakes latched on to his fingers.

Mitch continued to pull. The snake didn't come free. He pulled harder.

32

Mr. Bullsnake kept his hold on the flap. If he wasn't turned loose he planned to hang on. He was willing to turn loose if this other critter was but wasn't about to give up until that happened.

Mrs. Bullsnake and sack combined landed under the feet of Bart's horse.

Mrs. Bullsnake struggled to get clear of the sack. It proved to be difficult. She pushed on the sack to free herself.

Bart's horse didn't like snakes either, especially ones waving sacks around. He decided the best way to show his displeasure was see how high he could jump. It gave a wild snort and went into action. Taking several jumps would get him away from this mess. He was a good hand at bucking.

Bart was caught by surprise at this sudden turn of events. He dropped his pistol and grabbed the saddle horn with both hands in order to stay aboard. He was very busy clawing leather for a spell.

Mitch was still pulling with all his might.

Somewhat recovered from the shock of almost being blown out of the saddle, Toad glanced over at Mitch. He decided he had better help. He moved over that way.

"Here, Mitch let go of that thing. You're about to throttle yourself." His suggestion did not get through. "Crazy galoot. He's gone plumb nutty."

Mitch was beyond listening. He pulled harder trying to rid himself of this thing. His eyes bugged out that much more. They looked like they were on stems. His breath was coming in gasps. His face was now beginning to take on a tinge of purple.

"Turn loose I tell you." Toad yelled at the top of his lungs. "Let go before you choke. I guess he's gone completely daffy."

Mitch kept on pulling. His efforts were becoming weaker however.

Bart was busy pulling leather to keep from being dumped. He was beginning to have doubts about his ability as a bronc stomper.

Mr. Bullsnake wanted to escape but couldn't because he was wrapped completely around Mitch's neck and was being held in place by the pull. All he could do was bite at the

33

flap of hide sticking out near him. He was beginning to have another problem too.

While in Mary's henhouse he had feasted on several eggs after gobbling down two fat mice and one small rat. His digestive system had been full enough to last him for days when Virg had so rudely removed him. Now the pressure from the pull that Mitch was exerting hastened the completion of the natural progression of these items. Nature took it's toll.

Mitch was the beneficiary of this conclusion. His shirt took on some added color.

"Dang fool." Toad muttered as he forced his horse toward Mitch's mount. He grabbed both of Mitch's wrists and began to squeeze with all his strength. Slowly the hands began to open. "Let go of the danged thing, or he's going to chew your ear off." He made sure, as best as he could, to keep clear of certain material on Mitch's shirt.

Mitch's eyes still bugged out like they were on stems and he was gasping for breath. His tongue now lolled out. The spoken words had no effect but the pressure on his wrists worked. His hands opened.

When Mitch turned loose the snake slithered around his neck, dropped to the ground and headed for the brush. It gulped down something and joined it's mate there.

Bart was still having horse trouble.

Mitch reeled in the saddle while he gasped for more air. His eyes returned to their normal position in their sockets. His color began to improve. He licked his lips then spit several times then brushed the back of his hand across his mouth. He didn't notice some of the same stuff on his shirt being on that hand.

"Phoey, hrack, potuey, Ooh I think I'm gonna be sick." Seems there was a bad taste in Mitch's mouth all of a sudden. He had trouble holding on to his last meal.

"Where's the kid?" Bart, quit the bronc-busting."

Mitch had regained his senses after a few moments and had his gun ready for action after retrieving it from where he had dropped it. The side of his head was covered with blood. His neck and shirt front showed the effect of other material that he had accumulated.

Bart soon had the horse somewhat calmed. "I don't know. This darned bronc came unwound when I shot that snake off of Toad's saddle." He dismounted and picked up his pistol.

"Quit calling me Toad, I tell you."

"Shut up." Mitch snarled. "Shame you didn't shoot him instead, Bart. He threw that thing on me."

"I wus just trying to git rid of it."

"You didn't need to grab it to begin with."

"I didn't. It grabbed me."

The three horses were still nervous from all the excitement.

Virg was no where to be seen. He hadn't stayed to watch the show. Maw's youngest knew when to make tracks.

The two snakes peared out from under a dead branch. One of them appeared to be about six inches longer than he had been. He was sure a lot slimmer. He would also need to seek out some more things to eat pretty soon if that foul tasting piece he had swallowed after hitting the ground didn't kill him.

Crazy humans, what would they try next.

Virg was headed for home. "What's the country coming to. A person can't even take something home to catch mice without some robber grabbing it." He chuckled. "Best snakes I ever met. I mean the ones I had in the sack. Am I glad Jim didn't shoot them."

The three toughs had finally managed to get their horses settled.

"You better do something about that ear Mitch." Bart advised him. "It's sure bleeding. What's that other stuff all over you?"

"Yeah, you look like you were marked for the trail with a swallow-fork. They'll probably call you gotch-ear from now on." Toad added. "That other stuff looks like snake s-

"Shut your fool mouth before I put a bullet in it." Mitch snarled, cutting Toad off. "Throwing a snake on a man, I ought to shoot you anyway."

"Yeah, you started this whole mess when you took that sack away from the kid." Bart growled. "From now on let us do the thinking."

They were not in a very good mood as they headed for the Averill headquarters.

Toad rode along a few paces behind the others. If they had listened carefully they might have heard him complaining about the ungratefulness of certain people. Gun-slicks, ha. He laughed a little as he recalled the look on Mitch's face when he had the snake around his neck.

"Let them do the thinking, ha, I shudda let him go ahead and choke himself." He grinned again. "To stupid to get a snake from around his neck. That Bart ain't much better. That idjet almost shot me. I oughta take his gun away from him and cram it down his lousy throat, let them do the thinking, ha."

Mitch and Bart looked back at Toad when he began to laugh.

"I wonder how that stuff tasted to him?" Toad laughed to himself. "Maybe I better not ask him about it right now though."

Chap 6

"Is supper ready?" Virg asked as he came into the house after putting his horse away and doing some chores.

"You walk in after being gone two days and the first words are about eating. What's going on in town? Did you see any of the Freezes?

"Maw, you have to give me a chance to answer one question before you ask another one. I might forget some of them."

"Well, start answering then. Did you do anything about a way to get rid of the mice?"

"Another question. I had the mouse problem all but solved when something came up causing me to lose my mousers." He then proceeded to tell them about Dan Hale and the cattle.

"And I didn't see any of the Freeze family. I did visit with Jim and Mary. They are doing fine. She sure is a good cook. Almost as good as you, Maw. Of course that would take some doing."

"You sure know how to get the talk back around to eating. Get your hands washed and I'll put it on. You'll probably come up with some wild story about trying to solve the problem of the mice. That still needs to be done you know."

"I'll see what I can come up with. I need to stay on the good side of you if I want to eat." He decided not to tell them about his encounter with the three Averill hands even though he knew they would enjoy a good laugh. She would wind up worrying about him when he rode around the area. He didn't want to be the cause of her worrying.

Ab had been chuckling as the two exchanged their barbs. He had no doubt about the love that existed between mother and son. They just enjoyed the sparring.

"That story about Dan Hale is a strange one. It would sure be hard for anyone to convince me that he stole cattle." Ab had finished his supper and brought up the subject during their discussion.

"I've found out something that needs looking into so I better go back to Paden in the morning and have a visit with Newt and Joe Hale. We need to keep Joe from doing anything foolish before we have a chance to check things out."

"Just be sure to watch out for yourself. You know that bad things can happen. Don't take any wild chances." His mother was concerned because she knew he would be willing to jump in if his friends were threatened.

"I try to do that." He answered. "I mean the watching out for myself part not the taking wild chances part."

"That could be debated I believe." Ab gave his opinion on the subject.

"Virg, are you sure you should get mixed up in this thing about Dan Hale?" Maw Rankin asked. "People are pretty touchy about what happens to their cattle."

"They may use this as an excuse to get even."

"They may be touchy about their cattle, but should we just sit by and let them do this to Dan?" He wanted to know. "As for getting even, some of them are more than willing to do that now. Some of our old friends too."

"What makes you say that? Have you had any trouble with that bunch that tried to run us off our place? I thought they were all gone from here." She had a worried look on her face.

"I saw Toad Slater yesterday. He acted like he was still a little mad at me. He was with two of the new hands working for Alex Averill. One of them was upset because Buck kinda kicked him. I ran on to them on my way home. I thought they were going to give me a bad time but they decided they'd rather play with snakes." He kind of grinned as he told her this. "So I hurried on home."

"Some of your devilment is going to get you into trouble one of these days. Try to stay out of things. I worry all the time."

"You know me, Maw. I never bother anyone unless they force it on me. I'll do my best to stay out of trouble."

"That's what bothers me. I know you."

"I wouldn't want to have you embarrassed by things I do. You wouldn't be proud of me if I stood by and let them do Dan in if something could be done."

"Just be careful. I guess I'll still claim you." She gave him a smile. "I guess you will always be my baby boy."

"Gosh sakes, Maw. Don't say that where anybody can hear you. They'd laugh me out of the country." He mounted his horse. "I better get into town and tell Newt this new stuff."

She was still standing in the yard when he rode out of sight. He waved his hat in the air as he went into the trees.

"The idea of saying I wouldn't be proud of him after the things that have happened." She blinked away a tear. She then began to sing her favorite hymn.

The words drifted to Virg before he moved out of hearing. A smile lighted his face.

"Buck, old boy, we got a bit careless on our way home yesterday. Good thing I had those mouse catchers with me.

You better help me stay alert because that one guy may not have a very friendly attitude where you're concerned." Virg patted his favorite horse as he talked.

This morning he had included his bow when he had rolled his things to take along. He was a pretty good hand with the bow and it had the advantage of being shot without a lot of noise. The training he had received in the art of stalking and concealment while with the Cherokees had come in handy several times. Combining all these talents he could make him dangerous to tangle with in the woods.

He was riding along keeping a sharp watch but he hadn'd observed anything to cause alarm when suddenly Buck pricked his ears forward and turned his head toward the right. He gave a little extra puff of air out his nose.

"Easy boy. I see you're on the job. Don't know what's there but I get the message." Virg took a long look at the surrounding area. They would soon pop out in the open and make a good target for an ambusher. If the opportunity was missed there they would go through some trees and come out into an even better target area. "Looked like something moved up there. Didn't rightly locate it, just saw something out of the corner of my eye." He decided to be cautious.

"Probably doesn't amount to anything but If you're dead you don't get a second chance to find out. Better be safe than sorry according to Maw. Buck let's try one of our little tricks. I don't hanker to be ambushed again."

As he started into the open space Buck suddenly started jumping sideways as if something had startled him.

"Dog gone your hide, cut that out. You must be afraid of your shadow." Virg leaned forward and to the left as if about to fall out of the saddle. He slapped Buck with the reins a little.

Buck responded by hopping in the other direction. This caused Virg to lean the other direction. This would be a difficult target if anyone was wanting one. A bobbing object would be hard to hit.

He had experienced the feeling of being shot out of the saddle about a year before when they were having trouble with the cattlemen.

That was enough to make him wary after the run in the day before. He didn't want to take any chances now.

Buck had proven to be good at giving him advance warnings from time to time. He was from mustang stock and could spot trouble where a good dog might miss it.

39

Buck and Virg had something special between them. Virg's mother marveled at the pair. She often said they even thought alike.

"You rascal. Are you trying to dump me?" So saying he returned to a position upright in the saddle and then leaned forward over Buck's neck. As he did he raked his left heel along the flank. Buck responded by bolting forward.

"Now you're going to have a runaway. You knot head I'm going to stop here in this shade and let you know who's boss." He said in a loud voice so that any listeners could hear.

Pulling into the trees he dismounted and picking up some dead sticks broke a couple of them and then threw one back out into the clearing.

"Quit dodging. You're as hard to hit as a scared dog." He yelled. "You dog gone jug head, quit trying to get away."

Buck gave a small squeal and jumped a couple of times as if he was being worked over. It had taken some time to train him to do the many tricks he was capable of.

"You just cool your heels there while I get a bait of these berries." Virg yelled, grabbed his bow and a handful of arrows, doned his moccasins and moved off through the woods. He knew Buck wouldn't move away from where he left him. He would come galloping at a whistle.

It would be possible to make it back to the wooded area they had come out of by going away from the area that Buck had indicated first and then cutting back toward home.

If he was not mistaken about the area any ambusher would be up higher and to the right of the trail as they rode along. That way he could have a good view of both open spaces.

"He would probably be on this side of the crest of the ridge so as not to skyline himself." Virg muttered. "Here I go jumping at shadows but one time is enough for this boy to be shot in the back."

He moved at a fast trot after reaching a place which he was sure would be hidden from anyone on the ridge. Using every advantage of cover and shadowed area he soon covered a good quarter mile.

Cutting to his left he soon was over the crest of the hill. "I better slow down and start being careful. I don't want to step on anyone if he's there. It would be stupid to go to all this trouble and then give someone a chance so they couldn't miss." He moved back left again. It had been a while since he had stalked anyone for real. Better work extra hard at it now.

He suddenly stopped and stood dead still behind a small bush. It didn't appear to furnish much cover but he had learned that small cover could be used effectively. He could remember times when a half-dozen Indian boys had hidden from him, practically under his feet.

What was it he'd heard? Or had he heard anything at all? He remained frozen in place. Better not to move when in doubt. Still he couldn't take all day. It would arouse suspicion. He decided to move on.

Before he had time to ease out of his concealment the sound came again. A horse scraping his bit on the side of a tree. Then a small snort. It was off to the right a little. Better check it out. Didn't want to be given away by a horse. They could be a good watch dog.

This indicated that someone was on the ridge.

"I better drop back and come up from behind." He moved back the way he had come and then made his way toward where he had heard the sound. "There he is. Someone sure knows how to leave a horse where he won't be spotted."

The horse was tied to a tree with other trees in front, behind and both sides. A person would have to almost bump into him to make the discovery.

Chap 7

"Why would you hide your horse? Must have a good reason."

Virg studied the situation for a minute. The good job of hiding the animal could be used to his advantage. The fact that the horse could not be seen would also keep him from easily seeing things about him. He didn't act as if he

41

was from mustang stock. Didn't look it either.

Moving off to the side where the woods appeared to be the heaviest he made his way to where he was just below the crest of the ridge. A pretty good view of the area ahead was available from there.

"Where would a person be?" He ran a picture of the area through his mind, from where he had left Buck to where he was now. "In order to cover both open spots he would have to be a bit further up the trail." He studied the area from his present place.

"The only place I see is that dead tree with the brush around it. Have to watch my step. If I'm wrong it may be trouble. Have to move though. I couldn't eat berries all day, besides there aren't any down there." He smiled at the thought. "I hope that fellow doesn't know that."

Virg moved back down the side of the ridge. He could still make out the top of the brush where the dead tree was. Looked like the best bet might be to go past the spot and work back. He moved to a spot even with the brush and stopped again to listen. Not a sound. He made sure he kept cover between himself and the area in mind.

"Well, I made it to here, now what? I'll just move up higher again and take a look." Soon he could see the dead tree and brush from the other side. Still no one in sight. "Let's see what happens to that woodpecker. He's headed right toward that dead tree. Hmm he lit and went right to work. Whoa. He was moving around, checking it over and suddenly left in a hurry. Something he didn't like."

Scanning the spot from side to side, forward and back, Virg could not make out anybody. He moved a few feet closer and to the side, then repeated his examination. Still nothing. "If he's in there he's mighty good at hiding."

A rabbit came hopping down the ridge. He hopped a few feet and stopped to nibble on a few grass blades. This was repeated several times. Each move brought it closer to the dead tree. Suddenly it stopped reared up on its haunches and flicked it's ears forward. It remained in this position and then dashed back along the way it had come then swerved down the back side of the ridge.

"I know I didn't spook that fellow. He didn't look in

42

my direction at all, then he ran where I could see him for a good ways." Virg moved closer to the dead tree but froze when he heard a twig snap. Something had moved. He hoped he wasn't being watched himself. Especially over the sight of a rifle.

"If I am being watched I better move. I'd be harder to hit and the gun barrel would have to move to track me. Make it easier to spot." He thought he had the party located. The sound came from a spot right in front of him but he could see nothing yet. He eased forward a little more. A large limb had fallen off the dead tree, broken into two pieces, forming a pocket between the pieces.

Virg decided to risk raising his head a little. His efforts were rewarded.

"Well, well, a perfect spot. Hidden in both directions, front and back. The only problem is he can't see back here either. All I see is a boot. It moves so must have a foot in it. I have pretty good cover. Let's see how he reacts to a bit of noise." He made sure he would have an escape route if needed.

Taking a few pebbles he tossed them one at a time into some dry leaves. He spaced the spots to make it sound like something moving. He thought he heard a mutter then silence.

"I'll see what reaction this brings." Picking up a small limb about two feet long he brushed it over some dead leaves and then after a moment shook it back and forth. This produced a dry rattling sound.

"I wonder how long he's going to eat them blasted berries." A voice came from the space between the logs.

Virg rattled his stick again then tossed a pebble off to another pile of leaves. He was rewarded by seeing the exposed boot move.

"Sure is a nice place to watch the trail from." Virg spoke in a casual voice.

There was a period of silence.

"Who's there? Show yourself. What are you doing slipping up on people?"

"Just curious about why anyone would be watching the trail. Sure be a good place for a bushwhacker. Say, why

43

don't you come on out? I won't bite you."

"You can't see me either. I think I'll just stay put and you can move on off."

Virg rattled his stick in the dry leaves again. "I think I'll just sit here and see what happens when that big rattler joins you in there."

"What big rattler?" The voice was a bit shaky. "I didn't see any sign of snakes around here."

"Thought you might of heard him. He'd probably run from you if he spotted you in time but you never can tell about them. It may have a den under one of the limbs."

"Come on show yourself, then I'll get up and out of here." The voice coaxed.

"I'm not the one lying in a suspicious manner overlooking the trail so you get up and don't make any quick moves. Looks like we have a stand off. I know I won't shoot you but am not sure what you're up to."

There came a laugh from between the logs. "I'll just sit tight and you move on off and take your chances. If a rattler comes in here I can handle him."

Virg thought this over a minute.

"Wonder what would happen if some of these piles of leaves should catch fire. They look like they would burn right up to those logs. Do you reckon those logs would burn? Mister, I would suggest you come out if you don't want me to try them. I don't plan to wait very long, so you better decide in a hurry."

"You're bluffing. Start your fire."

Virg pulled a few tufts of dry grass and tied them around a handful of leaves, and fastened them to an arrow.

"Last chance, fellow."

"You're bluffing." The voice now had a sneer in it. "When you raise up to throw anything I'll see you."

"We'll see if you do." Virg replied.

Lighting a match Virg set the bundle on the end of the arrow afire. Barely pulling the bowstring back he looped the arrow into the space between the logs but away from the man.

He was soon rewarded by the sight of smoke rising from

the spot.

"You blasted heathen, you'd burn a man alive. Okay I'm coming out." He rose up from behind the log with his rifle ready for action. There was nothing to shoot at.

Virg had been anticipating some such action. This fellow didn't give up easy. He had moved from where he was and now was behind solid cover.

"Put the rifle down and then shuck that pistol and move away from them. I don't like bushwhackers."

"How do I know you won't shoot me?"

"If I'd wanted to shoot you, you'd be dead now, so do as I tell you or I will shoot and then we'll argue about it later."

The man glanced around. If he could only spot this one. They had said he was like an Indian.

"Last warning." Virg eared back the hammer on his pistol. The click was loud in the silence.

The man leaned his rifle against the log then placed his pistol on top of the log.

"Back away from them. I wouldn't want you to do anything foolish. Toss my arrow out here also."

When the man did as told, Virg stepped out into the open, walked over and picked up the two weapons keeping a close watch on the man.

"Now you can come out of your hiding place. As soon as my horse gets here we'll go get yours and head for town. You're lucky I don't just shoot you and leave you here for the buzzards." He gave a whistle and Buck popped out of the trees below and headed straight for them.

The man that stepped out was a surly looking fellow with narrow features. The most noticeable thing were his shifty eyes set deep in their sockets with heavy brows overshadowing them.

"I guess you have a name or do you want me to call you whatever comes to mind?" Virg had a smile on his face. "It might not be very complimentary."

"My name is Sutton if it's any of your business."

"Well Mr. Sutton, let's get your horse and take a ride into town."

"I wasn't planning on going to town."

45

"You're to jumpy to leave out here by yourself. I don't trust you enough to ride off and let you have that nice looking rifle. You might take a notion to shoot something. I wouldn't want that something to be me so just move ahead of me down to your horse. We'll ride into town. I'm not bad company when you get to know me. Keep your hands in sight."

"I'll go but there'll be some explaining for you to do when we get there."

They headed down toward the trees where the stranger had his horse. He seemed to be having trouble walking as he stumbled a couple of times on rocks and once as he stumped his toe on a dead limb.

"There's someone over there." Sutton said suddenly pointing with his left hand in that direction. He stumbled as he did and appeared to try to catch his balance bringing his right hand in front of his body. He went to one knee and turned with a small pistol in his hand. "Now we'll see." He snarled.

POW!

"Oooh. oaah. Blast you."

"You better learn to shoot first and talk later." Virg admonished him. "Those fake stumbles didn't fool me. I guess I should have warned you." He had seen the move and ended the problem with a bullet through the right shoulder of the bushwhacker. "I should've put it through your head but I'd like to know who you work for."

"I don't work for anybody right now." Sutton turned white and sagged onto a rock in the shade of a tree. "I need a doctor."

"Let's get you on your horse then it'll be a short trip to town. Someone there will know your boss."

"I told you. I don't have a boss."

"Here put this clean rag over that hole in your shoulder."

Virg gave him a boost into the saddle, mounted Buck and they headed toward Paden with Sutton in the lead.

Sutton almost fell a couple of times as they rode in. He was almost out of it by the time they arrived in Paden. He was reeling in the saddle.

46

"What the matter with this fellow?" Marshall Simmons asked as they pulled up in front of the doctor's office. His office was next door.

"Mr. Sutton ran into a bullet. He probably needs to see the doctor." Virg informed him.

"I was just sitting up there looking the country over and this kid sneaked up behind me. Then he shot me. I didn't do anything to him. You ought to arrest him, Marshall." Sutton could talk even though it took some effort.

Chap 8

"Is this true, Virg?" Simmons had a dark look on his face. "This could be serious. You can't just run around shooting people."

"Well, if you just tell pieces of a story it might be true but not tell the truth of the matter. He managed to leave out some pretty important information."

"Did you sneak up behind him?" Simmons asked.

"Sure did."

"Did you shoot him?"

"Sure did."

A small crowd had gathered. Newt Smith, Molly Brown and Joe Hale were among them. They all overheard the entire exchange including Sutton's story.

"Virg wouldn't shoot anyone without a reason. You know that, Marshall." Newt said quickly.

"That's right. We know Virg better than that." Molly chimed in. "We all do."

There was a murmur from the crowd.

"What's going on?" A man asked as he walked up to the crowd. "What's going on anyway?"

"Hold it a minute. I'll ask the questions." The marshal was getting a little red in the face. "This man said Virg sneaked up behind him and shot him. You just heard Virg admit the same thing. Now, in my book that makes it serious. We can't have people running around shooting folks, even Virg."

47

"You mean to tell me that you believe this wild story?"
Newt was furious. "Let me talk to Virg a minute while you
get this fellow patched up."

"Who needs patched up?" Doctor Dovell joined the
gathering crowd.

"I do." Sutton ground out. "This kid sneaked up
behind me and shot me."

"Somebody bring him on into the office. Molly you
can help me. You need some more nurse training." Doc
Dovell headed for his office.

Molly stepped over to Virg before going. "Don't you
worry, we'll help you."

"Ask Doc not to tell Sutton anything about the wound
but how to take care of it. It could be important." Virg told
her. "His story has some holes in it."

"Okay, I better get on over there." She hurried after the
Doctor who had stopped to talk to a couple of people.

Marshall Simmons walked over to where Newt and Joe
had joined Virg. "As soon as that man is patched up we'll
have a hearing about this in the courtroom. I'll get some
men together to decide. You could be in bad trouble so
don't go anywhere."

"I'll be here." Virg assured him. "I want to get the
straight truth of this out."

"Marshall, that bunch of men better be folks we can
count on to be fair." Newt told him. "We'll be there to
make sure of it."

It seemed like the whole town had turned out to listen
to the hearing. There was a lot of conversation going on.

Most of it favored Virg but there were some that had
their doubts about him.

"For a youngster, he's been in a few shootings. It
might be he's getting out of hand." One man offered his
thoughts.

"If you knew him you wouldn't say that." Another
responded. "That's a good family. He sure helped to save
all of us when that bunch tried to run us off our land."

"Sometimes good ones go bad."

"Wait until you hear the whole story."

48

Bang! Bang! Marshall Simmons rapped the table top with his gun butt. "Everybody be quiet so we can get this over with. Doc, is this Sutton fellow able to tell his story?"

"He should be, Marshal. He had a couple of drinks and he's ready I think."

"Are you ready, Sutton?" Marshal Simmons was enjoying the role of judge. He pointed to a group sitting in chairs to his left. "These six men will listen and then tell us what they think. Sit right up here in this chair and tell your story."

Sutton moved to the front and sat down. "You want me to tell it all, just like it happened?"

"That's right. Tell it all." Simmons answered.

"I was settin up on this ridge looking the country over when this kid sneaked up behind me. Then he shot me. I don't know why. You heard him admit it. I can't think of anything more that needs telling. From where I come from they put people in jail or hang them for doing stuff like that." He slowly surveyed the crowd.

There was some muttering as people started to discuss this information.

Bang! Marshal Simmons brought his gun butt down. "Keep it quiet. These six men will do the deciding."

Molly and Newt leaned their heads together. They had worried looks on their faces.

"Mr. Simmons, sir." Virg stood up and spoke to the Marshal.

"You'll get your chance when he's through." He turned to Sutton. "Anything else?"

"No. It's clear enough. I said he shot me and he says he shot me, I have this bullet hole in me so what more is there to tell? Let him have his say before we hang him." Sutton started to get up out of his chair. He made a sympathetic figure with his right shoulder tightly bound.

"Hold it. Stay right where you are." Virg was still standing. He turned to Marshal Simmons. "I want to ask him some questions."

Sutton had dropped back into his seat. "Do I have to answer his questions?"

49

Marshal Simmons looked over the crowd as a ripple went through it. "No but it'll look mighty odd if you don't. I'd suggest that you answer them."

"I'm not afraid of his questions. Let's get it over with." Sutton, though pale, had a smirk on his face.

Virg walked forward facing Sutton. "As I said outside a while ago. You can make some true statements that don't tell the truth of a matter. Let's see if we can fill in the parts you left out."

"I thought you were going to ask me some questions not make a speech."

"Okay, you say you were sitting up there admiring the country, is that right?"

"I told everybody that a while ago."

"You were sitting not lying up there?"

"That's right. Don't try to cross me up. I know what I was doing."

"A man telling the truth can't be crossed up. Just wanted to make sure."

"Well now you're sure."

"Maybe, maybe not, what was in front of you?"

"A log. A dead log."

"What was in back of you."

"Nothing."

"Better be sure. We have some pretty good sign readers around here. We can send some of them up there to take a look. Think it over carefully." Virg paused. "What was behind you? It was a big rock wasn't it?" He shot the question at Sutton, pointing his finger and stamping his foot with a bang.

"No it was the other part of the log." A startled Sutton dropped his eyes as he realized his error.

"Another piece of the same log?"

"Yeah, another piece of the log." Sutton snarled. The effects of the bullet were wearing off.

The crowd buzzed. Eyebrows raised.

"Could you see the trail?" Virg asked in a calm voice. "Remember we can go up there and check."

"Yeah, I could see the trail."

"Pretty good?"

50

"Yeah, good enough."

"Could anyone on the trail see you?"

"How would I know?" Sutton retorted. " I didn't go down there to check it out."

"So you didn't check it out. Okay where did you leave your horse?"

"Tied to a tree."

"Could it be seen from the trail? Think it over."

"I guess it couldn't."

"It was pretty well hidden wasn't it?

"I just tied it to a tree."

"Don't forget, that can be checked."

"It was in the shade. It could be overlooked."

"What did you have with you while you were admiring the country from a spot where you could watch the trail?"

"I told you I was just settin there."

"You weren't afraid that your horse would move against a tree and break your rifle while you were up there admiring the country? Seems real careless to me. Most fellows would be smarter than that." Virg gave Sutton a scornful look

"I'm not that dumb. I had the rifle with me."

"Not much of a rifle is it?"

"Lot you know. You won't find a better one. I can hit what I shoot at no matter what the distance."

"You were just sitting up there with that fine rifle, minding your own business and I sneaked up on you and shot you. Is that right?"

"That's right."

"You didn't try to shoot me with that fancy rifle?"

"You know I didn't. If I had you wouldn't be here."

"How could I shoot you if you had that good rifle?"

"You know you sneaked up behind me and shot me. You admitted that."

"Let's see. I sneaked up behind you and shot you. Did I give you any warning?"

"You didn't say a thing. Just shot me."

"From behind?"

"That's right you sneak. You sneaked up behind me

51

and shot me. I didn't know you were anywhere around."

"I must have shot you in the back."

"That's right you back shooter."

The crowd buzzed. Looks were exchanged.

Newt and Molly really looked worried.

Virg shrugged his shoulders. "Guess we have your story pretty straight don't we?"

"You sure do." Sutton said with a satisfied smirk. "Is that all?"

"All the information I want." Virg told him.

"Well men, what do you say?" Marshal Simmons asked the six.

"Wait just a minute." Virg said. "Now I'll tell it as I saw it. That's his story. I say it was a bit different."

"Let's hear Virg's version." Newt shouted. He was quickly joined by others.

"All right, we'll let him have his say." The marshal agreed. He thought he had heard enough. He was ready to arrest this young badman.

"You folks know I might be a bit skittish after being shot from ambush a while back. As I was coming to town Buck and I decided someone was up on this ridge with the trail in his sights. We hopped into some brush and I made my way up to the most likely spot."

"You mean you just walked up there to the place? If this fellow meant to shoot you looks like he could have done it while you made your way up the ridge." Marshal Simmons looked around the crowd. "How about it?"

There was a murmur from the crowd.

"Marshal, I'm not the smartest person in the world but I know better than that. You heard him say that I sneaked up behind him." Virg explained. "He was right about that part. Everybody here knows I can move fairly well in the woods."

There were many nods of agreement.

"Doesn't look like you are helping your cause much." Simmons responded. "Admitting that you slipped up behind him like he says."

"Let Virg tell the story and quit butting in unless you are trying to keep the truth from coming out." Newt was red

52

faced as he spoke.

"Okay, finish your story." Simmons snapped with a frown.

"Well I used some of my skills to get up the hill and then locate Mr. Sutton's horse on the back side of the slope. It was pretty well hidden. I eased on up the ridge from there until I was behind the place where I thought he was. I couldn't locate him so I made my way to the other side of the spot. Still couldn't locate him for sure. He hides pretty good."

"You mean you did all that shuffling about and he didn't see you or hear you? Surely you don't expect us to believe that." The marshal frowned as he said this.

Newt stood up again. "You want to go out and check his ability in the woods, Marshal?"

"All right let him continue." Simmons was pretty surly with his statement.

"I did all that moving around. He must have been looking the other way. The trail was down that direction. Some things told me where he was so I moved back directly behind him. I spotted his foot. It was on the ground like he was lying down."

"He said he was sitting down. Okay, Okay, go ahead." Simmons sat back down.

"I did some things to get him to move or maybe come out. He didn't so I spoke up. After we talked a while he decided to come on out."

"He tried to set me afire. The heathen." Sutton snapped. I could have been burned alive."

"Thought I just shot you without warning?"

Sutton didn't answer but realized he'd made another mistake. He drew several curious looks.

Virg Continued "I'll admit I had to persuade him some. He gave me his rifle and pistol to hold while we walked down to his horse so we could ride on into town together." Virg paused. He looked over the crowd.

Some had puzzled expressions. Evidently they weren't used to this kind of testimony about a gun fight between two people.

"You mean he gave you his guns? Just like that? If he

53

wanted to shoot you why didn't he do it?"

"He couldn't see me at the time. Well, I kinda talked him into giving the guns to me. He walked in front of me down to his horse."

They all looked a bit skeptical about him talking Sutton into giving up his guns. They had never heard of such a thing. This was getting interesting.

"Is that when you shot him?" Someone in the back of the room called.

"Yes, but not in the back. He didn't give me all his guns as he had one under his shirt I guess. He jerked it out as he pretended to stumble, whirled around and yelled 'now we'll see' as he pointed the thing at me. I shot him before he could shoot me. We came on into town and you know the rest."

Marshal Simmons stood up. "Sutton repeat your statement"

"He slipped up behind me and shot me without a warning. He shot me in the back." Sutton shot a confident look at the crowd. "Now you can hang him or put him in jail so he can't be ambushing people."

"We heard both sides. Looks like one's word against the other. Sutton was shot. Virg admits shooting him. Simple enough I guess." Simmons turned to the six men. "I guess it's--"

"Not so fast, Marshal Simmons." Virg interrupted. "He says I shot him in the back. I say I didn't. Let's hear what Doctor Dovell has to say. He's familiar with gunshot wounds."

"If you men think that will help any, we'll hear the Doctor. Come on up Doc." The Marshal sat back down.

Doctor Dovell was a heavy built man in his late forties. He stood facing the crowd. "I need a man to come up here so I can show you about the wound." He soon had Newt seated in front of him with his shirt off.

"The bullet went through the lower part of the shoulder from up here to a place down the back. If he was shot in the back it would have had to have been like this." He took a string and traced the path of the bullet as Newt assumed almost every conceivable position.

54

"Looks like he would've had to be up a tree to get a wound like that or lying down with his head a lot lower than his feet." One of the men on the panel exclaimed.

"He could have been sitting on a high place and been shot from below." Another added.

"The bullet didn't take that path." The doctor told them. "I said if he was shot in the back that would have been the way it was. He was shot from the front."

"How do you know that?" Simmons asked.

"A bullet will carry pieces of cloth into a wound where it enters. There won't be any in the wound where it comes out. Molly can back me up when I say that we cleaned cloth out of the front of his shoulder. He was shot from the front from a position from above." He had Newt take a crouching position and then traced the path of the bullet from the front. "No doubt about it." Doc was quite pleased with his little demonstration. "Put your shirt on Newt, we're through."

"Is that all, Doc."

"No. You should see the fancy little holster Mr. Sutton has inside his shirt."

Sutton turned a few shades lighter in color.

"Well men?" The marshal asked.

"Sutton lied." The spokesman of the group said. "Maybe we should find out why he was up there."

The rest of the men nodded in agreement.

"I guess you are free to go." Marshal Simmons told Virg.

"One of these days I'd like to hear more about how you talked him out of all those things." The spokesman of the jury called after Virg as he turned to go. "It beats all. He says the man couldn't see him."

"Thanks Marshal." Virg said as he accompanied Newt and Molly out to the front of the building.

"Boy, I thought you were in trouble for a while there. That Doc sure straightened things out." Newt told him.

"I knew all along that it would be fine." Molly informed Newt.

"Gosh, women know everything to hear them tell it." Newt threw up his hands as he said this.

"She's a pretty smart girl. She sticks pretty close to

you I see." Virg grinned at the blushing Newt.

"My time will come." A voice said. They turned to see Sutton glaring at Virg. He seemed almost recovered from the wound.

"My goodness!" Molly exclaimed.

Virg stepped up close to Sutton who gave a step backward. "If you want to declare war it's okay with me. The next time I catch sight of you I'll figure you want to shoot it out so I'll act accordingly. Might even decide to take the war to you."

"I might not be so easy the next time. I don't take to being made a fool of." Sutton snarled. "You better watch yourself. Things can happen to families."

"I'm going to take that as a threat to my folks so I guess the war is on. If you're still in this country in three days it will be all right to hunt you down like a mad dog." Virg smiled at him. "It might be fun to be on the other end of the game."

"I can't just quit my job and run. I need to work." Sutton didn't seem so confident all of a sudden.

"How do you have a job and no boss? Remember telling me that? Three days, starting now." Virg's eyes fairly shot fire at him.

Sutton stalked off mumbling to himself.

"Come on Newt. I have some things to talk over with you and Joe."

"Do you mean to start hunting him if he's still around?" Newt raised the question. "That doesn't sound at all like you, Virg"

"Men like him make life miserable for honest folks and don't seem to worry at all about their feelings. Maybe if he thinks he better keep an eye on his back trail it'll keep him on edge a bit. It might make him less efficient at his work." Virg grinned at Newt.

"I guess that's some kind of answer but I still don't know if you're taking after him or not."

"Maybe he won't know either. I just can't figure out right now why he's here."

"Maybe it has to do with some of the earlier problems. Someone of the old bunch may have hired him."

"And left the country? I doubt it. He may represent a new threat."

"Joe, that's the story. Zach can be relied on to tell it right. He's a pretty smart fellow and doesn't miss much." Virg had explained to Joe and Newt about the two settlers that had signed over their places and taken off. "The thing for all of us to do is keep hunting ways to find a weak spot in their armor."

"What about this trial that Dan faces?" Joe showed his agitation. "I won't stand by and let them send him to jail or maybe worse. The rest of the family want to take action. They don't like the idea of a Hale being in jail."

Newt glanced at Virg. "Joe, you folks don't do anything rash before you absolutely have to. You'll all wind up on the owl-hoot trail. Try to hold them down and give us a chance to get to the bottom of this mess. We'll all be doing our best."

"I don't know how long I can hold them in. You know how wild some of the boys can be, especially when they are being treated unfairly. Dad may be the worse one of the bunch."

"The most unfair thing that could happen would be for all of you to wind up as outlaws." Newt pointed out. "That's what'll happen if you do the wrong thing. Lets try it legally first. What do you think, Virg?"

"Well, let's take a look at what has happened so far. Two fellows give up without a fight. Now the same thing happens to the most honest guy in the territory. What do you think would be the result if he should be convicted?"

Newt and Joe looked at each other.

"If he was found guilty the rest of the people would probably figure they didn't have much chance if anything like that happened to them." Newt said. "We better not let that happen or we have big trouble on our hands."

"I say let's stop it before things go any further." Joe added. "We could hit back at them. That might back them

57

off and to look things over a bit."

"The problem with taking things into your own hands is that you're going outside the law. What could help the leaders of this more than to say to the authorities that they were trying to do everything legal and the settlers started a shooting war?" Virg paused and looked at both men.

"That's what I've been saying." Newt responded. "We need to stay inside the law."

"I guess you're right but it's going to be hard for us to stand by and let Dan down." Joe looked pretty discouraged. "The family won't stand for it. Deke is spoiling for a fight. He's been ready every since Zeb was killed by that back shooter."

"Joe, let's do all we can to follow the legal path. Think what would have happened to me if I hadn't faced this Sutton. If we can beat them in court things will favor us. Right now we need time. Let's make a deal to get Dan out until the trial. He can put up something to satisfy the owner of the cattle to guarantee him showing up." Virg was thinking of a plan. He smiled as he contemplated the reaction from Averill if it worked.

"What are you thinking about? You get that silly grin on your mug, then usually come up with some wild scheme." Newt shook his head and grimaced. "I'll admit that sometimes they work out all right. Do you think Mr. Averill is the man behind this?"

"I'm not sure but I'm fairly well convinced that he's the one we have to deal with even if there is someone behind him. After the last push by that judge, anybody behind the scenes will be extra careful. Let's get something organized to keep an eye on them."

"How are we going to do that?" Joe wanted to know. "They'll probably shoot any of our people caught spying on them. We don't have anybody good enough at scouting to keep out of sight."

"Yeah, we need some scouts that can keep under cover but would not cause a great deal of alarm if spotted." Newt added. "Virg, you could probably do the spying but they would be on guard if they ever spotted you. Any other ideas?"

"I believe we can get John Billy, one of the Sands boys and maybe one of the Harjos. They are all Creeks so it wouldn't be unusual for them to be hunting in this area. The Creeks are interested in keeping the settlers here. That is part of their larger plan. They don't want the cattlemen to get a foothold."

"This may take some time and Dan is waiting to be tried. We can't leave him in jail to much longer or our bunch will break him out." Joe reminded them. "They're getting restless."

Newt scratched his head. "How can we get Dan out until the trial? I can't think of anything."

"Me neither." Joe added. "I guess we'll just have to break him out."

"Quit talking like that. Remember the idea I suggested just a few minutes back? I've read about people putting up something valuable to guarantee that they would show up for their trial. If they don't show up they lose the thing."

"Dan doesn't have anything valuable." Joe stated. "He sure doesn't have any money and no one would lend him any under the present circumstances."

Newt just shrugged his shoulders.

"You two surprise me. You could be standing on the biggest thing around and not see it. What does Dan have that certain parties want to get their hands on? What have all of us been struggling to hold onto?"

Joe and Newt shouted. "Land! Gosh sakes. How blind can we be?"

"That's right. That's what they want so it'll be risky. They'll do all they can to make sure he doesn't show up until it's to late."

"We need to come up with some way of messing up their plans if that happens. Say, Joe, you get to visit with Dan. Wonder what would happen if Dan had done a lot of bad things to people and he had promised to pay them for these bad things? Three or four would be enough. And just suppose that he had done these things before these stolen cattle showed up. Get the idea?"

"Virg, one of your wild schemes is going to blow up in your face one of these days." Newt laughed. "Let's give it

59

a try. Joe get Dan to sign some papers and we'll round up some fellows we can trust to help us pull it off."

"Marshal, are you telling me that this Hale is willing to sign over his place so that he forfeits it if he doesn't come in at the time of his trial?" Averill could hardly keep from showing his satisfaction. He had been having his men spread the idea that he could be persuaded to drop the charges. "We have to word this paper right so he can't back out."

"That's what he said. You can come over and make sure the statement is properly written out as you're the one that the cattle belonged to." Marshal Simmons explained. "We can do it any time. Now if you like."

"I'll be over in about thirty minutes. We better get that lawyer to draw up the paper."

"What lawyer? Nelson's not here right now."

"That's okay. I just saw that fellow, Garrison in the office he uses when he has business over here."

"Good, I'll get him and we'll all meet in the jail in thirty minutes." Simmons hurried out.

Averill stepped into the next room. "Bart, you and Mitch heard the deal. Now I want you to scout around and see if you can catch some of the others that are stealing our cattle."

"Okay, Boss." Bart motioned to Mitch.

"When do I get to take that kid out? Nobody makes a fool out of me and gets away with it." Mitch turned red as he recalled the results of his encounters with Virg.

"We have more important things to do right now." Averill informed him. "You won't be much good to me if you are in jail for shooting some kid. Besides you haven't done very well so far when you took after him."

"I'll show him something for sure." Mitch snarled. "You just wait and see."

"Yeah, I owe him too." Bart put in.

"Now you two get this straight, we are not out to settle personal scores. You can do that when the time comes but right now you follow orders. If you foul this up by flying off the handle I'll deal with you myself and you know I can do

60

it too."

"Right, we'll do it your way. I can wait."

Averill gave them a slight sneer. "Three of you had him didn't you?"

Mitch and Bart stomped out of the room. Averill gave them a long look. Three grown men against one kid and they came out looking like they were fighting each other. Under his breath he said. "These are my best? Have mercy on me."

He called after them. "Hey, come along and see how things are supposed to be handled." The two gunmen followed him as he headed for the courthouse.

Averill's crew walked into the courtroom next to the jail. Marshal Simmons had his shotgun and was keeping a close eye on Dan Hale who sat in a chair drawn up at the table. Garrison, the lawyer, sat at the side of the table. Joe Hale, Virg and Newt Smith stood to one side.

Garrison cleared his throat. "Gentlemen, I understand Mr. Hale wants to guarantee his appearance in court by putting up his property for forfeit in case he fails to appear. Is that right, Mr. Hale?"

"That's right." Dan Hale answered. "I'll put it up but I don't think it's right to make a man risk everything he owns. His word should be enough for anybody."

"Now, Mr. Averill, you have an interrest in this case so if you object to this you just say so." Garrison looked up.

"Just make the title out to me and everything will be fine with me." Averill informed him.

"I want to put up my place to guarantee I'll be here. I won't have anything if it's signed over to him. If I show up the place is still mine so I don't want some other name on the title. I'll just stay in jail until this is cleared up."

Averill was seeing his chance slip away. "I'm not willing to see him freed if there's not some way I can be sure I don't come out holding the sack. An empty sack at that."

"Could it be worded so that if Dan forfeits his place that those having claims against him could have the judge settle it by giving them the property?" Virg asked. "Dan doesn't owe money to anybody does he, Joe?"

Averill cast a questioning look in his direction.

61

"Dan is to hard headed to borrow money. It sure keeps him from building up his herd." Joe looked down at the floor as if he had made a big mistake. This was about stealing cows. "Everybody knows about him not borrowing money."

Garrison glanced from Averill to Dan Hale. "I can make it out so that he forfeits his land to anybody having a claim against him for his wrong doing, if he doesn't show up. That way it won't look like I have given you a reason to keep him from getting here."

"I don't much like it but I could sign in a case like that." Dan muttered. "If I've done anybody harm I guess I ought to pay for it."

Averill could hardly keep a straight face. This was the one that never did anything to anybody. "But I have been wronged by him. If he fails to show upI win. If he shows he'll be found guilty and I'll have a claim anyway." He thought to himself.

"Mr. Averill?" Garrison asked. "It's up to you."

Averill acted as if he was thinking it over. Finally he said. "It's not entirely the way it should be but I'll go along with it. That place is mine though if he doesn't show. Might be better if he was hung. I'd rather see that done."

Joe growled something and started to move forward.

Mitch and Bart stepped apart with hands on their guns.

"Well that settles that." Newt said as he quickly stepped in front of Joe, blocking his way. "Nothing like settling everything peacefully."

The paper was soon prepared and signed by Dan. Averill and Newt signed as witnesses.

Chap 10

The mood had become fairly jovial with small talk being exchanged.

"Mr. Averill, I bet you have quite a bit of trouble with people that steal your cattle. What is the proper proceedure for dealing with people that steal your property?" Virg asked. He looked puzzled.

"Take them to court and let the law handle them. That's what I've done. You have to stay within the law. We can't have people taking the law into their own hands." Averill was pleased to be able to establish his position of observing the law. "Anybody steals from me will pay the price in a court of law."

"Thank you sir. It's good to have honorable men in the neighborhood. Say, I noticed one of your men had one of his ears hurt. He must be really unlucky because my horse kicked him the other day. Now this. Looks like something bit him." Virg acted as if he was completely innocent and deeply concerned about Mitch's welfare.

Mitch was about to explode.

Averill could hardly keep from laughing. He shot a restraining look at Mitch and shook his head. The nerve of this kid baiting Mitch, or was it stupidity. He wasn't sure which.

"He ran into some difficulty the other day. I didn't get a full explanation but my bet is that Mitch can take care of the problem if it comes up again." Averill put a lot of emphasis on 'take care' and 'the problem'.

"Must remember to do it in court though. That's the legal thing to do isn't it?" Virg reminded him. "We have to do things according to the law. I believe what you said was something like that. At least close."

Averill lifted an eyebrow. "This kid may not be as dumb as I first thought." He said to himself. He motioned to his men and they swaggered out of the room. He had things where he wanted them. "Maybe Hale won't show up."

Virg walked out with Newt and Joe.

"Did you get some fellows signed up with claims agains Dan?" He asked.

"Yep, and they're dated before this paper he just signed. We even put the time of day on them." Newt responded. "Might be interesting for a judge to decide if it comes to that."

"Boss, I've taken about all I can stand off that smart mouthed kid. He opens his mouth again and he's going to get smoked." Mitch was still steamed about the reference to being horse kicked and having a snake take a chunk out of his ear.

"You can have your fun but hold it up for a while. At least don't do it out in front of everybody. We don't want the whole territory up in arms. You and Bart go on with the plan to catch cattle thieves. You know what I mean." Averill was really pleased by the recent developments.

"He just gets under my skin somehow."

"Mitch, you'll get your chance. Right now we better do what the boss says. When we get the job done we can have our fun." Bart was having trouble keeping a straight face as he remembered Mitch's problem with the snake.

The three mounted and headed for headquarters. When they reached there Averill dispatched a man to go after a judge. "No need putting this off." He told his crew. He called the man aside that was to ride to Okmulgee for the judge.

"The man we want is Judge Harvey. I know him and he's tough on cow thieves. Look him up and tell him there will be a good fee for him to hold some trials over here. Let him know that there may be several cases." Averill informed him. "And Dobe, don't do any talking to anybody else about this."

"Boss, you're sending the right man." Dobe said as he rode off. "I know how to keep my lip buttoned so don't worry about it."

"Virg, you're going to get into trouble one of these days. That Mitch looked like he could happily shoot you on sight." Newt was busy admonishing his friend to be more careful in his dealings with the gun hands.

"A person doesn't think as well if he is busy being mad about something." Virg explained. "Those fellows will be more dangerous to us if they stick to their orders. They're more likely to make mistakes if they're trying to prove how tough they are."

"I better get Dan out to the place so we can keep our eyes on him." Joe Hale informed them. "We better come up with something to prove that he's not guilty when he has

64

to stand this framed up trial."

"We need to do something to stir them up some."
Virg told him. "Newt and I'll see if we can come up with
something. You just look after Dan."

Joe and Dan soon rode off toward the Hale family home
place.

"What are we going to do to stir them up? They'll
have a judge here in a few days and he'll set a date for the
trial. Can we do anything but wait?" Newt was racking his
brain for any possible out.

"People have a high opinion of that old man, Arthur
Higgins, don't they?" Virg asked. "He doesn't often speak
out but when he does they listen. I wonder if we could plant
an idea with him. I believe he's interested in seeing that the
settlers are treated fairly."

"Yeah, he's well thought of and is ready to help in
anyway he can. It must be something that wouldn't make
folks doubt him. He might be willing to take part in a little
harmless skullduggery as he has been known to take the
wind out of some pompous windbag now and then. He has
a pretty good sense of humor." Newt looked at his
companion with a question on his face.

"We might be able to delay things a bit if he'll go
along with what I'm thinking. Let's go have a visit with
him." Virg said as he headed for the favorite hangout of Mr.
Higgins.

They found him sitting under a tree on his favorite
bench.

"Hello there, young fellers. What kinda mischief are
you up to? I've been hoping to have some company. By
the way you sure handled that Sutton in fine shape the other
day. I also saw that little deal you had with the Gannon
crew a while back. For a sprout you get around some." Mr.
Higgins indicated seats available on the bench. "Set and
visit a spell."

"Mr. Higgins, you know about Dan Hale and the
charges against him." Virg said. "I was wondering what
you think about it. Most people say you're pretty well
informed about things."

"That's a trumped up charge and most know it. But I

don't know what we're going to do to keep him from being hung." Higgins burst out. "I hope we can come up with something. He's a good man. All of the Hales are good people. He's the best of them in my opinion."

"If we could get some evidence to show doubt that he did it." Newt told him. "We've tried but haven't found anything yet."

"Mr. Higgins, you know about these trials and things. We would like for you to advise us about how to go about gaining time so we can look around some more. I have an idea but you know more about these things than we do."

Higgins looked pleased at the compliment. "Have to be honest. No crooked stuff. I won't be a party to anything crooked."

Virg spent a few minutes outlining his idea.

As he went on with the plan a grin began to spread across Higgin's face. He was laughing openly when Virg stopped talking.

"That could delay things all right. And no real harm done except to a few egos. Nothing crooked about it either. By golly, I'll even do my part by bringing it up. Ha, Ha. It'll be worth it to see the looks on their faces."

Might only delay things a few minutes but on the other hand." Higgins chuckled again as he ran the idea through his mind. "Count on me, now you fellows start hunting some way to free Dan Hale for good. He's a fine young man."

Virg and Newt left him chuckling to himself as they made their way to Newt's place.

"Well where do we start?" Newt asked. "You seem to be full of ideas."

"I'll go get John Billy and the Sands boy. I believe the Harjo boy will help also."

"That means you'll be gone for about two days." Newt said as he stood outside his door. "I'll keep in touch with Mr. Higgins and see if I can find out anything else."

"Just don't let our scheme out about delaying things. We want it to be a complete surprise." Virg grinned. "That Mr. Higgins acted like he would enjoy himself. To many people think that the ordinary folks don't have enough thinking ability to do anything. People can't survive in this country without being able to do some thinking. You have to be pretty sharp just to stay alive. I'll be back as quick as I can."

He mounted Buck and rode off.

Chap 11

"Mr. Rankin, I really appreciate you giving me this work. Mandy and the kids were wondering how we were going to get money enough to buy supplies." Zach Vaughn looked up at Ab. When he smiled his pearly white teeth were like a flash of light in the middle of his black face. "You folks have been good neighbors to us."

"Zach, we consider you our best neighbor. Anything we have is yours for the asking." Ab had gotten over his reluctance to deal with black people.

"Don't you dare fail to call on us if you need help." Maw Rankin had come up as the two men talked. "By the way, Virg came by here on his way to Bill Smith's and he was saying that the Hales would hire some men to do some work pretty soon. I'll have to tell him to recommend you."

"I sure would be happy if you would, mam. I sure have made friends with the proper folks. That Virg is top notch with us. He treats us like regular folks." Zach said. "I better head for home."

"As much free work as he has done for us it gives me a good feeling to be able to pay him a little. We need lots of families like the Vaughns." Ab said as he watched Zach go out of sight.

Maw smiled at Ab. It was good to see the change in his attitude toward Zach and his family. "He's a good friend to all of us, especially Virg." She looked off into the distance. "I wonder what that boy is up to now? He said something about John Billy. Something to do with the Hales problems I bet. I can't help but worry about him."

"He does a pretty good job of looking after himself most of the time." Ab reminded her. "He sure has helped solve some of our problems."

67

"Anyway I'm going to say an extra prayer for him. He can use His help."

Ab knew who she referred to when she mentioned His help.

"Hello there, Bill. Don't you have anything to do but sit in the shade?" Virg had ridden up as Bill Smith stopped under a tree for a short rest.

"Dad-gum your hide. I take a minute to rest after working like a dog all day and some loafer that has nothing to do but ride around the country comes up and starts asking dumb questions." Bill gave a big laugh as he finished. "What brings you over this way? That is besides hunting a free meal. I see you're still riding that runt you call a horse. Why not get a real horse?"

"Guess I couldn't expect to be greeted friendly like by kin folk. I suppose they know me to well. But you'd think Buck would get some respect." Virg slid off of Buck and sat down next to Bill. They chuckled as they sat there looking at each other. They were both probably recalling the race against Harl Stone's prize horses. There was no doubt about strong family ties. These two were like brothers.

"How are the other Smith boys doing?" Virg asked. "Any more run ins with the Slaters?"

"No. People think the problems with the cattlemen are over since we had that big set to with them. You sure did a job for us in that mess."

"I hope it's over but we have a strange thing happening over our way." Virg went on to explain about the cattle stealing problems. "That's why I came over. We would like to get John Billy and that Sands boy to do some scouting for us. One of the Harjo's also if one's available."

"The way I heard it you didn't need any help to do your scouting. John says you're as good as any Indian. You must be good for him to say that."

"The people we want to keep an eye on would be suspicious of me. John and his friends wouldn't be suspected as they often go hunting. Besides I plan to be busy at something else." He grinned at Bill.

"That something probably spells misery for someone."

"If the time comes we may need some of you fellows to come over and back John Billy. You know most of the people won't accept an Indian's word in legal things unless he is backed by others. We also know that Indians and blacks are like all people. You have to take them as individuals. Most are good folks."

Bill laughed as he recalled the part John Billy and Zach Vaughn had played in their effort to trap a killer and bring a crooked judge to justice. "You're right there. I can get Seth James or Joe Nolan to come anytime. They still talk about how that Judge Holbrook was caught."

"I'll be back in time to eat. John Billy should be easy to find. He's probably been watching me for the last hour anyway."

"We can count on you being here at meal time. Boy I don't know how you keep from getting any bigger." Bill smiled as Virg rode off toward where he knew John Billy could be found, if he wanted you to find him.

"He'll find me instead of me finding him." Virg mused as he rode along. "Maybe I'll surprise him and slip up on him." He decided to do a little stalking. He removed Buck's bridle so he could graze freely then told him to stay there. Buck would come running at a signal.

He had gone but a short distance when he came to a small creek. He slid down the bank and moved up the stream looking for sign. He smiled to himself then said out loud. "I wonder where I could find that John Billy? I see his tracks here in this damp place." He moved silently on up the creek, making sure he would not be spotted if anyone was watching. This was managed by staying near the bank under overhanging brush.

Virg kept a watch for any birds or animals making strange moves. When he saw a bird he would stop and remain absolutely still while he checked the bird's movements. If it continues it's normal behavior he moved on. If it showed alarm he stayed still until he discovered what alarmed it.

"There's a red bird. I think I'll keep an eye on him for a while." He said under his breath. "They're pretty jittery but this one is staying low in the trees. He'll spot anything in the area. Lucky for me he came up ahead of me and moved in that direction."

He continued to watch the bird. It showed no alarm so he decided to follow it. "I better not get so involved with that bird that I forget to watch for the real danger. A fellow could lose his scalp that way." He mused.

Some folks had followed a sure watch dog right into a trap set by some cleverly hidden enemy.

The bird stopped his movements and sat still near the trunk of a tree. It kept moving it's head back and forth and was now completely quiet. It had been chirping at times as it moved along.

Virg was in a good position to watch so he remained still. "That bird is not bothered by me. Something else has him a bit spooked. He's not sure of it however. I'll just wait him out."

The bird remained still for several minutes then moved on but took a path to the right of the one followed previously.

"Might not mean a thing but when stalking enemies you better not make any mistakes. Let's try something." Picking up a couple of small pebbles and a dead stick about two feet long he placed one of the small stones on the end of the stick. Using this as a catapult he flipped the stone up through a small opening in the foliage. "We'll see if this gets any response." He had directed the projectile toward a good sized clump of shrubs to his left.

The bird stopped again when the pebble hit with a click. It could have been a foot striking a dry leaf or a dislodged object.

Virg heard a slight rustle in the area to the right of where the rock had landed. He remained frozen in place. There was no more movement or noise from there. "Could I have been mistaken?" He thought. "Some nerve of me trying to stalk a full blood Creek Indian. I'll go on with it though. The practice might come in handy."

There was the rustle again. He flipped another pebble in the same place as before. The bush moved a bit this time.

Virg moved away from the bush that had moved. He followed the path of the red bird for a short distance and then

70

moved silently to bring himself into a position where he could observe the bush . Nothing to be seen. Could the other party have moved. He looked both right and left.

"He didn't come back this way or we would have run into each other. He'll have to be where he was or to the right. He would have exposed himself if he moved anywhere besides there." Virg decided to wait him out.

Crash! A big rock landed in almost the same place that Virg had thrown the pebble.

"Come on out before a rock lands on your head. I know you're in there and you've no place to go." It was John Billy. He was right, anyone in the spot he had thrown the rock would have been at a bad disadvantage.

"John, you're getting a bit careless. I'm over here behind you." Virg spoke up but remained hidden.

"Dang you, Virg, you're getting to be more of an Indian than I am. I fell for your trick. What was it?" A sheepish looking John stepped out of the cover.

"I never was in that place. I flipped a couple of pebbles in there and moved in the opposite direction." He stepped out too. "I could never have done this if you had really thought you were in any danger."

"It's good of you to say that. I better remember this lesson though. It might be an enemy the next time. You didn't think you were in danger?"

"I knew that the country would be safe with you on the job." Virg said as he grasped both forearms of the young man that grinned at him.

They spent some time discussing what had been going on in the area. Virg filled him in about the problem concerning stolen cattle.

"We would like for you and a couple of your friends to come over our way and be scouts for us. John, I know your chief depends on you to keep your eyes on things around here."

"Nobody is supposed to know that. Not even my Indian friends. How did you find out?"

"Don't worry. It isn't known to others. I just figured it out. We want you and your friends to go on a hunting trip over our way. If you happen to spot anything useful to

71

us it would help." He gave John Billy a big grin.

"We'd like to do some hunting and that's a good place to start. Maybe I can improve my skill in the woods while I hunt."

"It might be useful if you practiced up on that skill you have with a pencil and paper too." Virg referred to John's ability to draw a picture of anything he saw.

"We'll be there. I may not be so easy to find the next time. Anyway I hope not."

Virg gave him a smile and a friendly punch on the shoulder. "I'd bet on that. Well I better get back to Bill's place or he won't feed me. You can leave any information for me at my folks. Newt Smith in Paden is someone you can trust too. See you in a few days."

John Billy had disappeared when he looked back.

"Is supper ready?" Virg asked as he rode up to where Bill was fastening his lot gate.

"I'm sure Doris has a bite ready. We thought you might do us a favor and not make it back." Bill laughed as he said this. "People say a bunch of things about you but none of them includes missing a meal, especially a free one."

"I knew you would be terribly disappointed if my company was missed at the table."

Buck was soon unsaddled and made happy with some oats to munch on. Then they headed for the house.

"Hi Doris, I sure hurried so I could get back for some of your good cooking. If anybody can cook better than Maw it has to be you."

"Virg, don't try to flatter me. You probably tell all the women that." Doris was obviously pleased by the remarks however. "We don't have anything fancy but it's good to have you here to share it."

Bill returned thanks and they spent the next few minutes enjoying a fine meal.

"It may not be fancy but it sure is good. It seems to agree with Bill all right. Can't remember when I ate better."

"Thank you. Come over and eat with us anytime you have a chance." Doris smiled as she gathered up the dishes.

"Dad-gum, Virg, you'll fix it where all us guys will

have to be passing out compliments right and left to our wives in order to keep on the good side of them." Bill laughed as he finished. "Now tell me more about this cattle stealing business."

Virg went over it again. "If any of your settlers in this area are charged with stealing cattle you need to examine the case carefully. It could be a new strategy to get our land. It may not be that at all. Maw says I am always suspicious of everything that has any thing different about it."

"Won't hurt to be prepared for any move that might be made. The land is such a big stake they may not give up easy. We whipped them down pretty good before but we can't count on them just tucking tail and running."

"Right. Those people don't lack for nerve or desire. Put the two together and they form a basis for a tough fight."

"I'll let Seth and Joe in on the idea and we'll keep our eyes and ears open."

"Good. I think I'll hit the road even though it is about dark. I want to go by Barney's and check with him. Nelda fixes a mighty good breakfast if I can remember right. She might even have some left overs for a late snack."

"I wouldn't think you'd mention food for a day or two after the way you put it away just now. We thought you'd spend the night and were worried about where we were going to find stuff to fix for breakfast." Bill gave a big laugh. "We'd be happy to have you stay though. You could take off early in the morning before we eat if you need to get back that soon. I was just kidding. Doris would cook half the day after the way you bragged on her food."

Chap 12

"I'll head on to Barney's place. I need to get back to Paden so we can get busy looking for ways to get Dan Hale out of his mess."

Virg soon had Buck saddled and headed across the country. It was pretty dark. The moon was up but a thin layer of clouds kept it from providing it's full light.

He had been moving along at a fair clip for some time.

73

"Their place is right over the next hill. It shouldn't take me long to get there now. I better make a little noise as I ride up as they could still be jumpy about night riders."

Suddenly Buck lifted his head and turned it to the left. His ears both shot forward. He gave a short snort. Something sure had his attention. Being part mustang, he didn't miss very many things that were out of the ordinary. His actions were not to be overlooked.

"What is it, boy? Let's pull up here in these trees and wait a spell." He reined Buck into a clump of trees and stopped with the horse facing in the direction he had looked. "Easy fellow. You still appear to be interested." They sat still for a few minutes.

He started to urge the horse on but then recalled other times when Buck had spotted things long before he was aware of them. He decided to wait a while longer. Then he heard it. Cattle moving. Would never have heard them if he hadn't stopped. "Good boy, Buck. Guess you're worth your oats after all."

Now why would cattle be moving at night. They wouldn't unless they were being driven. It was a rare thing for honest people to drive cattle at night.

"People that drive cattle at night can almost be counted on to be up to no good." Virg observed. "They're headed in Barney's direction. I don't think he'd welcome a bunch of cows eating his crops right now. I think I'll see what I can do to side track them."

Virg started off to get in front of the bunch. He planned to surprise them and break up the drive. His idea was to scatter the cattle and head them back where they came from.

"They don't seem to be headed toward the house or even where they will be heard from there. I wonder what's up." He said in a puzzled tone. "Barney doesn't have anything planted down that way." He sat still doing some thinking about the strange behavior of the drovers. Suddenly an idea hit him. "I'll bet that's it. Same deal."

"Maybe instead of a stampede we might fix up another little surprise if they plan what it looks like. I'll just trail along and see what's going on." He wasn't at all worried about them hearing him because of the noise of the cattle plus the fact of Buck's ability to move quietly. "I need to make sure of what they're up to anyway."

The small herd moved on. The riders were being as quiet as possible but it was an easy job to discover that only two were involved.

"That pen is just past that next bunch of trees. Move up to the right and then check to see if the gate is still open." One man gave instructions in a low voice.

"Keep your voice down."

"Okay, no need to yell."

The other man moved away and then pushed on ahead. He soon returned. "It's open. They're headed right for it." They kept the cattle moving.

Virg was trailing along in the tracks of the herd knowing the men would be watching to the front and sides. His danger of discovery would be greatest when they had the cattle penned and moved off. If this was done as he suspected, they would come back over the trail of the cows. He overheard their conversation.

"Let's get em in and make tracks."

"They're all in. I'll shut the gate."

"Don't forget how we're to leave our tracks heading for the house after following the trail back for a spell."

"How are we going to keep em from hearing us? We better not get to close."

"Won't matter if they do hear us. We just want to get our tracks covered by the trail. They won't show past his place. We'll follow his road out. "

Now Virg was satisfied about their plan. He eased off the trail the cattle had come down and sat still until the riders rode past and were out of hearing.

"Now, Buck old boy, if you and I work hard enough we may have a little surprise for these fellows. This is Barney's place but those aren't his cows. I'm sure no one around here is generous enough to make him a present of them either."

The next two hours were busy ones for Virg and Buck. Sometimes Virg worked on foot while Buck did his part as a member of the team. Finally their task was finished. They were both ready to settle down and rest for a while.

75

"Maybe Barney will offer us a bite when we get there."
They were now back on track to go on with their visit. He
decided to sing a little.

"I'm just a lonesome cowboy,
Riding along the trail.
Hoping for a friendly welcome
When you hear my weary wail."

"Hello the house. Hey Barney. Are you at home? I'm
tired and hungry."

"Never saw you when you weren't hungry, Virg. What
are you doing out at this gosh-awful hour? Don't you ever
sleep? Come on in but cut that gosh-awful noise out before
my horses stampede. I'll slip my shoes on and we'll put
your pony up. You are still riding that runt that runs like a
scared rabbit aren't you?"

"Yep, I still have Buck and we're kinda tired. I'll fill
you in on a little surprise that may come your way. You
have some mighty generous neighbors around here. Yes sir,
mighty generous."

"What the devil are you talking about? I have some
good neighbors but to call them generous, my foot."

"I'll tell you about your generous friends."

They put Buck into the shed and fed him some of
Barney's best hay. Virg explained the reason for the late
arrival. "Let's wait and see what happens. This might be
fun."

"No use upsetting Nelda about it right now" Barney
said. "We'll wait and see. Right now you better get a
little sleep."

"Boy, I sure did the right thing coming on over here for
breakfast." Virg said as he rubbed his full stomach. " Oh,
oh I forgot. Your cooking is supposed to be dangerous."

"It's dangerous all right. You might eat enough to
explode." Nelda laughed as she cleared the table. "Say,
here comes a bunch of riders."

"Looks like that new lawman from over at the small
town of Arlington." Barney stated as he started toward the
front porch. "I believe that's the new man that took over the
Harl Stone place with him."

There were five in the party. They drew up at the porch.

"You two stay in here and I'll see what they have in mind." Barney told Virg and Nelda. He stepped out on the porch.

"Nelda, don't get to excited about what they say." Virg told her. "Things may not be what they think."

"What are you talking about? We don't have anything to worry about from the law."

"Well, I think they had a little scheme in mind." He grinned at her. "The bait is out of the trap you might say. Barney can explain later. I think I'll step out and join the party."

She stared after him as he went through the door.

"I wonder what the devil he's talking about. It's probably some devilment he's been up to." Nelda moved closer to the front door in order to hear what was being said.

Virg eased out on the porch and leaned against one of the posts. He had placed himself in a strategic position.

"Go through that again." Barney was speaking to the man with the badge. "Mr. Taggert is missing some cattle, you say? I don't see what that has to do with me."

"I'm saying that someone stole cattle from my place and you have some tall explaining to do." A tall hook nosed man that must be Taggert said in a forceful manner. He was flanked by three men.

"Yeah, we're calling you a thief. What are you going to do about it?" One of the hands flanking Taggert moved to one side and shifted in the saddle making his intent obvious. He was of medium height and build. His most outstanding feature was a pair of icy green eyes. He looked like he could shoot a person without a qualm. There was no doubt what his job was.

"Bonior, you just hold on. We didn't come over here to start a fight." The marshal looked nervously at Taggert.

Taggert only smiled at him then glanced over at Bonior and shook his head slightly.

Virg had moved out on the porch and taken a position away from Barney. The men on horseback had to turn their heads away from Barney in order to see him clearly. He was

77

also partially behind a porch post. He knew what he planned if that Bonior fellow went for his six gun.

"Let's quit the stalling around and arrest Smith for stealing cattle, Jackson." Taggert addressed the marshal. "This kid was probably involved also so just take him along. Who is he anyway?"

"A cousin of mine." Barney informed him.

"Were you talking about me?" Virg asked.

"I'd say you were one of the two that drove them off." Bonior snarled.

"Gee, you're sure a friendly fellow. I bet that's why they brought you along." Virg chuckled and winked at Bonior.

"I don't see any cattle. Marshal, don't you have to have evidence before you arrest people?" Barney asked. "I thought that was the way it worked."

"Yes I do. These fellows claim they can show me the evidence so you two get your horses and come along." The marshal ordered. "That's the only way to clear it up."

"Always glad to cooperate with an officer of the law." Barney told him. "Come on Virg, let's show them that we respect the law."

"I'm ready to give the law a hand any time." Virg agreed. "We better get our horses. No telling how far these fellows want us to go."

Barney and Virg soon had their horses saddled and were ready to go.

"We'll be back in a little while, Nelda." Barney called as they rode off. "Don't worry about us."

"Jack, you and Ed lead the way." Taggert said to the two men that were with them. "Bonior, you can see that these two don't decide to skip out. You know what do do if they try it."

"Skip out and deprive ourselves of such delightful company? Why we wouldn't think of it. I don't often get to ride around with a nice friendly fellow like Mr. Bonior." Virg assured them with a grin. "I sure hope you find your cattle, Mr. Taggert."

Bonior glared at Virg and placed his hand on the butt of his pistol. "I wish you would try to skip. It would be my

78

pleasure."

Taggert looked at Virg with a puzzled expression. He was wondering what was wrong with this kid. He must be a little daft to bait Bonior this way.

"Marshal, the cattle are in a pen right past that bunch of trees just ahead." The man called Jack pointed in the direction he was headed.

They rode around the trees. The pen was in sight.

Virg grinned at Barney.

"I don't see any cattle." Marshal Jackson said as he moved on toward the pen. "The place looks empty to me."

"They are probably bedded down in that bunch of bushes at the back of the pen." Jack informed them. "You can be sure that they're here."

"There aren't any cows here." Jackson repeated. He looked at Taggert. "As you can plainly see, the place is empty. Not a single head of stock."

"Look at the tracks all over the place. I say arrest them because of that." Taggert demanded. "That's all the evidence you need."

Marshal Jackson looked a little doubtful.

"Are you telling him to arrest us for stealing cow tracks?" Virg asked. "Barney, have you been stealing this man's cow tracks? Shame on you if you have."

Barney was having a time keeping a straight face. "I never stole a cow track in my life." He said in a mild dead panned voice. "Never thought of them being worth much."

"Marshal, have you ever jailed any cow track thieves?" Virg asked.

"No, I never have." He was getting tired of the whole affair. "Don't plan to start neither."

Taggert pushed forward. "Them tracks mean that there have been cows here." He was getting pretty red in the face.

"Yeah, what more proof do you need?" Bonior chimed in. "Cows have been here and this is on Smith's place." His agitation was plain to see.

"Marshal, they're right. When you find cow tracks you can almost be sure that cows have been around. That's one of the sure signs. There are other signs they sometimes leave but they haven't accused us of stealing that, yet. You know what I mean don't you?" Virg was enjoying the looks passing among the Taggert crew. "May not be any around. My mistake, there's a pile of it right over there."

"You're right, Virg. Cows always leave tracks." Barney said with a chuckle. "I see that other evidence too. There's another bunch of it."

"If they can prove it's theirs, would you let them take it along with them, Barney?"

"Yeah, they can take it if they want to. It's good for putting on gardens and flower beds."

"They might take you to court, Barney. I wonder what argument they would put forth when the judge asked them what they were doing with it before you stole it." Virg looked as Taggert. "Mr. Bonior might suggest something to say in that case. He might be an authority on that kind of stuff. He was slinging some around earlier."

"I'll shut that smart mouth." Bonior was fairly fuming. "Why don't you run or are you to scared to run? When I get through with him I'll take care of you too, Smith."

"Why would anybody be scared of a nice fellow like you?" Virg asked him. "I might learn something by staying around. Like cows leaving tracks and things like that. It's not often you run into somebody that has knowledge about this kind of stuff."

Taggert signaled for Bonior to hold up on any action. Jackson was an honest lawman so they couldn't just shoot these two down unless they were ready to finish him also. He wasn't all that sure of Jack and Ed either.

Bonior was having difficulty containing himself. He wasn't used to people making smart talk to him without suffering the consequences.

Marshal Jackson turned to Taggert. "I can't arrest them on the things I see here. We might as well ride back to Arlington."

"They might want to take a shovel full of that evidence along to take to court." Virg offered.

"Shut your smart mouth." Bonior snarled.

Taggert was still fuming about the failure to find his cattle. "I suppose you're right, marshal. Jack, I want to talk to you and Ed when we get back to the ranch." His voice had a tone that did not encourage his men.

"Yes sir, boss." The two said in unison. They headed their horses back along the trail the cattle had used getting here. They didn't wait for Taggert and Bonior. It could be that they weren't interested in trailing along with them.

Marshal Jackson breathed a sigh of relief and followed Jack and Ed.

Taggert and Bonior had moved to the side and were holding a conference in muted tones. They rode back to where Barney and Virg sat their horses under the shade of a tree.

"Smith, you got out of this somehow but I'll nail your hide the next time you run some of my cattle off." Taggert warned. "Stone warned me about you."

"I guess you'll plan a next time." Barney said. "I'll try to be more careful."

"I'm going to slap some sense into this smart mouth." Bonior growled. "A pistol barrel up side the head may unscramble his brains. He's probably not smart enough to know what danger he's in." He eased his horse toward Virg.

Barney was between Taggert and Virg. This kept Taggert from seeing what transpired.

Bonior reached for his pistol. He would show this farmer a thing or two. Suddenly he froze and eased his hand away from the butt of his gun. His mouth dropped open and a look of fear was on his face. He was staring into the muzzle of a pistol. The face before him had a slight smile on it.

"I would appreciate it if you would ride off and not try to hit anybody with that pistol." Virg told him. He had been sitting relaxed as if he didn't have a care when suddenly he had a pistol in his hand. "The jar of being hit might make my pistol go off and no telling where the bullet would go. You might even get hit by it. As you see it's pointed your way."

"Well, I'll let you off this time." Bonior snarled. "Don't count on always getting off so easy."

"Thank you. I knew you were a nice man when I first set my eyes on you."

Bonior turned and headed up the trail. Taggert followed

81

him with a frown on his brow.

"What happened back there, Bonior? I expected you to slap him around a little. They might have started something and we could have finished them."

"That kid had a pistol in his hand when I reached for mine. He looked just crazy enough to shoot me if I tried anything."

"He didn't have it in his hand when you started over there. When did he get it out?"

"I don't know. He must have had it behind him. He better stay clear of me after this."

Taggert gave him a peculiar look. Bonior didn't sound to eager to go after the kid. "What was this kid's name? I never caught it."

"I don't think it was ever mentioned. If I meet him again he won't need one anymore."

Virg and Barney sat their horses and watched Taggert and Bonior ride off.

They broke into a laugh when Virg looked at Barney and said. "You danged cow-track thief."

"I guess I better be careful from now on." Barney said. "If I steal anything I'll try for something more valuable."

"Yeah, like cow piles, if they come after you for rustling their cow-piles you could be in for real trouble." This brought a roar of laughter from them both.

"I thought for a minute we were going to have some big trouble. What made that Bonior change his mind about slapping you up side the head with his pistol?"

"He just saw something that changed his mind. He decided to be nice for a change. A friendly smile has that effect on some people. I do have a friendly smile, you know."

"Yeah, sure. I'm sure he just saw your smile and felt like he had to be nice. He's a cold blooded killer if I ever saw one. I'd bet he'd as soon shoot you as look at you. Maybe rather."

"Well, he didn't shoot us, so I guess we can head back to the house and see if dinner is ready."

"I guess we owe you a feed for driving those cattle off.

82

If you hadn't spotted them I could be in a real pickle now."

They soon made it to the house and were seated around the table enjoying a good meal.

"I was worried half to death. You just rode off with those people as if there was nothing to worry about." Nelda scolded them.

Barney filled her in on the affair. "Virg spotted them last night and ran the cows back to where they came from. That's why he was so late getting here."

"I don't think they'll try that again very soon but you could tell the other settlers to be on guard. I let Bill know about our problem at Paden. I think I better make tracks for home before Joe Hale takes things into his own hands."

"Thanks. We owe you for another favor. Maybe we can repay you one of these days." Barney and Nelda were standing on the porch as Virg led Buck up and prepared to ride off.

"That's what families and friends are supposed to do for each other. You guys are both to me. Just keep the skillet hot when I come this way."

"I'll try not to poison you." Nelda laughed as he rode off.

Chap 13

About an hour later Virg paused at the top of the ridge overlooking his home.

"I wonder how long it'll take." He said to his horse. "She seems to have a sense of when I get back."

It didn't take very long. His mother stepped out the front door of the house and wasted no time before letting her eyes move up the slope.

The words of her favorite hymn soon drifted up to waiting ears. It brought a smile to his face. Coming home always produced a good feeling in a person.

"Hi Maw, what's going on around the place here? I hope my being gone so much hasn't caused you to feel lonesome." Virg grinned at his mother as he dropped off of his horse. "Guess you haven't had to cook so much so that

83

should have given you some rest."

"I knew you wouldn't make it through your first words without mentioning food." She fussed, but you could read the look of pleasure brought about by the sight of her youngest. "We still have that mouse problem. You promised to take care of it."

"I'll get right down there now and see what a dent I can make in their population. I'm sure it will make me hungry though."

"I don't doubt that. I'll see what can be found for supper."

Virg went down to the barn and entered the corn bin. Taking a short stick he began to move the ears of corn to a side of the bin where there was an empty space. He was raking the corn with his hands while keeping the stick handy. Every time a mouse was flushed out by the movement of the corn he tapped it with the stick. This took quickness and accuracy but he had done this before.

"Well, I see you are piling up a good number of the little rascals." Ab spoke from the doorway. "We might hire you out as a mouser." He gave a short laugh at this.

"I'm glad someone thinks I'm good for something. This keeps my hands and wrists loose." Virg smiled at Ab. He was really fond of his step-father. He had come into their lives when Maw's three sons needed a man's steady influence.

"That Zach Vaughn sure thinks you're okay. He never misses a chance to say good things about you." Ab said. "His wife and kids seem to share his sentiments."

"I just treat them like they deserve to be treated. I don't care if they are black, they're the right kind of people to have around."

"Sure can't complain about them so far." Ab agreed. "It took some getting used to on my part but he's turning into a pretty good neighbor."

"All you have to do is give them a chance. He sure opened some eyes over at Prague when that crooked judge tried to pull a fast one."

"Yeah, the idea that he couldn't read or write." Ab laughed as he recalled the episode. "Supper should be ready by the time you get through the rest of that corn."

Virg finished moving the rest of the corn around. Once in a while he would spook two or three mice at a time. This tested his skill with his stick. He managed to smack all three a couple of times. When he finished he got a shovel and buried the harvest in their garden spot.

"Did you do enough to earn any food?" Maw asked him. "I hate to have good food go to waste."

"I'll try to keep any of it from wasting." Virg assured her. "It'd sure be a shame to waste any of your good cooking. Haven't seen you throw much out yet."

Ab laughed at the two. "Don't think you are using the word waste with the same meaning." He added.

They all had a laugh about this as they dug into the bounty on the table. Hot biscuits, fried ham, gravy, mashed potatoes and home churned butter. There would be some of the famous, 'Vi's fried pies', later.

"I don't think the cattlemen have given up. This business of cattle showing up on places and then people being arrested as thieves is to pat. Ab, you and Maw better keep a lookout." He went on to tell about the attempt to frame Barney.

"We'll keep our eyes peeled. Where are you going to be?" Ab asked. "You're gone most of the time."

"Young man, you need to spend more time here at home with us instead of running around solving other people's problems." His mother scolded. "But I guess your Grandpa Smith and me taught you to help people when you got a chance. It looks to me like you hunt for chances though."

"That's right, Maw. I'm just putting your teaching into practice. You sure hammered that home pretty good." He gave her a smile. "I know you wouldn't have it any other way."

"When you put it that way." She shook her head conceding the point. "At least you will be here over night this time. I might even fix a good breakfast. That is, if you have time to eat it."

"Maw, you know that nothing could drag me away

85

when some of your cooking is available."

This brought a smile of satisfaction to her face. She was proud of her reputation as a cook.

Ab just sat back and enjoyed the exchange.

They were soon enjoying the pleasure of a restful sleep. Nothing like home to relax a person.

Virg had remained awake for a while thinking about the things that had happened to them since they had left Arkansas.

The problem with outlaws on the trip out west.

The time spent with the Cherokees at Tahlequah.

He smiled about the trades for the barrels.

Then there was the river crossing with Daisy.

He laughed out loud when he recalled the two dudes that had planned to hold them up.

Maw's joy when they had stopped on their land. He didn't recall a time in his life she had been so happy about anything. It was something to remember.

The trouble with the Gannon crew and then the shoot out with Seener, the back shooter, then the final showdown.

"The Good Lord has sure been keeping his hand on this family." He said to himself. "As for me I know how blessed I am to have such a wonderful family."

He had a smile on his face as he drifted off.

"I think I'll go by and see Zach on my way to Paden. He may know something for me to pass on to Newt and Joe." Virg was saddling Buck as he prepared to leave.

"Now you be careful. Don't be stirring that bunch up. Try to let the law handle things." Maw Rankin had a worried look on her face. "You take a way to many chances."

"Maw, you sure give good advice. That bit about letting the law take care of things is sure the way to do things. We can't take the law into our own hands but it doesn't hurt to help the law out now and then does it?"

"We should all be ready to help the law out." Ab joined the conversation. "That's the only way we're going to have a peaceful place to live."

"I just get worried when he talks about doing things the

ordinary way." Maw said. "It usually winds up with one of his wild schemes. Then someone gets caught in the deal and they don't like it."

"Maw you know I wouldn't do anything to upset folks. Not unless they needed it. I'll try not to do anything to reflect on the family."

"I just want you to be careful and not take any unnecessary chances."

"Don't worry. We'll have Dan cleared in no time and everything will be fine. I'll try to be home right away. I might even find some solution to the mouse problem."

"If you're going by the Vaughn's I have something for Nell and Jerimy"

"Okay Maw, If it's something you cooked they'll be happy to get it. Nobody cooks like you."

He mounted Buck and headed for Zach's. He turned and waved before he faded into the timber. His mother was still standing where he had left her. She returned his wave before she started humming her favorite hymn.

"Hi there. Didn't figure on seeing you for a while. Thought you were busy with that business concerning Dan Hale. Get down and have a cool drink." Zach Vaughn smiled as he greeted Virg. "What's in the sack?"

"A little something for Nell and Jerimy. Maw sent it over."

The two children had overheard the talk.

"What did Mrs. Rankin send us?" Nell yelled excitedly as she tried to out race Jerimy.

"Let me have it. She's liable to drop it and mess it up." Jerimy shouted as he caught up with his sister.

"Whoa up." Virg called out. He held the sack up in the air out of their reach. "It could be a toad or maybe a real jumping frog."

"It's not either. You said Mrs. Rankin sent it and she doesn't play tricks like you do." Nell told him. "Let me have it and I'll handle it carefully."

"Let her have it and if it's a frog we'll enjoy the show." Jerimy said with a grin.

Virg handed the sack to her. She opened it with some

87

show of caution and then let out a whoop when she saw the contents.

"Some of 'Vi's fried pies'". She exclaimed. "Anyway that's what Mr. Rankin calls them."

"Let's take them and show mama." Jerimy called as he started for the house. Nell moved to follow him.

"Haven't you two forgotten something?" Zach asked them.

"We sure have." Jerimy said. Both children turned to Virg.

"Thank you, Virg."

"And tell your mother, thank you too."

"You're more than welcome."

Zach had a big smile when Virg turned back to him. "Have to keep after them to remember their manners." He said.

"You folks have done a good job as far as I can tell. Say, Zach, I wondered if you had any more information about any cattle stealing problems?"

"No, I sure don't. The only thing I have heard is that Dan is out of jail while he waits for his trial. The Hale's want me to come over there and help them with some repairs. They may be doing some field work too."

"You can ride in with me if you're going now."

"They said they would let me know when to come over. Be about a week or more before they're ready I think."

"I think I better head on into town and see what's going on." Virg told him. "It's been a few days since I left." He told Zach about what had happened at Barney's place.

"Interesting, different people but the same type of problem. Makes you wonder, doesn't it?"

"Sure does. Maybe I'll see you at the Hale's place, Zach." Virg told him as he rode off.

As he rode toward Paden he kept a watch about him. It wouldn't do to get to careless now. He remembered that Averill's crew was still on the loose. "Hey, I almost forgot about that Sutton fellow. I wonder what happened to him? I'm getting pretty forgetful. Must be old age." He chuckled as he remembered the cake his mother had fixed for his seventeenth birthday a while back.

Buck flicked his ears forward as a rider came out of the woods several hundred yards up the trail. The rider waited for Virg to come on.

"It's either the Sands boy or one of the Harjo's. I don't know why we say Sands boy as he's a full grown warrior. Anyway he's friendly. I wouldn't like to run into him if he wasn't." He rode on up to the waiting rider. "Your name is Harjo isn't it?" He asked the man.

"That's right, I'm Sam Harjo and I know you. You're Virg. John Billy said for me to tell you we're here."

"Anything to report?"

"No, just say we're on the job. I have to go." He smiled and winked. "We're hunting, you know."

"Hope your luck is good. Thanks for coming. Tell John I'll be watching for him." He rode on toward Paden as the Indian disappeared into the woods.

He soon made it into town and spotted Molly Brown walking along the street.

"Hello, young lady. What brings a pretty thing like you out? Never mind. You are such a sight for anyone to see they don't need an explanation. I'll just sit here on my bronc and enjoy myself."

"Virg, you flatterer, I would be happy to hear that if I didn't know what a talker you are. I'm surprised you compliment anyone on anything besides their cooking."

"Say, can you cook? If you can I might try to give Newt a run for his money. Where is Newt anyway?"

"He said he was going to ride out to visit with Joe. They need to come up with something to help Dan."

"We sure need to do that. Did he say when he'd be back?"

"He should be back fairly soon. He left early. I have to check with the doctor to see if he wants me to help him."

"You'll probably become a top notch nurse. Any fellow that's hurting will look up and see you and think he has already made it to heaven."

"Go on with you. I just hope I don't have very many patients to look after."

"While I wait for Newt and you practice your medicine,

89

I think I'll have a visit with Mr. Higgins."

Virg rode over to the favorite gathering spot for the 'spit and whittle' club. This described the group that could often be found discussing the problems of the people.

"Hello, Mr. Higgins, I see you're in good company. Hi, Marshal Simmons. You fellows have everything settled?"

Simmons grinned at him. "Not everything, we need to find some way to keep the Hales from going outlaw. For the life of me I don't know how Dan can get out of this."

"It's a crooked deal. You can bet on that." Mr. Higgins offered his opinion.

"Several say that but the evidence is there. I had no choice but to arrest him after Averill swore out a complaint."

"How does that work?" Virg asked. "He swore out a complaint and then you had to arrest him?"

"That's right. He signs a paper and I have to arrest the person. Usually a judge or Justice of the Peace issues a warrant but we don't have any so I have to fill all the jobs temporarily. Then a judge comes in and holds a trial."

"But you were holding a trial with Sutton and me."

"No, that was just a hearing to check whether we should charge you with something to hold a trial about. Sutton claimed you did something to him. You agreed but said it didn't happen like he said. The story that came out indicated you were right, so no charges were filed."

"If he had signed a paper charging me with a crime what would have happened?"

"I would have had to arrest you. Then we would have a trial as soon as a judge showed up."

"Who can sign a paper charging someone with a crime?"

"Anybody can."

"Anybody?"

"That's right, anybody."

"Looks like there could be problems if people didn't use the law the way it is supposed to be used. We all need to live by the law however. Thanks, Marshal Simmons. It's good of you to take your time explaining things to a kid like me Not everybody would be willing to do this."

Virg looked around at the others. "Isn't that right, Mr. Higgins?"

"It sure is. Marshal Simmons takes his job seriously." Higgins spat a stream of tobacco juice at a fly that had the misfortune to light within range. "Got you, you pesky rascal."

The marshal stood up and proudly threw back his shoulders. He smiled at them. "I better get on with my rounds." He said. "Young man you handled that Sutton as well as any lawyer could have. Don't let one piece of good luck get the best of you though."

Mr. Higgins grinned at Virg as the marshal walked off. "Had to admit to the job you did but sounded a mite jealous to me. It won't hurt to butter him up a bit for the thing we have planned though."

"Be good to have him on our side for sure. I see Newt riding in. Better check with him. I'll bet they'll be fit to be tied if what you do goes over."

"Be fun trying it anyway." Mr. Higgins let go at another fly. "You never get anything done if you don't make a try at something."

"I agree with you there. Mr. Higgins, you're almost smart enough to be a member of the Smith clan." Virg chuckled as he winked at Higgins.

Higgins returned his grin and nailed another fly.

Newt had a worried look on his face as he rode up and dismounted..

"You look like Molly had told you to get lost." Virg told him. "Any news from out the Hale's way?"

"We can't seem to come up with anything to clear Dan. He's about ready to let them have his place in order to keep the rest of the bunch from hitting the owl hoot trail."

"Don't forget about our plan about his place. We have him pretty well signed up to stay around and help. I don't think this thing is just something about Dan Hale." Virg went on to tell him about the deal at Barney's and then reminded him of the two that Zach had mentioned. "Looks like a new threat to us."

"What are we going to do?"

"Stall for time while we continue to look. We have

three new helpers now. They'll come up with news if anything stirs." He told Newt that the three Indians were on the job. "Don't worry, they're smart fellows."

They looked up as a rider came galloping down the street. He pulled up in front of the marshal's office and went inside.

"We better go over there and see what the excitement is." Newt said as he headed toward the marshal's office. "He sure was in a hurry."

They walked up in time to hear the man say. "That's right, marshal, the judge will be here tomorrow. I better hustle on out and inform Averill." He almost bumped into Virg and Newt as he charged out of the office. "Guess we'll have some law and order around here pretty soon." He gave them a glare as he mounted and rode off.

Newt hurried into the marshal's office with Virg on his heels.

Virg stopped. "Newt, you look after things here I better get back to Mr. Higgins."

"What will be the procedure now?" Newt asked. "How are you going to handle everything?"

"The judge will get here, get my report and then announce when the trial will be." Marshal Simmons told him. "He'll be in charge then."

"Everybody will know about it I guess." Newt observed.

"It'll be mighty hard to keep from knowing about it if you are around here anywhere."

"Will you go out after Dan?"

"No, he said he would be here. It'll be up to him to come in on his own. He doesn't, he's an outlaw."

"Won't you have to make sure he knows about the judge getting here? Surely you wouldn't make an outlaw out of a man without giving him a chance. You can't just depend on the word drifting out there."

"I'll go out and notify him officially. It's up to him to come in though. You'll have to ask him if you want to know any more about it." Simmons indicated that the talk about the trial was over.

It was early afternoon when a buggy wheeled down the street and pulled up in front of the marshal's office. It was flanked by two riders with a big A-A brand on their horses right hips. Averill had changed the G-R brand to the A-A when he took over.

The man in the buggy got down and stood looking up and down the street. He was only about five feet eight inches tall and would weigh well over two hundred pounds. He wore a black coat that was rumpled from his journey. His hair appeared to be mostly dark brown but had streaks of white in it. Fairly long strands of it fell almost to his shoulders and looked like it might be a stranger to such a thing as a comb. The two most prominent features about him were his waist line and his nose.

Newt and Virg had just ridden up and joined Mr. Higgins.

"It would take a mite of cowhide to make a belt for that gentleman." Mr. Higgins said with a chuckle. "And if I'm not badly mistaken that nose was sniffing around for the nearest drinking establishment. It looks like one that has had close association with more than it's share of them from the size of it."

Newt and Virg exchanged grins.

"Are you telling us that he is a drinking man?" Newt asked.

"Yep. That nose sure didn't get that size from smelling the roses." Higgins replied with a laugh. "I'd say he's hoisted a few in his time."

"Newt, I see John Billy on his horse under a tree right down the road." Virg told him. "I better go see what he has on his mind. He didn't come this close to town to find a shade."

"Okay. I'll go over to the marshal's office and find out what I can. See you in a little while."

They both moved off.

Virg headed out of town but not in the direction John Billy was located. He knew John would spot Buck and could come to him if he wanted to.

93

"Better for John if I don't give him away." Virg said to himself. "If Averill's people see us meeting they might get suspicious of him."

Virg rode in the direction of Zach Vaughn's place. Everybody in the area knew he often visited the Vaughns. He was soon out of sight of town. He rode on a short distance and then moved off the trail into some fairly dense woods. He was completely hidden from view.

Buck pricked up his ears. Virg sat absolutely still. You could hardly hear them breathe. They both remained motionless for several minutes.

Finally Virg broke the silence. "Come on out John." He said in a low voice.

"I must be getting careless." John Billy said as he stepped out from behind a tree directly behind Virg. "Or maybe you're still more of an Indian than I am."

"You aren't and I'm not. I just took a chance. I'm sure you were looking for me so I headed out here. You're not losing your touch because you had me in no time."

"We have been watching the men you talked about. They do some funny things. They put cattle off in little bunches."

"It would sure be handy to have a small bunch ready if you wanted to move that many in a hurry. Sometimes it is hard to cut out a small group from a herd."

"That is what I thought about it." John Billy agreed. "For a Cherokee you think pretty good."

"Not as good as a Creek, huh? Anything else to tell me?"

"One man rides toward town almost every day but he never goes to town. Just circles it and rides on."

"What does he look like?"

John Billy gave a fairly thorough description of Sutton. "He sure carries a good looking rifle." He added.

"So he didn't leave the country after all. I know him and am pretty sure what his job is. Is there anything else? If not I better make tracks back to town."

"No other information right now. Do you want us to grab the man with the rifle? It would be easy for three Creeks."

94

"Thanks John, but no, you better not do that. If things went wrong it would make it impossible for you to continue your work for your chief. That's more important to the Creeks."

"We will help if you need us. Let us know. We might enjoy going on the warpath again."

"Try out that skill with a pencil and paper. That might be the best help you can give us. Thanks again."

They took off in different directions. Virg kept looking but never saw any sign of John. "And he worries about his skill slipping." He muttered. "I better get back to Newt in a hurry. If that Sutton gets done what he seems to be trying we could have a full blown war on our hands. The Hales are about ready to explode now."

"Hey, Newt, hold up a minute." Virg called as he rode into town.

Newt stopped and waited for him.

"What's the news from the judge?"

"He said this is late Friday so the trial will start at noon Monday." Newt looked worried. "We don't have much time."

"We have to make sure Dan gets here. Then we will put our plan into action."

"That's right." Newt said. "We don't want to forget what happens if Dan doesn't show."

"One thing for sure, nobody would be interested in what Mr. Higgins had to say. John Billy gave me some information about Sutton that might have something to do with keeping Dan from getting here. Who is supposed to tell him to come in Monday?"

"The marshal has that job. He's just going to tell him, not bring him in." Newt indicated with his thumb. "There he goes now. I'm sure Dan won't be in until Monday though. He doesn't enjoy sitting in jail."

"I better go out there myself and have a little talk with Joe and the other Hales. They're familiar with the trail into town. I might be of some use in checking some of the spots if anybody wanted to try his luck at ambushing him on the way in."

"Why don't you get your Indian friends to help?"

"I know that's a good idea, but just stop and think what would happen if they got into a shooting match with any of the cattlemen and wounded one of them."

"The country might get up in arms if an Indian shot a white man without a mighty good reason."

"You're right. And this bushwhacker, if there is one, could say he was trying to make sure Dan made it into town safely and was jumped by Indians. John and his friends can help us best if they keep right on with what they're doing. By the way he did offer to help." Virg mounted Buck.

"You be careful too. That man with the rifle acted like he didn't care much for you." Newt called after him. "Don't want you to get shot."

"Me either." Virg responded. "Come to think of it, he didn't act very friendly at that. I'll have to keep that in mind when I'm in his vicinity."

Virg soon overhauled the marshal who was riding at a leisurely pace. "Thought you might get lonesome riding out here by yourself." He said as he caught up.

"Glad to have company." Marshal Simmons informed him. "I'll be glad to get this over with. Boy you sure get involved in a lot of things for a young sprout."

"It takes all of us to make a go of it out here. We can't wait until we're full grown to pitch in and help. If we did we might never get full grown." He gave the marshal a grin as he said this. "Maw says that almost everybody has to work together to get things done."

"You seem to be willing to do your part. Maybe even more than your part."

"Everybody should put whatever skill he has to good use. Like you, you use your skill to be a marshal." Virg was studying the layout of the land as they rode along. "I just try to help where I can."

"Well, I'll say one thing, you're developing a pretty big reputation for being helpful. Some might think you're to helpful." Marshal Simmons noticed the way he kept studying the area. "What are you looking for? Nothing out there but trees."

"Sometimes there are things in among the trees." He smiled at the marshal. "Remember Sutton? He was in the trees that day."

The marshal gave him another look. It had a touch of awareness in it. "There's the Hale place now."

Virg had known that they had been watched for some time now. He had spotted one of the Hale boys keeping an eye on them. "Glad to see they have guards out."

"What do you mean?"

"They have been keeping track of us for a while now."

"I haven't seen any guards."

"They're there."

They rode up to the yard.

"Hello. Mr. Hale, Joe, anybody home?" The marshal called out.

"Get down, Marshal Simmons, you're a mite off your reservation aren't you? Joe's not here right now."

A tall, stout looking man came out of the house. His hair was almost white but you could still detect the fire that burned within by the light of his eyes. He might have a few years on him but it was obvious that he would be a force to reckon with in a scrap.

"I really came to see you and Dan anyway."

"I guess I don't need to ask what brings you out this way. Just tell us when. We'll be there. Can't guarantee what'll happen if that fellow tries to go on with this trumped up charge against Dan."

"I'm just to deliver a message. The trial will be starting at noon Monday. Dan agreed to be there. That's all I have to say about it for now. I'm supposed to tell him though."

"Dan, come out here, the marshal has something to tell you."

Dan Hale stepped out on the front stoop. "No need to repeat it, marshal. I heard. I'm to be there before noon on Monday."

"Enough about that. You fellows set down and relax a little while. We'll have a bite to eat soon. Never turn a man away from my table." Mr. Hale glanced over at Virg. "Is this your deputy? If it is, the law must be getting hard up for help." He had a twinkle in his eye as he said this. He knew who he was talking about.

"Not my deputy, just someone that tagged along for the ride. He says he spotted some guards you had out. I didn't see anybody."

"He might make you a fair deputy if he did that, because they're out there. I'll have to talk to the boys about being careless."

Virg had a big grin on his face as the marshal turned to look at him.

"I would like to stay and eat but need to get back to town and look after that judge. I'm sorry, knowing the way you spread the table. Later maybe." The marshal got aboard his horse and headed back toward town.

Virg made no move to follow.

"Guess we can count on you for supper. Won't be much of a strain from the looks of you." Mr. Hale chuckled. "We're used to big eaters."

"Most folks think I can hold my own when it comes to eating." Virg informed him. "I really came out to talk to you folks about Dan's trip into town though."

"Joe will be here pretty soon. He tells me that even though you don't look like much, you make a pretty good hand. Not being disrespectful but most people look for size when it comes to a scrap."

"Dad Hale, don't make remarks about people's size. It might hurt their feelings." Mrs. Hale scolded. "I'm surprised at you."

"I'm not touchy about my size, Mam. My family got me over that a long time back. Maw says everybody just reaches to the top of their head and using what you have is what's important. Lots of folks have a lot but never learn how to use it or are to lazy to."

"Pretty good advice. We'll see how you eat then go from there." Mr. Hale looked skeptical. "Everybody just comes to the top of their head. That's a pretty good one. I'll have to remember it. Course the top of your head's not far above the ground."

"Dad, don't you worry about Virg. He can handle his end of things. He has even been known to have a good idea now and then." Dan had been chuckling. He turned to Virg. "He kinda likes to jolly the young folks."

"Don't worry. I'm not about to take offence. He'd probably boot me good if I got sassy."

Mr. Hale fairly beamed. It was good to see a respectful youngster.

"I see you weren't just talking about your eating skill. Now if you can manage to haul it all around with you I'll really be surprised." Mr. Hale laughed as he turned to his wife. "Mom, you'll be expecting all of us to brag on your cooking like he's been doing. He didn't have to say a word. The way he lit into it you could tell he liked it. He eats like a full growed man."

"Dad Hale, let the boy eat. Growing boys need a lot of food. Besides I appreciated the compliments." She offered Virg another helping of apple pie.

"No thank you mam. Better give it to Mr. Hale or he's liable to get jealous of my eating ability. He's hardly touched his food."

This brought a round of laughter as Dad Hale had a reputation for his ability to eat. He had more than lived up to it during this meal.

"Dad, we better do some talking about the trip into town." Joe said as they gathered in the front room. "That bunch would be happy if Dan didn't show up. Virg here gave us an idea to foul things up in case he didn't but we aren't sure it would work. Be best if we get him there on time."

"We'll all ride in with him. That way he'll be in a crowd. Should be safe that way." Dad Hale looked around the circle of faces. All of the Hales nodded in agreement.

"Young fellow, I didn't see you do anything to show you agreed. You looked doubtful. Speak up if you have anything to say."

"Mr. Hale, if you wanted to stop one man and he was riding in a crowd what would keep you from putting a bullet in him as they all rode along?" Virg asked. He waited for an answer.

Mr. Hale considered this for a minute. He looked around the family. "Nothing, if I was willing for them to do me in after I did it. Doubt if they would chance it."

The rest of the family studied on it a minute. There was some muttering but no one came up with any suggestion.

"Well, everybody seems to go along with me." Dad Hale said. "What is it, Joe?"

"Let's hear what Virg would suggest. He's had some experience with bushwhackers."

"Go on, say your piece." Mr. Hale replied. "We'll give it fair consideration."

"Mr. Hale, you folks are used to fighting face to face. You're not accustomed to sneaks that shoot from ambush. I know you lost one boy that way but you aren't prepared to fight them on their own terms. A skilled marksman could shoot one of you and be gone before you knew where he'd been holed up."

"You talk pretty strong for a kid." One of the other Hale men offered.

"Let him talk." Joe interrupted. "It makes sense to me so far." They all fell silent.

"Mr. Hale how would you shoot your man if you couldn't pick him out of the bunch?"

"Be mighty hard to do."

"That's one thing can be done. The other is to let me scout ahead to try to locate any bushwhacker and see if maybe he can be persuaded not to bother folks."

"What if there is another one put in place to do the job if the first one fails?" Dan asked. "Virg, why are you willing to do this for me? Looks like you're taking a big risk yourself."

"You folks would do the same for us. Also, if this is what I think it is, we're all involved. You aren't the only one involved in stealing cattle." He went on to tell of the other cases. "It looks like a new threat aimed at the settlers. We all have to stand together."

"It still seems odd to let a kid take so much risk." Mr. Hale mused. "A new threat, hmmm."

"We have to use everybody's skills. I just happen to have some that are useful in this case."

"I guess you're right about that. We don't ask a good carpenter to do the cooking. If you do some things better

100

than others that's what you do."

"Mr. Hale, Zach Vaughn said you might have some work for him. He's a good man. My mother knew the family back in Arkansas. They're good people and need a chance to be a part of the community. He'll work hard and you can trust him with anything."

"I told him that we might need some help in a few days. If you say so I'll sure give him a chance." He looked at his family. "We don't mistreat anyone. We'll give him a fair shake."

"That's all anyone can ask for." Virg told them. "I bet you folks will be telling others about Zach before it's over."

"All he has to do is carry his share."

They all nodded in agreement.

"We'd better hit the hay. Big day tomorrow. We have a lot of things to do before we're ready to ride in Monday morning."

Virg and Buck hit the trail toward Paden after an early breakfast the next morning.

"I hope John and his friends are where I can find them. It'll keep me on the run to check with them and then get back to scout the trail." Virg was talking to himself as he studied the area. "Buck, old boy, we need to make a lot of tracks in the next two days."

He wanted to take off on a direct line for the place where he could find John Billy or one of the other Indians but decided he'd better take some time to examine the trail between the Hale place and Paden.

"I'll have some idea of the places that might be the handiest for a bushwhacker by taking a little time now while I'm here." He rode off the trail and moved up on a knoll. Stopping Buck he dismounted and climbed up a tree so that he had a better view. Satisfied that this place would not be a threat he remounted and moved on.

"Shucks, it'll work out better if I don't try to do everything myself. John said they would help. I'll get one or two of them to come on over here and look the place over. They can find a logical place for an ambush much better than

101

I can." He put Buck into a lope and rode toward the area where he was sure he could find the three. "I'll mess around Paden some and ride toward home in case anybody is keeping an eye on me."

Although he kept a sharp lookout he did not spot the lone horseman watching him from a distance.

Sutton sat in some brush well off the trail and watched as Virg rode through. He had not spotted him earlier when he had been looking part of the trail over.

"I sure would like to put a slug in that heathen" He muttered. "But the boss made it clear that Hale was the important one."

He continued to remain in the spot he had picked. He was well concealed and had a good place to observe the trail. He just wanted to check who showed up in the area. This would give him an idea of how much effort was being put into the protection of Dan Hale.

Sutton took pride in his ability to do his job. Most people had a very low opinion of this kind of work but he only thought of it as a way of earning a living.

"It's the same as ridding the country of any other pest. You don't give a cougar or a bear, or even a deer an even break. You just plug them without warning." He was speaking in a voice that was barely audible. Sounded like he was making an effort to fully convince himself. "In fact I like what I'm doing. It sure beats working six ways from Sunday."

After watching the trail for at least another hour he faded back into the brush and left the area. "Better have another visit with the boss. At least this bunch hasn't spotted me. That kid everybody talks about being so good in the woods rode right on by." He was regaining the convidence he had lost when caught by Virg earlier. "That was just an accident. He won't get by with anything like that again."

Sutton wouldn't have been quite so confident had he spotted the pair of dark eyes watching every move he made.

Isaac Sands smiled as he watched the efforts of the man to move through the woods with stealth. He probably wouldn't win many stalking contests if he was pitted against a few Creek Indian warriors.

"I doubt if he could even fool a Cherokee." He chuckled as he recalled some of the friendly meetings between the two tribes. Back in earlier times, friendly was a term that wouldn't have been used. Wars weren't very friendly.

"I better go let John in on things. He said we were supposed to keep out of sight. That's not very hard to do with this bunch." He set out at a fast trot. His horse had been left behind while he did his scouting work. It was hard to keep a horse out of sight. They were noisy too.

John Billy and Sam Harjo were waiting when Sands trotted into the small glade where they had made their hunting camp. A person could have ridden by the place on any side without seeing them. They were skilled in the art of concealment. It helped to learn certain skills if your life was at stake.

Issac made his report to the others.

John looked at his two companions. "Did you see Virg?" He asked.

Harjo shook his head.

"I saw him." Isaac Sands replied. He went on to explain about watching as Virg came by and then how he had kept an eye on Sutton until he rode off. He had followed Sutton into the area earlier.

"I better pass the word along to him." John said. "You fellows go back to your scouting. Don't let them see you following them. Sorry, I didn't need to say that."

Sands and Harjo rode off. John sat for a few minutes and then headed for the spot where he had met Virg two days earlier.

He had been concealed in the meeting place for about an hour when he saw a bird suddenly take off. "He's going to try that on me, I guess." He thought as he remembered the previous meeting where he had stalked Virg. He continued

103

to remain still. His horse was trained to stay as still as he did.

Suddenly a bush gave a quiver and some rattling noise as if something had bumped against it.

John faced that way but still could see nothing. He decided to take the same chance that had led him out. "Come on out, Virg, I've got you spotted." He waited for a reply.

"John, I'm over here." The voice came from behind him. Virg stepped out with a big grin. It was unusual to successfully stalk a Creek warrior or to catch him off guard.

"I better move to the village and stay there if I'm getting this easy. Maybe I can help the squaws." John was obviously disturbed.

"Don't worry about your skills slipping. I used a trick with this string." Virg showed him the string that he had tied to the bush and then run along the grass and leaves so that he could pull it from a distance. "I knew you would come back here so I set it up. Might come in handy some other time."

"What was the rattling noise?"

"I put some pebbles in the forks of some limbs. They fell when I moved the bush."

"I'll have to remember that one. You're getting mighty tricky for a Cherokee." He laughed as he said this.

"We've learned a lot from the Creeks." This brought a smile of satisfaction from John. "I came looking for you to find out about the area between town and the Hale place. Dan is staying at Dad Hale's. They will all escort him into town Monday morning."

"A good man, or a bad man, could shoot one man in a crowd before they know he was around." John paused. "They might get him but if he is good at the job he will be gone before they locate him."

"I need to know where the best ambushes are. There's not time for one person to check out the whole trail before Monday."

"We thought you might want to know this so we have already been checking it out. Fact is, Isaac watched the one you called Sutton go over some of it."

104

They sat and talked for almost an hour. John Billy gave Virg the location of four places. Indicating in order, from the best to the least desirable location. He described each place as to advantages and disadvantages.

Virg sat pondering the information. He was also thinking in terms of the person laying the ambush.

"It isn't a successful ambush if you don't get away. So that probably rules out the last place you described. He would surely be caught and killed if he used it."

John smiled at him. "That's the way I see things. You keep working on this and you might become a fair Creek warrior."

"I'm thinking that little statement over. Go on with your story. I'm all ears."

John grinned at this. "The place nearest the Hales is the best place but they may be aware of it also, so would be on guard. If they got past there they might relax a little. The next two places are almost as good as the first one."

"Thanks John, with this information I'll have time to check them out as I don't have to examine the whole trail. I'm honored to be thought of as almost having skill like a Creek. "

"We will keep watch and try to let you know if anything happens."

"Just don't take any chances. You'll do your best work if nobody suspects what you're doing."

Virg decided to make another pass by and check with Zach Vaughn. This wasn't much out of his way because the route he took away from where he had met John led in that direction.

"Hello, what brings you out here? I thought you were busy helping Dan Hale." Zach Vaughn swung the ax in his hand at the piece of wood he had been in the process of splitting. "I've got to get this done so I'll be ready to go over to Dad Hale's Wednesday and work some for them. One of the young boys came by here and told me a while ago. May be three or four days work. It'll sure help out."

"We have to make sure that Dan gets to town. He has plenty of help to guard him. I'm doing a little scouting around. If this cattle stealing thing works with Dan we could all be in a bundle of trouble."

"It seems that everywhere we turn there are people wanting to take our property away from us. I guess it's always been that way. Folks have to fight to hold on to what they have."

"Zach, I'm glad you're getting to work for the Hales. I'm sure they'll treat you right."

"I'll have to get around the days I'm over there. It's quite a trip there and back each day and I have my chores to do here. I don't mind though. We can use what I make. Jeremy is getting big enough to help out here. Mandy can do as much work as I can in a pinch."

"I better make tracks. Tell Jeremy and Nell hello. Mandy will probably be relieved because I didn't stay over for supper."

They both laughed.

Newt and Molly were the first ones Virg saw as he rode into town. They appeared to be headed toward the marshal's office.

"Where are you two headed?" Virg asked as he pulled Buck to a stop between them and their destination.

"My goodness, you sure stir up a mess of dust. I guess if we hadn't stopped you'd have run right over us." Molly was pretending anger but could hardly suppress the smile that was about to break out on her face. "Newt, say something to him about his actions."

"There you go again, telling me what to do." He turned back to Virg. "We didn't see the marshal when he came in last night so wanted to find out about his trip to the Hales. You can probably tell us more than he would about that, anyway."

"I can do that all right. The Hales are all going to come in with Dan. You might as well get used to being told what to do. They say it goes with the deal." He laughed as Newt turned a little red.

"Your turn will come." Newt said.

Molly stood silently looking innocent.

"I don't know. If they're all as fussy and bossy as what

106

I've observed so far I think I'll pass. Imagine trying to cause trouble between best friends over a mite of dust."

"It's hard to believe all right. Some folks seem to enjoy a good argument." Newt grinned as he winked at Virg.

"You two are impossible. I think I'll go on over and visit with the marshal. At least he's nice to ladies." Molly walked across the street using every opportunity to glance back at the two who kept a conversation going as if she didn't exist.

"Newt, I'm going to go on out in the direction of the Hale place and scout around. You keep things going here. Especially try to keep Molly in line." He laughed as he headed toward home. Anybody watching him would think that was where he was going..

"I'll just take a right here and then head toward the Hale place." Virg didn't figure it would hurt to keep his movements somewhat concealed. He soon made it to the area he wanted to examine.

Buck was left in a small glade where he wasn't likely to be discovered. This spot was nearly a mile off the trail. The saddle and bridle were removed. A small meal was prepared.

"Not much to eat but it will keep me alert if I'm not stuffed." Virg said to himself as he took off on foot for the spots to be scouted. The three places to be checked were not that far apart. He had donned his moccasins and left his hat behind.

He decided to check the place closest to the Hales first. When he reached the area the first order of business was to make a complete circle around the spot checking for get away routes. This was an ideal spot for an ambush as it had plenty of cover and a good escape route.

"If I used this, how would I take off?" He decided to follow the escape route for some distance.

"If the enemy was in hot pursuit you could have a problem here as this leads across an open space." He paused to consider the idea. "Sutton won't be interested in taking any chances." That along with the idea that the Hales would still be on high alert as they passed this place tended to make it less likely to be used.

He followed much the same procedure at the next two places. Now all he had to do was wait. Tomorrow morning he would repeat the check in full daylight. He lay down and was soon asleep.

As daylight broke over the land he was well on his way back to the first spot he had examined. He quickly repeated the action of the preceding night.

"I still think the second spot will be the one." He mused. "Just have to take the chance. Maybe I'll get lucky and spot him as he comes in. Might better take a look at number three first though."

He examined the next two areas and then headed back to check on Buck. He found him contentedly nipping off tufts of grass and slowly chewing them.

"You'll get so fat and lazy that you won't be able to out run a fat cow." Virg smiled at his favorite horse.

Buck raised his head, took a look at Virg and then went on about the business of grazing.

Virg settled down for a few hours of rest. The problem ahead appeared to be a fairly simple one. He would get into position during the night, spot the man as he came in, let him get located, then move in on him. Didn't seem like a very difficult problem. If things went right. You could never tell when dealing with men though.

Saddling Buck, he headed on foot for what he considered the best position to keep an eye and ear on the two spots. He had decided to take a chance that the first location would not be used.

Leaving Buck in what he considered a safe place he moved on a short distance. "If I don't get away from him all I'll be able to hear is him chomping grass." He settled down to wait. "Buck will stay there until I yell. Nobody will slip up on him either unless he's mighty good."

The sounds of the night carried to him. A couple of owls flew overhead. They flew on what had been described as silent wings. He heard them however. Several other night creatures could be identified as they made their way about the woods.

"I hope a skunk doesn't decide he wants my place." He

108

grinned at the thought of it. He would just have to move if that happened.

Suddenly the night sounds changed. Things around the third possible spot were different. Nothing to be seen but the sounds were different. Then he heard a stick snap. The sound carried clearly in the still night. Another stick snapped, then a stone was dislodged and rattled down a bank and rustled the dry leaves. After that things became quiet again. Some but not all of the regular night sounds returned.

"Well, I guess I know where he is. I'll get in the best place then make my move when I can see." He had his pistol, knife, and the bow. He had only brought three arrows held on his back with buckskin strings. This would give him greater freedom of movement.

Virg moved carefully through the woods stopping often to listen. He didn't want to stumble into the other man's horse in the dark. He was sure it had been left close by for a quick getaway. That narrowed the choices to two places. Daylight would have to come before he checked them.

It was going to be a late daylight. There were wisps of fog everywhere. This would clear in time for the ambusher to do his job but made for delay in locating the horse and then the man himself.

"I know where he is but don't want to spook him. I'd like to deliver him to town all in one piece." He cast a concerned look around. He might not have time to do the job right.

The area began to clear. Virg decided he could take a chance on trying to locate the horse. Then he heard a sound that was familiar. The scrape of a horse rubbing his neck against a tree trunk. It was close by. If it had been a mustang he would have been discovered. Maybe things were going to go his way.

Better get on with the job. He didn't want to be caught spending his time thinking while the Hales rode into an ambush. Time was slipping by.

Cautiously he moved to the base of the small knoll where Sutton had to be located. "Have to be extra careful or he'll be waiting for me." He thought as he moved through

109

the brush. His Cherokee training began to take over to a higher degree. Move silently, then check all surroundings. Be on the watch for Sutton to make a move or sound.

Suddenly he froze. He hardly breathed. There it was again. A sound right in front of him.

He still didn't see any sign of Sutton. He had to be there. Then he remembered. This was the place with the slight depression. It was deep enough for a man to lie down in and be completely hidden.

"I better not poke my nose in there without knowing for sure what his position is." He was sure that Sutton would be watching the trail most of the time. He would check his surroundings from time to time though.

He checked the time. The Hales would be along pretty soon but he probably still had ample time. Hurrying this type of business could put you out of it.

He heard the sound of movement. Sutton must be extra confident. He usually was not one to be careless.

Virg decided to give his eyes a rest from the strain by looking back toward Paden. He saw what looked like a puff of smoke. Then there was another one. Smoke signals? Surely not. Who would be doing that? John or one of the others? Hmm. He turned his attention back to stalking.

Moving to his right a short distance he began to scan the place. Examining everything as he moved his eyes from one side to the other. He was looking for anything that didn't fit. He saw something that looked out of place. He moved to one side and examined it again. A rock that looked different. No help.

He decided to try some leaf noise. Taking some loose dirt he tossed small bits of it into some dry leaves. He continued this as a pattern. It sounded like some creature moving along. No result. Sutton wasn't falling for that this time.

"Time is moving on. I better try something else." He picked up a piece of stick about six inches long and taking a small pebble he aimed it at a bush several feet away. Click, rattle, click. The pebble struck the bush, trickled down it and landed in some leaves.

A head popped up and then back down again. He heard

a low mutter. Now he knew where Sutton was and how he was concealed. He had only seen the back of his head. He was puzzled. Something different.

Virg moved up and to his right again. This put him directly behind Sutton. He had him located now. He pulled his pistol and moved so that he could see the head and shoulders of his man.

Click! The cocking sound of the pistol was loud in the quiet. Anyone familiar with guns would know the sound. The figure before Virg froze. He was not about to do anything stupid. There was something about him.

"You're smart not to move. Slip that rifle over to the right and then put your pistol with it. When that's done, slide a bit to the left and get up facing the way you are now. Quick before my thumb slips."

The man hastened to comply. He moved his rifle and pistol to the right and then slid to the left, then got to his feet.

Virg was feeling pretty good about the job he'd done. Dan Hale would be able to ride in safely. He caught sight of Sutton's profile in the increasing light. He snapped to attention.

It wasn't Sutton! He had his man but it wasn't Sutton. His mind began to race. If Sutton wasn't here, where was he?

Dan Hale's situation had returned to it's original status. Time was short.

Virg was stunned. He was sure from the reports from his Indian friends that Sutton would make the attack if it came. Now he was here with this guy.

"What are you doing, sneaking up on people?" The man demanded. He began to flex his fingers.

"Put your hands on top of your head." Virg spoke softly. "Be careful. I wouldn't want to get excited and shoot you but I'll sure do it if you make a wrong move."

The man obeyed. It was doubtful that he had any other weapons unless it was a knife.

"Where's Hatton?" Virg snapped the question.

"You mean Su-. I don't know what you're talking about."

111

Virg had heard enough. The little slip had been the tip. This guy knew Sutton all right but there was not time to get it out of him. The Hales would be here soon. He had to get a move on.

Now he recalled the smoke signal. Two puffs. It now had meaning. John Billy had been trying to send a message. Two bushwhackers. He'd better get a move on.

"Back up here but don't look back. I'll tell you when to stop. Be careful not to make any false moves." Virg instructed. He was still concerned about Sutton. He figured he knew where that gentleman was. It posed a big problem. Was there time enough to do anything about it.

"How far are going to have me back up? I'm against a tree now."

"I know who you are now. You're Lem, one of Averill's hands. Turn to your right and walk slowly down to your horse. I'll be right behind you in case you have any wild ideas."

When they reached the horse Virg instructed Lem to get his rope and toss it aside.

"Now lay down on your belly and put your hands behind your neck. If you try any quick moves my knife will slide right between your ribs. I don't want you wandering around for the next few minutes. You lay real still now because I'm in a hurry. Might be better if I just stuck a knife in you."

He soon had Lem tied with a slip loop around his neck.

"You just wait til I get loose. I'll fix you." Lem snarled just before his mouth was filled with his own bandanna fixed to stay there.

"Don't try to hard to get loose or you may choke yourself. Probably save a hanging. I don't have time right now to visit or we could have a nice chat about what you were doing here." Virg took off at a trot. He didn't have much time left. The Hales were surely on their way by now. They were depending on him.

As he came within sight of the second spot he cut to his left in order to approach in the best cover for a person on foot. He would have to slow down soon as he didn't want to risk alerting Sutton.

"What if he isn't here? Gosh, I hope there aren't three. I'll just to have to figure on two. There were only two puffs of smoke. At least I only saw two. I better quit bringing up doubts and concentrate on the job at hand." He knew that a mind that was jumping from problem to problem didn't work at it's best.

"Dad gum, here come the Hales." He had spotted a group of horsemen in the distance. "There's not enough time to ease up on the spot. Have to think of something else."

Chap 16

He moved forward quickly. Even if spotted he was pretty sure that Sutton wouldn't risk a shot at him because that would alert the Hales.

"If I have to I'll try to force him to fire that rifle anyway. If he doesn't I'll have to use my pistol to warn them." He smiled to himself. "I don't cotton much to tempt him to shoot at me."

Sutton looked pleased. Here came the whole bunch. "All dressed alike are they? Bet they think that makes the one guy safe in the crowd." He raised a small telescope and studied the approaching horsemen. He didn't see the figure that moved through the brush behind and below him.

"Dust the one, jump my horse and be gone. They'll never see me." Sutton yawned. This was boring because it was going to be so easy.

"I already know my man." He glanced back behind him. "Nothing there but I wonder what those puffs of smoke meant. Probably some Indian talk."

Virg began to circle the knoll. Time was sure getting short. He looked toward the Hales again. They would soon be in rifle range for an expert marksman. He was sure that Sutton would fit that bill. He would have really been worried if he had known about the telescope.

"Joe, I tell you if there was going to be an ambush it would have been back there. I think he would rather I stand trial and lose." Dan Hale was trying to make a case for riding on into Paden without all the extra precautions.

"That's possible but we still need to keep alert." Joe replied. "What do you think, Dad?"

"We'll stay on our toes but Dan may be right. I'm used to people fighting you face to face. That kid may have been a bit to edgy, talking about bushwhackers."

There were four other Hales in the party. They usually followed Dad's lead. Nothing had happened as they rode by the place they considered the only good place for an ambush.

Probably nothing to worry about. They would just ride on into town and straighten this whole mess out then get back to their work. If it wasn't settled they were ready to go to war.

"None of mine are going to hang as long as I'm loose with a gun in my hand." Dad Hale cast a look around at his boys. He knew that they would be right behind him.

"Say, this might work better than anything else." Virg muttered as he looked at the horse tied at the base of the knoll. It had taken him only a few minutes to locate it. "Anyway it's all I have time to do. Decide what's the best or only course and then take action. That's what Maw always told us to do. She usually knows what she's talking about. I sure hope it works."

He walked casually up to the animal, keeping an eye on the top of the rise. "Easy, boy." He said in a low voice. He quickly untied it. "Come go with me, boy." Leading the horse he set off for a clear spot to the left of the trail. He would be in plain sight of both the trail and anybody at the top of the ridge when he made the clearing. He'd have to be on his toes if someone on the ridge decided to take a shot at him.

"I'll worry about that when the time comes. He's probably worrying about the Hales."

He hurried on toward the clear spot.

"I hope I figured Mr. Sutton right. I don't think he's the kind to take the risk of shooting if he's sure he'll be

114

caught as soon as he does." Virg said to himself. "I'd bet
on it. In fact I am betting on it. I wonder if Dan Hale
would be happy with what I put on the line."

Sutton was already taking practice sights. A little
closer and it would all be over. "I thought I heard my horse
a minute ago. He's probably stomping at flies." He
lowered the rifle and closed his eyes to clear them. He still
had the pleased look on his face.

When he opened them he would draw a bead and get off
his shot. "Then that bronc and me'll leave them flies
behind. The boss man can send the judge home."

He raised the rifle into position and opened his eyes.
The target was there. There was no way to miss. This job
was almost to easy. He began to prepare for the shot. "It's
almost a shame to collect pay for this. I think I'd be happy
to do it for nothing. However, it's good to be paid for
something you like doing."

The Hales were riding along at an easy pace. They were
somewhat more relaxed now that they had passed the most
obvious spot for an ambush.

Most of them were in agreement with Dan in his
insistence that the danger was probably past if it ever existed
at all.

"He'd rather convict me and make outlaws out of all
us." Dan continued the argument.

"That does make some sense." Dad Hale agreed.

"Let's not go to sleep, completely ." Joe Hale warned
as they broke out into the clear. "They know we'll go on
the warpath anyway if Dan is downed."

"Yo-Ho, Mr. Hale, look over here." Virg waved his
hand over his head as he yelled. He was standing with the
horse between him and the top of the rise. He didn't want
to get shot because some fool lost his head.

The Hales all stopped. Joe pushed his horse in front of
Dan in order to shield him.

"It's that kid." Dad Hale exclaimed. "What's he up
to?"

Sutton's head jerked to the left at the sound of the shout. "What the devil's going on? Say, that's my horse. How'd he get out there. That sorry, heathen half breed kid has him. I ought to put a bullet in him." He shifted his rifle. "But how would I get away with the Hales right on top of me?" He did have the ability to think fast when his hide was involved. His rifle sagged.

"You might as well forget it, Sutton." Virg called out. "You might make the shot but they'd have you on the end of a rope in no time. Of course you could run down here and get your horse. You could make it if he doesn't stampede. Want to take the chance?"

"I'll ride over and see." Joe Hale said. "Dan, drop off your horse and stay behind him. Be a good idea for all of you." He kicked his mount into a gallop toward Virg. The rest of the Hales took his advice.

Virg waited for him to ride up. He kept his eye on the top of the knoll. He was in position to catch any movement going off the back side. He called out. "Mr. Sutton if you try to sneak out of there I'm willing to shoot you in the back this time."

"What's going on?" Joe asked as he rode up. "You could get shot popping out of the woods like that without a warning."

"I was counting on that not happening. I think there's someone on top of that ridge that wants to ride into town with you. He's been waiting for quite a while for you to come along."

"Who is it? Maybe we should just shoot him or string him up."

"Be better for the Hales if you don't. Take a dead one in and people will wonder about you." Virg made a suggestion. "What do you think about it?"

Joe broke into laughter. "Dad would love to do that."

"I'll see if I can get your company to join us." Virg told him. "Hey, Sutton, you better come down and get your horse. Mr. Hale wants you to take a ride into town with him. My advice is to take his offer. He's not a very patient man so you better move quick. Give him time to think it over and he might decide to hang you. He's a

116

might touchy where his boys are concerned."

A very sullen and angry Sutton walked out of the brush at the top of the ridge and made his way toward them. "I'll get that heathen yet." He muttered to himself in a low voice.

Virg had been right, Sutton wasn't willing to risk his neck to do the job.

Dad Hale and his boys joined them on the trail. Joe took his father aside and explained about taking Sutton in with them. A big grin began to spread across Dad Hale's face as he began to think of things to say when he took Sutton in.

Sutton was invited to ride beside Dad Hale at the head of the column. His fully loaded rifle and pistol were still in his possession. He could almost feel the eyes boring into his back however.

"Let's stop here and let this other fellow ride in with you too." Virg said as they came up to the place where he had left Lem.

Lem was untied and invited to join the group. He was given a place of honor in the center of the cavalcade. His weapons were also returned. As he looked the Hales over he decided it wouldn't be healthy to let his hands even get close to a gun.

"Now that you have two extra hands to make sure you get to town safely I think I'll get Buck and come on in pretty soon." Virg told them.

"It's good to have all the help we can get." Joe laughed as he glanced at Lem. "Wouldn't want you fellows to think we don't appreciate your help."

As all of the Hales joined the laughter, Sutton and Lem seemed to fail to catch on to the general feeling of good fellowship. They couldn't see anything to laugh about right now.

Dad Hale looked at Virg for a moment. "Young man, I take back any thoughts about you not being big enough to do any fighting. You can join my army anytime you've a mind to. Where's your horse?"

Virg smiled, turned, and gave a piercing whistle. He then stood waiting.

117

"Do you see that?" One of the Hales asked in amazement when Buck broke out of the woods and came at a gallop toward them.

Buck came to a sliding halt with his nose almost against Virg's chest then nipped at him playfully. He was rewarded by having his ears scratched.

The town of Paden was crowded. It wasn't often they had a trial and everybody wanted to be sure they were part of the festivities.

Alex Averill and his men were off to one side watching the crowd. Averill had a satisfied look on his face. He walked over to the marshal's office.

"Is Dan Hale here yet?" Someone shouted. "It ain't long til noon."

"No, I'll bet he doesn't come. Be a fool to come in here and stick his neck in a noose."

"He'll be here. Bet on it. The Hales won't run from a fight or anything else."

The crowd was enjoying the banter. Some even offered to go along with the idea of bets.

They kept looking down the south road.

"Here they come now. The whole crew is riding in. At least enough of them to fight a war."

"Is Dan with them?"

"Yeah, he's there and they have a couple of others with them. Don't rightly recognize them."

"Maybe they hired some extra hands for more protection."

"Could be but they usually fight their own battles."

The crowd parted as the Hales rode up to the marshal's office.

Marshal Simmons stepped out front.

Alex Averill came out right behind him.

"Marshal, here's Dan just like we told you." Dad Hale said in a loud voice. "Oh, Mr. Averill, I want to thank you for sending a couple of your men out to help us make it in safely. Doubt if we'd of made it without them." This brought a laugh from the crowd. Turning to Sutton and Lem he added. "I believe it's safe enough now, so you

118

fellows can join your boss." This produced another round of laughs. "Thanks for the help. We really appreciate it"

A very crestfallen pair of would be bushwhackers eased their horses out of the pack and moved down the street where the rest of Averill's crew waited. Everybody could see that the two were fully armed.

Averill was on the verge of denying that they were his men but stopped when Sutton and Lem joined the rest of his bunch. He had already suffered the embarrassment of Hale's thanks for sending help. He stood staring at Dad Hale.

"Let's see what Judge Harvey has to say." Marshal Simmons wanted to get this bunch inside before trouble started. "We might get things started early."

Judge Harvey stepped out on the front porch of the meeting room where the trial was to be held. His nose gave evidence that he had been successful in locating some refreshments. He moved with some measure of unsteadiness.

"Judge, is it possible to get things started?" The marshal asked. "All the people involved are here. We better get it over with before anything happens."

"Har-rumph. That's a mite unusual. Things are supposed to be done at the proper time." Harvey raised himself up to full height and looked over the crowd with an official stare. "If there is no real disagreement to that arrangement I guess we could dispense with the absolute formalities of the occasion. Court will be in session in ten minutes."

He turned with a flourish to step back into the courtroom. He almost stumbled and fell when his foot failed to clear the threshold.

"My boy has to stand trial before a drunk, posing as a judge." Dad Hale grumbled. "Let's get it started."

A snicker ran through the crowd.

The place was soon crowded with people. All seats were occupied. The walls were lined with people standing. Some leaned in the windows from outside.

"Art, have a seat here by me." A man spoke to Mr. Higgins. "We'll have a good place to watch things."

"Thanks. Don't mind if I do. Been a while since I seen a trial." Higgins was talking pretty loud.

"I guess you've seen your fair share of them?" The man asked. "I suppose they are mostly all alike."

"Cain't always count on that." Higgins responded. "They can be different at times. They're not all so much the same."

"What can be so different about trials as long as a judge runs things? Ain't they all about the same? Judges I mean."

"Funny thing, this reminds me of a time back in Tennessee. This feller wanted to get rid of a rival of his, so he went out and found somebody to pose as a judge. Pretty imposing looking feller too. He brought this phony judge in and had his rival arrested and tried on a trumped up charge." Mr. Higgins was still talking rather loud. He paused and looked around the room. He seemed to have forgotten his story.

"Well, what happened? Tell the rest of it." The man that had offered him the seat urged. "Don't stop now. Tell the rest of it."

"Finish the story. Don't stop in the middle of it." Another added. "You tell some pretty good ones."

"Not much more to tell. They hung the poor guy."

"That's terrible. Nothing more happened about it I guess."

"Found out later it was a mistake but it didn't help the man they hung." Higgins grinned at them. "He was still just as dead."

"That could never happen here."

"You might be right but I'm glad it's not me on trial before this sot."

"What have you done to be arrested for?"

"Nothing. How would you feel if they came back here and arrested you, tried you and found you guilty?"

"I haven't done anything to be arrested for neither."

"Neither had that man in Tennessee. I always thought Dan Hale was an honest man too."

"That was a frame up, back in Tennessee, like you said."

"Do you know this judge? I wonder if the marshal knows him." Mr. Higgins shrugged his shoulders. "Maybe they'll hang this Hale feller. We can find out later if he's guilty of anything. It ain't nothing to me I guess."

"You cold blooded old coot." Came a voice from behind them. "You'd let them hang an innocent man"

"Quiet everybody, here's the judge." Marshal Simmons called out. "Simmer down."

Rap Rap! Judge Harvey pounded the table with a hammer that someone had handed him. "Court is in shession. Everybody get quiet." He proclaimed. "Lesh start the trial. Whersh the prisoner? What is he sharged with? Marshal do your duty. Anybody have any questions before we proceed?"

Marshal Simmons had risen and stepped out in front ready to make his statement of charges against Dan Hale who was seated at the front. He was flanked by most of the rest of the Hales.

"How do we know this is legal? He may not be a judge at all."

"Who said that?" Harvey roared. He was partially hidden behind the marshal.

"I did." The man with Mr. Higgins stood up and looked around the crowd. The seed of doubt had been sown in the right place.

"Are you ready to repeat it?" Harvey asked. The place had become very quiet.

"Yes I am. How do we know that you're a judge?" Higgin's friend replied. Sometimes a few words had great effect. You could almost feel the idea spread through the crowd.

"Everybody knows he's a judge." Snapped Averill. He had almost jumped up to push the man down when the question came.

"I don't know that." The man said. He thrust out his chin. He wasn't going to back down now.

"Me neither." Came another voice.

The place was soon in an uproar as everyone seemed to be trying to cast his vote. Doubt had spread.

"Be mighty handy to bring in a phony judge and hold a trial. No doubt about the outcome then." A settler who had overheard the conversation between Mr. Higgins and the

121

man seated with him shouted this out. "He looks like some old drunk to me."

Rap! Rap! Rap! "Order, Order, marshal get thish bunch quiet. Thish is the most preposterous thing I've ever heard of." Judge Harvey was livid. "Questioning my integrity. It's preposterous I say."

"Them thar big words don't prove nothin."

Chap 17

Marshall Simmons stepped back to the front and held up both hands, palm forward. "Folks, we have to have it quiet if we are going to settle anything."

The room became relatively quiet. There was still the rumble of murmuring making the rounds.

"Thash better. Now we can procheed." Judge Harvey adjusted his chair and looked out over the faces that appeared less friendly than before. "The audacity of some ignoramus plebian questioning the veracity of thish court."

"Won't do you any good saying nice things about us. It won't turn our heads any a tall." Higgins answered in a voice that carried all over the room. "We been bragged on before this and by some mighty fine folks."

This brought a roar of laughter.

"We're not going to proceed with anything until we make sure we're going to get a fair deal." Dad Hale said in a firm voice. "I'm not letting my boy be given a raw deal by some drunk old coot that calls himself a judge."

He had been given the responsibility of defending Dan as there were no lawyers available in Paden at this time. He didn't know if he was ready to trust Newt with the job.

"Let him prove he's a judge." Came a shout from the back of the room. "That's all's needed. Averill made the charges."

"Yeah, Averill's man brought him in."

"He's been drinking Averill's liquor ever since he arrived."

"Looks kinda fishy if you ask me."

Marshal Simmons signaled again for order. "Does

anybody know the judge besides Averill? Who can vouch for him?"

A man standing against the far wall held up his hand. No other offers came.

"He's gonna vouch for him." A man leaning in a window shook his head. "When did Rufus ever stay sober long enough to know what was going on?" Several people laughed.

Simmons gave him a scowl. "Go on Rufus, Tell us what you know."

"I can vouch for him. His ability to put snake bite medicine away is the best I ever seed. I wus over east a while back and he drank me right under the table. Now you know that takes some doin. The folks there said he was a champion for sure."

The room erupted in laughter again.

Harvey appeared to be about to explode.

The marshal again called for order.

"Go on Rufus, tell us about him being a judge."

"Oh, I don't know nothin aboot him being a judge. You asked if anyone could vouch for him about anything. I told you all I know. If he can judge as good as he can drink, he's a dandy. I'll vouch for that."

Pandemonium broke out. People were slapping each other on the back and were having trouble catching their breath.

It took some time to restore order.

"Marshal. all the judge has to do is show his credentials." Averill told Simmons.

Simmons turned to the judge. "Your Honor would you be kind enough to present your appointment papers."

Judge Harvey had a hard time raising his eyes. "We took off in sush a hurry I left them in Okmulgee. Nobody ever questioned me before. I'd advise you to clear the room of spectators and then we can get on with thish trial."

"Are you crazy? If we tried that, these people might string us all up." Simmons looked him straight in the eye. "You better put it off until you get your papers here."

Judge Harvey thought about this a minute then rose to his feet, slammed the hammer down on the table and

123

pronounced. "Thish trial will be postponed until a week from today. I'll warn you right now." He paused. The past few minutes had sobered him a lot. "Anybody that interrupts my court at that time will pay a big fine or spend some time in jail."

With an attempt at dignity he turned and left the room by the back door. He was still a bit unsteady.

Averill stalked out behind the judge. He soon overtook him. They conferred for a few moments. It was clear that Averill was upset with the judge.

Virg and Newt had been leaning against the back wall. Molly was seated in front of them.

"By Golly, it worked." Newt exclaimed as he grabbed Virg and shook his hand. They both started laughing.

"What do you mean by that?" Molly asked. "Did you two have anything to do with this?"

"Why Molly, you know we wouldn't do anything to mess with the wheels of justice." Virg assured her with a grin.

Newt just grinned at her.

"You two are impossible. I think I'll go see if Marshal Simmons will tell me anything."

"We better go thank Mr. Higgins. He sure stirred up a hornet's nest" Virg suggested. "Went even better than expected."

Mr. Higgins was busy enjoying himself when they joined him. "Yes sir, one time back in Tennessee--."

"Marshal, I want to talk to you. If that judge is going after some papers I want Joe to go with him to make sure it's not a phony deal." Dad Hale had stopped the marshal as they left the courthouse. "He better have the proper papers when he comes back."

"Sounds fair enough to me. Let's see if Averill wants his man to go along with them." Simmons replied. "Hey, Mr. Averill, hold up a minute."

Averill had retrieved his horse and was prepared to ride out of town with his crew.

Marshal Simmons explained Hale's proposal.

"I better send a man along to make sure the judge

124

makes it back in one piece. This thing has been delayed long enough. I wouldn't put anything past that bunch because I think they were behind this deal today." Averill rode over to his crew and after a short discussion returned with Dobe.

"There's another thing, Marshal Simmons, I want somebody to keep an eye on the Hales until the judge gets back. They might waylay him on the way."

Dad Hale overheard the remark. "Send a couple of your hands out if you want. We'll put them to some honest work, for a change."

"I'll just take you up on that." Averill snapped. He rode off to where his crew sat waiting. After a short exchange Toad Slater and another man rode over to join Dad Hale. and the marshal.

"We're to spend a few days with you." Toad offered. "I hear you feed pretty good."

"You're welcome but everybody at our place works." Dad Hale informed him. "You do look like you've been putting away a few vittles all right. Maybe we can work some of that lard off."

Some of the men overhearing the remark were heard laughing.

Toad had a scowl on his face as they rode out of town. Being reminded of his build didn't make him all that happy. He thought again of the chance to be able to eat well and his disposition improved somewhat. The food at Averill's spread wasn't all that good.

Averill assembled his entire crew as soon as he reached the ranch. The outcome of the morning had left him in a foul mood.

"That old fool forgot to bring his credentials. He sure fits this bunch. I wonder if I can count on any of you to do a job right. I want a report and don't try to make any excuses. We'll start with you Lem."

"I was laying there in my position ready to do my job if it became necessary when suddenly that heathen kid was behind me with a pistol in his hand. He had the drop. No excuse, I guess I got careless."

125

Averill glared at him in disgust. "Well at least you admit it." He turned to Sutton. "So you're supposed to be the best. Here you come riding into town with the Hales crew like you were the best of friends. Care to explain?"

Sutton turned red. He wasn't used to people questioning his work. He started to speak. "Well--."

Averill interrupted him. "Don't forget anything. I remember you being brought in by that kid one time before. Then he made a fool of you when you tried that business of making them believe he backshot you."

"Do you want the information or not?" Sutton snarled. "I had my spot picked out and was ready to shoot when that blasted heathen stole my horse."

"Stole your horse. You didn't plan to shoot Hale with a horse did you? You should have gone ahead and done the job you were sent out there to do. He stole your horse. Good gosh!" Averill was disgusted.

"No I didn't plan to shoot him with a horse. I didn't plan to commit suicide either. That bunch would have had me in no time if I'd shot at them. He stole my horse and I didn't have a way to get away." Sutton let his eyes traveled defiantly around the circle of men to see if anyone disapproved his action.

"Every time I ask for information all I get is a report on 'that kid'. Can't any of you handle a half pint half-breed?"

"He said he was only about a quarter or less Cherokee." Bart offered. He looked a bit sheepish when Averill glared at him. His eyes dropped to study something on the ground.

"Boss, you better watch out for that one. I've seen him in action. I tried to warn Gannon. He didn't listen." Gomez spoke up. "I want no part of him."

"Shut up unless I call on you." Averill stormed. "Here's what I want you men to do. Deliver some of those cattle in the next two or three days. We want plenty of business when the judge returns. Sutton, you take care of that kid, that is if you still have the stomach for it."

"I'll get him. You can count on it." Sutton walked off with a pleased look. He didn't fail very often.

"Boss, I wanted that job." Mitch volunteered. He glared at Gomez. "He needs to see a real hand use an iron."

"He's seen some. He's still here." Gomez replied. "Better leave him alone."

"Wait'll I get him in front of me." Mitch smirked. "A little lead will make him easier to find. That'll stop that sneaking around. I want you there to see it."

"You're going to be busy with cattle, Mitch. If Sutton misses, he's yours. You didn't do so well the last time you tried him if I remember right. Almost got your guts kicked out."

"I better not find out who that was." Mitch snarled as he eyed the crew. Averill's last remark had brought a snicker from somebody. He suspected Bart.

"Get started and I want it done right. I don't even want to know where they are being delivered." Averill turned to walk off. He paused.

"He does seem to be involved in everything that goes wrong. Maybe we are underestimating him. But he's just a kid." He was almost talking to himself.

"King David, in the Bible, wasn't very old when he did some mighty things." Gomez informed him.

Averill gave him a peculiar look as he strode off. "Now we start Bible talk. That's all we need around here. One thing's sure. He's no king."

Averill decided to go to town and stir the marshal up a bit. "He better get on the job. He'll probably be more than happy to do what I tell him some day pretty soon when I get things cleared up."

"I suppose the nesters think they can steal me blind after that deal with Hale. They're in for a surprise. Judge Harvey will have fire in his eye when he comes back." Averill was reporting the loss of several cattle. "Marshal, I want some arrests made."

"Show me the men and the evidence and I'll make the arrests. You'll have to sign the warrants."

"Don't worry. That'll all be taken care of." Averill said as he walked out. "Anybody that steals at all will be tried for it."

Things were working out fine. Looked like plenty of work for the judge.

127

"They move several bunches. It's hard to keep track of all of them." John Billy was telling Virg about the activities of the A-A crew.

"Do you have any idea where they are planning to put them?" Virg asked. "If they have a bunch in a certain area there would be a limit as to where they moved them to."

"Two bunches are close to where you live." John went on to indicate the locations.

"The best place to leave them is either there or Jim's. Course they could give some to Zach." Virg thought for a minute. "John do you have your pencil and some paper?"

"I keep it handy. I'll draw you a picture."

"Good, If you find a chance do your best. If possible see if you can save the real thing." He grinned at John's puzzled expression. "You'll figure out a way."

"Okay, I'll work on it." John was highly pleased by the confidence placed in him.

"Where are the other cattle?" Virg asked.

"Some south of town." John answered. "Don't know the spot yet. Isaac and Sam checking it."

"Thanks John, you fellows are sure doing a job. I better go by the house and check on Maw and Ab. She'd die if anybody accused any of her's of stealing."

The two friends parted. One minute they were there and the next it would have been difficult to tell if anybody was anywhere in the area.

"I'll drop by Jim's on the way back to Paden. I guess Ab can go over and alert Zach. I could stay at home but Newt needs to know what's up." Virg put Buck into a lope.

Chap 18

Sutton was determined not to fail a third time. He knew the place. It would just be a matter of waiting for the opportunity. He gave a chuckle and a twisted smile appeared on his face as he thought of the irony of it.

"Lightening may strike twice in the same place." He said half aloud as he made his way along. "It'll sure be a pleasure."

He planed to use the same spot that had proved so be handy for a fellow named Camden. It might take some time but everybody came home sooner or later.

Sutton would just get into position and wait. Most people weren't as alert around their home place. Make the job that much easier for him.

"When I finish he won't be leaving home again." He boasted. "If Gannon had put me on the job instead of that bumbling Camden he might still be around here with a fist full of land.

"I'm surprised that Averill is able to keep that bunch of his in check. Not that I'm disappointed." Virg mused as he rode toward home. "If he can do the job in court though, it'll be harder to undo it."

"We have to come up with some way to turn the tables." He smiled as a thought came to him. "I better quit talking to myself or I'll be locked up in the looney bin."

He began to imagine what Maw would have cooked. It had been a while since he had been home. The very thought of food made his mouth water.

"Buck, my boy, you can roll in the dust and then eat a bait of those oats. I might get a chance to loaf a few minutes myself."

Buck gave a small snort.

They proceeded on toward the home place.

Virg wouldn't have been so relaxed if he had been aware of the surprise waiting for him just around the corner.

Buck gave another small snort.

"Me too, Buck. I shudder every time I go by this place. That guy almost finished me for sure. Averill seems to be holding Sutton in though. Wonder what he was doing when I caught him that day?" That was still a puzzle to him. "Could he have been after me?"

"Well right up there is where it happened. Lucky for me something was on the ground. If I hadn't leaned over to look at it that slug would have gone right through the middle of me instead of being off to the side some. It sure took me a while to get over it though."

Sutton figured he would have a day or two to wait. It didn't matter, he was used to that. He tied his horse out of sight behind the hill and made his way to the top to find the best spot. He leaned his rifle against a tree.

"That place over to my right looks like the best." He moved over and took a look. "Good cover but best of all a clear view of the road." He was more than satisfied. "Anybody riding through there lives or dies depending on my decision."

He soon had the ideal spot picked out. Probably the same one that Camden had used. That had been an interesting story. He'd never heard of anyone just disappearing like the kid did after he was hit. He glanced down the trail.

"My gosh. I can't believe my luck. I better get my rifle in a hurry. That buckskin will be along in a few minutes. Easiest job I ever had." He almost ran to the spot where he had left his rifle. "Talk about luck. He won't sneak up behind me this time."

"I get the willies when I ride through here. I guess a person can't expect to be shot every time he rides past a place. I just can't help it though. I get uneasy." Virg looked up he slope. "Quit looking for spooks. You'll get afraid of your shadow. Think of the pies Maw may have ready."

He forced himself to relax as he rode up to the place he had been shot out of the saddle. He looked down to see if he could spot the shiny object that had saved his life before. He leaned forward and to the right.

Sutton could hardly believe it. "He's going to ride right up there for a perfect shot. It couldn't be better if I was telling him what to do."

He began to try some experimental sights as Virg approached. "I'll let him slide by and then it'll be perfect."

He took another sight. Some limbs were in the way now. Just a few more feet. His back was in view. He'd be clear of the limb then. Nothing to deflect the bullet. A clear shot and it would all be over.

130

"Now you meddler, take this." Sutton took a deep breath, let most of it out, sighted carefully along the rifle barrel and his finger squeezed the trigger. The rifle was steady as a rock when the hammer fell.

"It's still there." Virg leaned over to look. "Hey!" He yelped as he tumbled out of the saddle. He left so fast it looked like he had jumped.

'Crack! The shot came loud and clear.

Virg hit the ground and rolled over. He was in the same depression that he had fallen in when Camden had shot him. He had a burning sensation in his back. He had sighted a wisp of smoke up the ridge as he rolled over into the lowest area of the ditch. Question was could he do anything about it.

Buck bolted into the trees just ahead. A small rabbit beat him there.

"Got him. Saw it hit." Sutton exclaimed. "I just wished he'd known what hit him and who delivered the slug." He was a cautious man however, so did not expose himself.

"Don't want some nester to see me. I'll wait a minute and ease around where I can see him. He fell in that draw." He tried his best to make out any sign of Virg. "That must be deeper than I thought it was."

He decided to hold his position.

"At least that heathen won't sneak up on anybody else. I wonder what smart remark he'd have now."

Buck looked back toward the spot where Virg had left the saddle. After bolting into the trees he stopped. This was a part of his training. He saw some movement in the small gulley. He held his position and waited.

"I don't think I better lay here and take any naps. Man, that stings." Virg shrugged his shoulders and flexed his arms. Everything seemed to be working. The only discomfort was the stinging on his back. "The good Lord must be watching over me. Good thing because I wasn't doing a very good job of it myself."

Moving as quickly as he could without exposing himself he worked his way into the trees. This required him to crawl with his head and backside down. It was not an easy task but time spent among the Cherokees had taught him many skills. He remembered crawling out of this same place some time back when he was in much worse shape.

The low place ran slightly away from the trail but provided cover all the way to the brush.

He soon joined Buck. "Good boy, you tried to warn me but I was to busy thinking about my stomach. I knew you wouldn't leave me. Now to get my rifle and we'll see if we can give this guy a little of his own medicine."

"There you are you little rascal. If I hadn't tumbled out off the saddle to grab you I'd be a goner now." He said as a small rabbit scuttled out of a small brush pile. "Don't worry, you've earned your freedom. I may never bother a rabbit again."

He was sure he knew where the shot came from. The problem was to get around behind the place without being spotted.

"I'll send Buck on home. Maybe he'll see him and think I'm still in that gully. It's worth a try." He headed Buck up the road toward home.

"Go on home, boy." He patted him on the hip and Buck set off at a fast walk. "Now for a little game of war. He won't leave until he's sure."

Virg set off through the brush back the way he had come. He still had that stinging in his back but it didn't hamper his movements.

"There's no doubt that I got him." Sutton wanted to make sure of his kill though so he remained in place. "He's in that low place I know. I'll wait a minute. If by some chance he raises up I'll put another slug in him." He kept a sharp watch on the spot.

The time drug on. He'd have to move soon so that he could see into the low place.

"I better get my horse before I move around to much." He still watched for some movement. He considered getting his horse and leaving.

"Darn, just my luck he'd fall in a hole. If by chance he's not dead and I go back and report he is they'll laugh me out of the country. I better make sure of it."

Virg was soon out of sight of the clearing. He wouldn't be in sight from the ambush spot either. Turning to his right he trotted up the ridge, keeping in the trees and brush. When he reached the top he turned to the right again and headed back.

"I better start being a little more cautious. Be stupid to luck out back there then run right into a bullet when I know it's waiting for me."

He began to move toward the spot where the shot had come from. He moved with utmost caution but was compelled by the need to move quickly. The rifleman had had ample time to change position. He could have gone to his horse and left the area. He hadn't heard the sound of it leaving however.

"I better check out his horse." There was an area of sparse cover that he had to cross. If he moved quickly he was more likely to attract attention. He went down on his hands and knees and started to crawl. This afforded more concealment.

Suddenly he stopped. Had that been movement? He was in a poor place to engage in a battle with rifles. His only hope would be in concealment so he slid a bit to his left where cover was better.

"Something moved up there. I just wished it would move again." Virg was pretty confident that he was hidden well enough but it would be difficult to make any progress in the direction he wanted to go. He continued to scan the hillside. "Sure still now. Nothing moving. That's not normal." In ordinary circumstances birds and things would be moving about.

Sutton continued to watch the place where Virg had disappeared. "It sure looks like he would still be in that low spot. There's no way for him to leave there without me seeing him. He's probably finished."

If he had been an experienced woodsman his confidence would have been little lower. He had spent a lot of time at his present occupation but had not had the training that Indian warriors routinely went through.

"That blasted horse will reach home soon so I better get

133

my horse and make sure, then be on my way." He began to ease back toward the crest of the ridge.

This was the movement that Virg had spotted.

"That's him all right. He's moving over the top, probably headed for his horse." Virg moved quickly now. He had to get there fast or the man might be gone. "I'll just have to chance it." When the hat disappeared he jumped to his feet and made a dash for the spot. It would be to bad if the fellow looked this direction.

"Made it." Virg breathed. "Now to ease up and check the back side of this place." He made his way, on his hands and knees to the crest. This was tough going while carrying a rifle.

"There he is. It's my old friend, Mr. Sutton." He considered the situation. "He'll mount and ride off before I can get to him. Not a chance to ease up on him."

Sutton moved directly to his horse untied it and mounted while keeping his rifle in his hand. He would need it when he spotted his victim. He'd just put another slug in him and be on his way.

"He's moving out I believe. To many trees and limbs to get a clear shot at him." Virg was disappointed in a way. He wanted to get this over with. "No telling who's next on his list. He may have been turned loose on the settlers. Might even be some of the family. Can't have that."

He could still keep track of Sutton through the trees. There was something puzzling about his direction.

"Hey, he's going to move around where he can get a better look." Virg mused. "Maybe I can help him see his target. I better be careful that he doesn't get to good a look." He took off at a fast trot to get into position.

When Sutton found his quarry missing he was sure to take off at a run. He decided to be ready to stop that.

"Be a lot better to settle things here and now. If not, he'll still be out there. There's not enough time to spend hunting him down." Virg moved on.

"I can see most of the hollow. He should be right in there. I'm sure that's where he hit the ground. I'll just ease to my left a bit." Sutton nudged his horse. He had his rifle

134

in a ready position.

"You looking for somebody, Mr. Sutton?" Virg asked. He was well concealed.

Crack! A bullet whistled past Virg's ear. Sutton had shot from the hip and at the sound. He was good. A few inches different and he would have accomplished the job.

Crack! Virg also shot from the hip. He had been carrying his rifle ready in case he needed it in a hurry. He had planned to give Sutton a chance to surrender. Now he mentally scolded himself for not having his pistol ready. At this range it would be pretty handy. The bullets from it would be more easily deflected by a limb, however. Better stick to the rifle.

Sutton fell off the side of his horse and rolled down the front side of the ridge. His descent was stopped when he bumped into a tree. His rifle was still clutched in his hand. He worked the lever with his one hand as he moved behind the tree. The left one was useless. Virg's shot hadn't missed completely.

"Let him stick his head over that hill." Sutton readied his rifle. His left shoulder was numb. It would soon began to hurt.

Virg was not about to do what was expected. Most people would charge straight up and over. Cherokees taught better lessons than that. He moved to his right and then up to the top.

"He's right handed. If he's behind a tree it will be in his way." Virg said as he moved.

Crack! Sutton fired again. "That'l show him." He had seen movement and fired at it. "He's a smart one. Didn't come over where I expected."

Everything got quiet. Sutton reloaded. He got no return fire. This puzzled him. "Maybe my luck has improved some." He muttered.

Virg lay still. He looked like he was done for.

If Sutton had known the damage the last shot had done he would have been on his feet finishing things.

Virg blinked his eyes trying to clear his sight. The bullet hadn't hit him but had filled his eyes full of grit. "If

135

that guy jumps now I'll have to do some blind shooting myself. That business with the tree sure saved my hide."

Sutton was still undecided as to what move to make next. If he had both hands available he'd be able to maneuver better.

Virg continued to rapidly blink his eyes. They were clearing up somewhat. If Sutton didn't make a move to quickly maybe he could see him when he did.

The silence grew and held for an eternity.

There was movement.

Crack! A rifle sounded in the stillness. "Oohh-". The groan followed the shot.

The sound of a rifle being reloaded sounded.

Crack! The rifle spoke again.

"Ooohh-- Oohh--". There wasn't any doubt about the pain it represented.

A clattering noise was heard. Sounded like a rifle sliding away.

This was followed by gasping breath and two long sighs. It sounded like somebody was out of business.

A deep silence fell over the area. It held for several minutes.

One pair of eyes watched to see if another shot was needed.

Another pair flitted about and waited for the next piece of lead to strike. He figured it would bring the end of things. He was defenseless.

Finally a voice sounded.

" Can you hear me?"

"Yeah. Ohhh."

"Don't try for that pistol on your hip or I'll put a bullet right below your belt." Virg had moved so that he could see the weapon. Sutton's rifle was off to the side and down the grade several feet. "And I remember that hold out so don't try for it either."

"I don't have any hands left to use a gun." Sutton groaned. "I'm shot to pieces."

"Well, I'm not taking any chances. I'll shoot you dead center if you move a hair." Virg stood up and moved to a position where he could watch any move made. "I'll just remove the temptation in case you're not telling the whole truth. You've been known to leave out some facts at times."

Sutton was on his stomach so Virg eased up to him keeping on the alert for any sudden movement. He now held his pistol.

He studied Sutton for a couple of minutes then picked the pistol from his holster. When he was satisfied that Sutton was out of action he reached under him and removed the weapon under his shirt.

"Slick little arrangement you have there." The front of Sutton's shirt was fixed for easy access to the pistol under it.

Virg could see what Sutton meant about being shot to pieces. The last two shots had been fired by Virg. The first had blown a hole in the upper leg and the second had smashed through Sutton't right hand. That along with the hole in his left shoulder put both hands out of action.

"I'm trying to figure out what to do with you, Mr. Sutton" Virg told him. "Maybe I'll just leave you here for the varmints."

"Oohh-, That would be the same as murder." Sutton moaned. "It ain't human to do that."

"I kinda wonder what you would call your little game." Virg stopped and listened. "I think I hear someone. Maybe that's human."

Sure enough it came again. "Heyyy. Virrrg. Hey."

"Virrg. Where are you? Answer me." It was Maw and Ab. Guess Buck had made it home.

"Right up here on the ridge." Virg yelled. "Come on up."

They scrambled up the slope.

"We heard a lot of shooting." Ab said as they came close. "What you after? Oh, I see."

"What was all the shooting? Who is this man? What happened to him? Did you do this?" Maw fired the questions in rapid fire order. "Are you going to answer me? Are you all right?"

Virg grinned at her. "Which question are you most interested in?"

"You know the answer to that. It just came out last."

"I know."

She grabbed him and hugged him. "You know what's important to me."

"I'll explain this whole thing but we better do something for him before he kicks off."

Sutton was getting pale and was shivering. His breathing was irregular.

"You two take care of him. I'll go get the wagon to haul him in." Ab volunteered. "I'll be back in a hurry."

Virg and Maw began to do what they could to stop the bleeding and ease Sutton into a better position.

Ab soon returned with the wagon filled with hay and they loaded Sutton and headed for the house.

"That's how it happened." Virg said as he finished telling them about his duel with Sutton.

"We ought to hang the worthless good-for-nothing." Maw snapped. "The idea of shooting innocent people from ambush. And you're only a kid too."

"Maw, I'm not a kid anymore." Virg protested. "Maybe we can make him good for something. He might be willing to do some talking in order to keep from hanging."

Ab had been silent as Virg and his mother talked. Now he spoke up. "That's an idea but we'll have to keep him alive and out of sight for a while."

"I think I have an idea where we can stake him out." Virg replied. " Believe I know just the place."

They soon had Sutton in a spare bedroom. His clothing were removed so as to treat his wounds.

"He's pretty well messed up. His shoulder is busted. That arm may not work as well after this. His leg should heal up all right but that right hand won't ever be worth much." Ab was reporting his findings. "One eye also has some problems. Looks like some bark hit him in the face. He looks like he'll recover though."

"Virg, I've told you that nothing good will come of using guns. Just look at this man." Maw Rankin fussed.

"I know but Maw, this man as you call him was trying to kill me. A little while ago you were ready to hang him." Virg shook his head. "If some of those cattlemen rode up and started shooting and wanted to run us off our land."

He paused "What would you do then?"

"I'd get the shotgun and shoot the skunks." She snapped. "I see what you mean. Might as well forget about arguing with you."

"Maw, I've got to head back to town and let Newt and them in on the cattle movement. I need to stop by and warn Jim too." Virg told them about the movement of several bunches of cattle. "We need to check on the ones south of town also."

"I just wish you could stay around here. Seems like you're gone all the time."

"If we don't put an end to this we'll all lose our land and maybe wind up in jail if we don't hang. Then we'd all be gone, all the time."

"Trouble, trouble always trouble. I wish we could live in peace." She looked at him. "Well, I guess everybody has to do what they must. You do kinda have a knack for getting involved though."

"Just doing what you taught me, Maw. Help your neighbors. Do onto others as you would have them do unto you. As you say, it's from the Bible. The Golden Rule, if I remember right."

"I can never win. I guess you were paying more attention than I thought when I told you those things."

"It's not what you said, Maw, it's what I've seen you do." He smiled at her. "I'll be back in a day or two. I'll send John Billy by after Mr. Sutton."

Maw wiped a couple of tears away as he rode off. "It's a chore, raising boys." She said. "Don't know if girls would be as much of a problem."

She stared after him. "Guess I won't ever know. I'm stuck with what I've got and I'm not complaining, Lord. I wouldn't trade them for anything." She added hastily before bursting out in a hymn.

Chap 19

"Jim, I'm telling you to keep a sharp lookout. This bunch mean business." Virg went on to tell Jim about the trouble with Sutton.

"Maybe he was just trying to settle the score with you." Jim suggested. "He was pretty mad about the other times I hear. You have made some people pretty mad."

"He takes orders, you can be sure of that. I doubt if he spends much time running around settling scores. Anyway it'll be a long time before he does that kind of work again, score settling or otherwise. You keep your eyes peeled. We don't want Mary left with a jailbird husband or one at a necktie party."

"That makes sense. I don't either. I'll be on the alert. You be careful too, we don't want to lose you even if you are somewhat of a pest occasionally." He gave Virg a big grin. "Sorry you don't have time to stop and eat."

"I'll bet you are. I'll try to make time to do that the next time I'm by here. Wouldn't want you to be disappointed every time." Virg waved as he turned Buck and loped off.

"He sure must be in a hurry to turn down a meal without having to work for it." Jim laughed as he finished. "Mary sure won't believe it."

"Marshal, you told me that if anyone signed the papers then you had no choice but to arrest them."

"You're supposed to have evidence. I can't arrest someone on your say so."

"I remember exactly what you said. If Sutton had signed a complaint against me you would have arrested me. When a judge showed up we would have had a trial."

"That's right, Marshal. That's what you told him. I was right there with you." Mr. Higgins informed him. "We have to treat everybody alike don't we or are some better than others?"

Simmons scowled at Higgins but didn't answer. He then turned to Virg.

"Well, I did say that but you're just a kid."

"You mean I don't have to obey the law?"

"You sure do. Everybody has to obey the law or suffer the consequences."

"Then I'll sign the papers and you do the rest. We'll

140

let the judge decide."

"I don't know."

"I'll just tell everybody that the marshals office is only for the big shots." Mr. Higgins said as he headed for the door.

"Hold on a minute, Higgins. Go ahead and sign the papers then we'll see about it."

The papers were soon signed.

"Marshal Simmons I would rather you didn't warn these people about this." Virg urged. "Might make them harder to round up."

"You don't have to worry about me telling anyone about this deal." Marshal Simmons responded. "I'd be branded as ready for the loony bin."

Virg walked out with Mr. Higgins. He was pleased with the marshal's statement.

"Virg, you're going to stir up a mess if you keep on. This may be fun at that. It'll be something to watch 'his honor' handle this case. Okay, I'll keep it under my lid even if it will be hard to do." Higgins was laughing as he headed back to his favorite spot.

Virg set off to locate Newt. He saw him come out of the doctor's office.

"Hi Newt, I've been looking for you. If the doc keeps his nurse I guess you'll be sick all the time." Virg grinned as Newt turned a light red. "How is Molly anyway?"

"She's okay. I wanted to talk to the doctor about something."

"I'll take your word for it. Say, it's Wednesday and that judge will be back Monday according to him. We better get popping if we're going to come up with anything at all."

Newt scratched his head. "I'm at my wits end. I can't think of a thing. What did your Indian buddies tell you?"

"We may have stirred the bunch up when we messed up that trial the other day. They're moving several bunches of cattle."

"You don't reckon they plan to have some more cases ready for the judge when he gets back?"

"By golly Newt, you're beginning to think a little bit.

Virg said. "See when you get your mind off of the nurse, your head works pretty good."

"Where are they moving the cattle to?"

"Two bunches are out toward our place. Some more are south of town and back west. I need to check with my friends to find out just where they are."

"You go on and do that, Virg, and I'll stay close to the marshal. I'll try to find out if anything comes his way."

"Okay. Let me know if anything happens that I need to know about. I'm going down toward the Hale place and scout around a little."

Virg was about halfway to the Dad Hale's when he saw one of the Indian scouts sitting astride his horse off to the side of the trail. He was sure that he had moved out in the open to get his attention so he rode toward him.

The Indian sat waiting for him to approach. As he drew near he recognized Sam Harjo.

"Hello, Sam. You're getting a little careless sitting out here where anyone happening along could spot you aren't you?"

Sam grinned at him. "You just slipped right up on me. I didn't know you were in miles of me. I'll have to learn to be more careful. If I let a Cherokee slip up and catch me I'd be ruined with the Creeks. Probably the only way one could do it was if I let him."

"I'll bet you did. I wouldn't have known you were here if you didn't want me to." Virg moved over and shook his hand. "You fellows are doing twice as much as all the rest of us. Anything to report?"

"They have cattle in a place almost west of here. Only two men with them now. Four drove them. I don't think they'll be moved until the others return." He went on to describe the place and how to get there without being seen by the herders.

"Thanks, Sam. You and Isaac can turn the job over to some of us now. I have a favor to ask of you fellows." Virg went on to explain about Sutton and the need to keep him hidden for a while.

"We'll take him to the Chief. He won't leave the village."

142

"He'll need some doctoring. I want him in shape to come back to Paden while the judge is there if we need him."

"Don't worry. Just let us know when you want him."

"I'll see some of you fellows in about a week if not sooner. Sam, tell Isaac and John to keep up the good work. You might get John to show you that stuff he can do with a pencil and paper."

The two friends waved as they rode off. A few seconds later neither was in sight.

"He let a Cherokee slip up and catch him. Ha!" Virg smiled as he said this. "The only way one could, I believe he said. I wonder."

"Get down, young fellow, we may have something to eat soon. What brings you out this way?" Dad Hale called out when Virg rode into the yard.

"Checking on stolen cattle. They tell me that you Hales need to be watched." Virg laughed as he slid to the ground. "The way you people eat it would take a cow every day or two. That would do away with a lot of evidence I imagine."

Dad Hale started to reply but was laughing so hard he couldn't get an answer out.

"Didn't mean to make you so mad, Mr. Hale." Virg joshed. "I'm usually pretty friendly."

Dad Hale finally recovered his breath. "You sure know how to bump a fellow's funny bone. Riding up here and practically calling us cow thieves. Have you seen your friend Sutton again? He didn't act like he liked you very much."

"Yeah, I saw him this morning. He had a little problem. He's going to take a few days off and rest up." Virg told about the episode with Sutton.

"He may just come after you again."

"I doubt if he'll be in any shape to go after anybody for a good long time, if ever." He outlined the nature of the wounds.

"And you didn't even get a scratch. Hard to figure."

"I got a burn across my back. Maw says it's not hard
143

to understand. She says the good Lord was watching over me."

"Glad to hear you say that." Dad Hale replied. "She must be quite a woman to let her youngen run all over the place helping folks."

"She is."

"You never did answer my question."

"I guess I better tell you or you'll probably refuse to feed me. And you know I don't eat much." Virg told him about the cattle staked out west of the Hale place.

"They surely know we'll be on the lookout." Mr. Hale had a puzzled expression. "You reckon they have their scheme aimed at some of my neighbors?"

"That might be but if I was going to do something like that I'd wait until the trial was going on. Not many will be on the lookout then."

"Dog gone it, that would work for sure. You're sure good at figuring crooked deals. Hope you don't turn into a wild one as I'd hate it if I had to help hang you. Probably save me a bunch of groceries though." Dad laughed as he enjoyed turning the tables on Virg a little.

"You'd probably do it too, if food was scarce." Virg countered. "I'd hate to take the chance."

It was a few minutes before Dad Hale got his breath and continued.

"We need to do something to buffalo their plans. We don't want to tip them off though." Dad Hale thought a moment. "Let's think on it some. What would be the best way?"

"Mr. Hale, Averill was sure surprised and bothered about the way you took Sutton and that Lem in according to Newt. I wonder what his reaction would be if you could do him another nice favor?"

"You have any ideas? You seem to be pretty good at this crooked stuff." Dad chuckled at the thought.

"There's something if you're willing to take the risk. It sure would be an eye opener for the people that have their doubts about you folks if we can pull it off." Virg went on to outline a plan.

Dad Hale began to laugh in a low voice then it

144

increased to a deep rumble. "By golly! We'll give it a try. That's a dandy idea. We'll be able to tell that story for years. We've just gotta do this right." He began to laugh again. He would stop and think a minute and then start laughing again.

"I'll need one of your boys to go with me to get the lay of the land." Virg told him. "I want your best hand in the woods. Don't want them to see us looking them over."

"That'll be Lanny. It's to late for today so let's eat and you can take off early in the morning."

"That's where you're wrong. Tonight is the time to look them over. Easier to keep out of sight and your hired help won't see Lanny drifting off."

"Well, I said you were good at crooked stuff." Hale chuckled. "That proves my point. Working at night so you won't be seen. You'll teach my boy bad habits."

"Mr. Hale, where are the men that Averill sent over here to keep an eye on you folks?"

"They're down at that little house, yonder." He pointed out a building a short distance away. "They don't come to the house much. During the day we all work and they join in or they don't eat."

"We'll need to do our little job without tipping them off. Then we'll let them help finish it." Virg chuckled at the thought. "That ought to make Mr. Averill a lot happier."

"I'll bet. He didn't seem so pleased when his bushwhackers rode in with us. If some of his men helped with this deal I'm sure he wouldn't be willing to pay them a bonus." Dad Hale had a big smile on his face. "It might be worth a bonus to watch his expression when we go in for the trial."

"We better not let them know about our little scouting trip tonight."

"That's easy as Lanny is just a kid and they don't pay much attention to him. He won't be missed for a few hours."

"I'm right over here, Lanny." Virg said in a low voice. He had eaten and then left the Hale place as if to return to Paden.

"Dad told me you'd be waiting for me so I caught up old Bess and came on. She was in a pasture away from the house so those two fellows don't know anything about me leaving."

Virg told him the location of the cattle. "We're really lucky to have this little haze settle in. It's light enough but not as bright as it would be with the moon out like it is if the night was clear. Make us harder to see."

"I know where the place is. There's a spot this side of there we can leave the horses." Lanny explained. "I guess you want to go on foot the last part."

"You lead the way. They haven't been there long so probably haven't moved." Virg told him. "We sure don't want to stumble over them though so be careful."

They rode toward the area keeping to the shadows as much as possible.

"I'll leave Buck here. You better tie your mare over there on the other side of that brush." Virg suggested. "We don't want them to make much noise."

They took off through the woods, moving fast but making almost no sound.

"Psst. Psst. Hey Virg." Lanny had stopped. He nervously looked around.

"What's the problem?" Virg whispered.

"I lost track of you. I've never seen anybody get through the woods like you do. It's hard to keep up with where you are." Came the whispered response. "It's like following a ghost."

"Hope there aren't any of them around." Virg laughed. "Spend some time with a bunch of Indians and you'll think I'm clumsy as an ox. I hear the cattle right over that little rise so we better be careful."

"I didn't hear anything."

"Sure you did. You just didn't notice the difference. Listen-- Hear that?"

"Gosh, I see what you mean." Lanny agreed. "You just have to pay attention and listen hard."

"Let's ease up there and take a look." Virg went into a crouch and moved up the slope keeping under cover of any available brush. He was careful not to brush against any of it

146

making unnecessary noise.

As he reached the crest of the ridge he held up his hand.

Lanny was close behind him and caught the signal. He was already improving his skills.

Down below was a campfire with two men seated next to it. They were both facing the fire with cups in their hands.

"That's good. Looking into the fire they won't pick up any chance movement away from it." He smiled as he observed the men. "No matter, I better stay on my toes."

Virg motioned for Lanny to stay where he was. He wanted to move around the ridge so that he could make sure that no one else was present. He checked the wind direction. He didn't want some bronc to get wind of him.

"This is the easiest work we've had to do for some time, Rance. Just lay around and loaf."

"I'd rather be doing something, Trip. This hiding out gives me the willies. No telling what kind of varmints are wandering around out there."

"Ah Rance, you're just jumpy. Don't start seeing spooks behind every tree. There's nobody in five miles of this place. Quit worrying about varmints. We only have to worry about the two legged kind."

"I don't like being out away from everybody. I just don't know how long I can handle this."

"You better handle it for a few days anyway or Averill will have your hide. We better not mess this job up. We'll be able to finish it in no time after Monday. Then we can watch the fun."

"I thought Mitch was the one that sent us down here."

"He did but you know who we're working for."

The two men kept up this line of talk. Rance would have really been bothered if he had known about the varmint that had moved around the camp and listened in on most of the conversation. He was a lot closer than five miles too.

"Come on Lanny, let's go."

"Whew! I almost jumped out of my skin. I didn't know you'd come back." Lanny whispered.

The two boys moved back off the ridge and made their way to the horses.

"Could I learn to move in the woods the way you do?" Lanny asked. "I thought I was already a pretty good hand in the woods but have I had my eyes opened."

"I imagine you could. The Cherokees say to use this idea as you move. One mistake and you're dead. That helps to keep your mind on what you are doing." Virg explained with a smile. "They had to live it all the time not just when they decided to practice it."

"I guess that would make a difference. I get to moving along pretty good then begin to think of something else. Usually wind up spooking the game I'm after."

"That's the idea. If your hide was on the line you wouldn't be thinking of anything else. You did all right tonight though."

"Thanks, Virg. What do we do now?"

"Lanny, you report to your dad. Averill's bunch will think I'm gone so it would look odd if I showed up at breakfast. I'll head back to Paden. By the way isn't Zach Vaughn supposed to come over and work for you folks?"

"He's going to get an early start the day after tomorrow. Anyway I hope he does."

"Good. See you, Lanny."

Each headed for his destination. Virg was satisfied that Lanny would give Mr. Hale all the information he needed.

Chap 20

"I am afraid we may be fighting a losing battle." Newt was saying. "Is there any reason to think that what you're reporting will have any effect on the outcome of Dan's trial?"

"I don't know." Virg replied. "All we can do is hope for the best. What do you think, Mr. Higgins?"

"A war is never won by a doughting army. If these things happen it might blow things wide open. People get mad they sometimes lose their heads and make bad mistakes." Mr. Higgins laughed. "I'm eager to see the outcome of that one little deal you hatched up."

"I've lost most of the day going over plans." Virg said. "We need to have some kind of plan though so we can make the most of our efforts."

"Now we all know what our jobs are. So let's be sure to do our best." Newt replied. "Virg, you go on and find your friends and see if they have anything more to report."

"I better move along because we only have two more days to get what we need." Virg walked over to Buck, mounted and rode out of town.

He rode into the campsite where John and his two helpers had been earlier. There was no sign of them. Examination of the evidence revealed they hadn't been there for some time.

"Where should I look next? They might be over by Jim's place. I'll try there then double back toward Zach's" Virg looked up at the sun. Not long until it would be dark "I better take a chance and ride out in the open so one of them can spot me."

He kept a sharp eye out for any sign of any of his friends. He was not in luck.

It was almost dark when he rode into the yard at Jim's place. There was no sign of life there, at least human life. The hen house door stood open and the last chicken was heading for the roost.

"Maybe I'm the only person left. If the rapture has come and left me behind I sure made a wrong turn somewhere along the line." Virg was making the rounds. He closed the door on the chickens and did another job or two that was needed to settle down for the night. He unsaddled Buck and fed him some oats and hay.

Going into the house he began to prepare a meal. He went about the work cheerfully but glanced out the window occasionally. From the amount of food he was fixing it looked like he was expecting company. Some people would have said that he planned to eat it all himself.

He had the food almost ready to serve when he heard a wagon approaching.

"Ho, hold up horse. Mary, I better see who's in the house. Well for gosh sakes, look what we have here. We leave for a few minutes and he tries to slip in and eat us out of house and home."

Virg stepped out the door.

"Get down and come in. Make yourself at home. You're just in time to share my supper." Virg called out. "I fixed a little something extra in case I had company show up."

"I was dreading the job of cooking supper this late so hope you have something that us normal people can eat." Mary said as she walked through the door. "Some of the things you think up to fix, well, I just don't know. I'll reserve my opinion until I see and smell it."

"Now Mary, you know I'm a good cook. I just try to copy what you fix. If I get anywhere close it's bound to be good."

"Don't try to flatter me. I'll bet my kitchen is a mess." She looked around and gave a look of approval. "At least it's pretty clean. That's one thing in your favor. Now if we can eat what you've come up with."

Jim came in from putting the team away. He walked over to the table and sat down.

"I'm ready to eat. When you're as hungry as I am you can eat anything. Hope it doesn't do me in." He kept a straight face as he spoke. "Have a seat, Mary, we've been invited to supper."

"That's right, we have." She took a seat. "Bring on the food." She snapped her fingers.

Virg served her. "Is everything satisfactory, mam?" He turned to Jim. "Here you are, sir, help yourself." He stepped back from the table. "Would it offend you if a lowly servant also ate?"

They all burst into laughter.

The meal was finished and the dishes were washed and dried. Virg had insisted on doing this chore while they visited.

"You're just doing that to ease your conscience in case we all die of food poisoning." Jim informed him.

"Now Jim, don't be to hard on him. Why just think how lucky the girl that gets him will be. He can do all the housework while she sits around and looks pretty. Speaking of that, I might let you try it a little."

"Danged if he doesn't bring trouble with him every time." Jim grimaced. "We better change the subject before I'm in deeper trouble."

"I guess a good brother isn't appreciated no matter how hard he tries." Virg complained. "Changing the subject suits me. Have you seen John, Isaac, or Sam in the last couple of days?"

"Isaac and Sam came by here day before yesterday. Seems they were going to take your friend Sutton to get some fixing up." Jim replied. "It's odd he would ask them to look after him. I didn't think they cared much for that character."

"You know better than that, Jim." Mary broke in. "If those fellows took him off you can bet that your brother had a hand in it."

"Now Mary, you know that they're friendly to me because they like me. Friends do favors for each other." Virg thought for a moment. "I better see if John is around. I'll bet he finds me in the morning. I sure hope he does."

Jim and Mary spent the next hour telling him about their trip to visit Ab and his mother.

"Maw and Mandy Vaughn have been working on a way to store food for the winter. That Mandy sure is a lot of company for Maw." Mary told Virg. "She enjoys those two kids too."

"I went over to help Ab fix some of the lot fence. We had to cut a bunch of new poles. We also replaced some around the garden while we were at it. They said the only other one that had time to help, spent all his time gadding about the country poking his nose into other people's business." Jim grinned as he said this.

"I better get some rest if I'm going to find some place to poke my nose tomorrow." Virg answered. "Otherwise I'll be so tired it might be cut off. I'd sure look funny without a nose."

"You look funny enough with one." Jim laughed.

They were all in a jolly mood as they went to bed.

When Jim and Mary woke up the next morning Virg was gone.

"I'm surprised he left before eating." Mary observed.

"Better check the food supply." Jim laughed.

Virg wanted to be out and about early in order to find John. Time was growing short. Something was needed to take the focus off of the case against Dan Hale.

If Averill's bunch would only make a mistake. Maybe Sutton could be pressured to talk if some other thing could be found to weaken Averill. It was all they had.

"Maw always told me to just keep on working at a thing if I believed in it. Things will usually work out in the end according to her." Virg could only hope she was right. "She says the Lord makes the final decision anyway but he expects us to do what we can in the meantime."

He rode back in the direction of the place he had met John before. Time was to valuable to use in their game of stalking each other. If John wanted to best him at it there would be no objection this time.

"I might have time to go by Zach's and check with him. He's probably gone but Mandy may know something. It won't hurt to check." Virg put Buck into a lope and headed straight for the Vaughn farm.

"Hello Mandy, I'm looking for John Billy or one of his friends. I'd like to ask Zach about some other things too if he's around."

"Zach has gone over to work for the Hales, Virg. He won't be back until late. I haven't seen any of the Indian boys and Zach didn't mention them."

"Well, I'm about out of ideas. Can't think of where to look next. They usually find me."

"I saw a Indian man when I was chasing the cow in." Jerimy Vaughn chimed in.

"An Indian, Jerimy." Mandy corrected him.

Jerimy grinned. "An Indian, was riding off at a distance."

"How did you know it was an Indian?" Mandy asked him.

"Virg showed me some things about watching people and how they act. Daddy also has taught me some things he learned from the Cherokees. I've been practicing. It was an

Indian all right." Jerimy's teeth fairly sparkled in his black face as he smiled at them.

"He's been slipping up on me and scaring me." Nell, the little sister exclaimed. "I'll have Virg or one of the Indians sneak up on him if he doesn't stop it."

"That's telling him, Nell. Say Jerimy, which way was he headed?" Virg asked.

"Kinda in the direction of Paden."

"Thanks, Jerimy. Nell, you might get even by slipping up on him and scaring him bad enough to slow down his growing." Virg turned his attention back to Mandy. "I better hit the trail in that direction. If one of those fellows show up tell them I'm hunting them."

"I'll do that." She called as he rode off.

"Come on children. Time for your lessons. Nell, you might try scaring him out of eating so much. He can eat as much as two men." Mandy hugged her two children as they went into the house. "Your daddy will want to know how you're doing as soon as he gets home. He'll be late getting in."

"It would be fun to drop off and engage John in our game of stalking but I can't see using that much time right now." Virg muttered as he rode into a wooded area. He decided to stay in the saddle and let John do the stalking.

"I better see if I can locate John instead of waiting for him to show up. He may not know where to find me when he tries." Virg grinned as he scratched his head. "Now that sure was an odd thought for me to have. John not know where to find me. How silly. I better not tell him that or he'll be insulted."

He rode into an area where he often found John and began to ride from one spot to another.

"He may not be in this place since I've asked him to keep his eye on cattle." Virg started to ride on to the next logical spot.

Crash! Something hit a bush off to Virg's right. He turned Buck so he faced that direction. The bush moved.

"Come on out. I see where you are. Can't fool me that easy." He said as he kept a close watch on the bush and it's

153

surroundings. He waited.

"I've got you. I'm behind you. Your string trick works pretty good." A grinning John Billy walked out of the brush behind Virg.

"You waylaid me for sure. Guess I better quit revealing my secrets or you might get as good as I am at this kind of thing."

"A Creek could never match a Cherokee. At least that's what you Cherokees say." John burst into laughter. "You ought to see the look on your face."

"It came as quite a shock to hear you admit that we Cherokees are so good." Virg said in mock surprise. "It makes me respect you a lot. You being man enough to admit that."

"Be more careful when you ride around in a place. Your horse almost stepped on me back there a ways."

This produced a laugh from both friends.

"John, what have you fellows found out since I saw you? We located the cattle south of Paden and we have a plan for them. Has anything happened to the bunches up here?"

"They just stay in the same place. The men sit and take it easy all the time. Looks like they're waiting for something." John glanced at Virg. "You have any idea about that?"

"I think so. They are probably waiting for the judge to come back. Then everybody's attention will be on the trial. Nobody watching things then. What do you think of that, John?"

John thought about it a minute. "You may be on to something. It sure might work if people weren't watching for it."

"When will Isaac and Sam be back?"

"Today, if nothing holds them up."

"It sure would be handy if you fellows kept a watch up here. Don't bother with the ones south of Paden unless they drive more down that way. Any luck with the pencil?"

"Not yet. It's going to rain though. That would probably help."

"If you have any luck with it, we need to get Bill

154

Smith and Joe Nolan to hurry over to Paden to back you up"

Virg looked around to see if he could detect any sign of clouds. He didn't see any.

"You look for rain?"

Virg laughed. "I guess there are still some other Indian skills for me to study."

"Maybe I'll teach you. I don't know though. I can't be giving all of the best Creek secrets to the Cherokees. Might make them equal to us."

"Like for you to do that. It would probably take us a while to catch up." Virg said before changing the subject. "I better get in and see if Newt knows anything more. If one of you go to get Bill, tell him how important it is for two of them to come over."

"Okay, we'll keep watch. I may still show you about rain one of these days."

Virg headed for Paden. They would need some luck to come out on top in this. Two more days.

The rest of that day and the next were spent checking back with various people.

The Hale place looked about as usual. Toad and his helper were still keeping an eye on them. Virg thought he saw Zach among the workers in the hay field. He decided he'd better not try to check with him because of the two Averill men.

"We still have our mind on that deal." Dad Hale told him. "They're still there."

Back in town Newt had no information at all.

Marshall Simmons only glared at him when he asked about how things were going.

Seeing Alex Averill talking with some townspeople and Mr. Higgins, Virg walked over to them.

"Hello, Mr Averill. How are you today?"

Averill gave him a strange look when he turned. "H-Hello young fellow, I'm surprised to see you in town."

"Oh, I come in now and then. Say that's a mighty nice looking horse there. Do you ever race him?"

Averill was surprised at the compliment on his horse. "No, I never have. He's pretty fast but is better at distances. He's a mustang, right out of the Rocky Mountains."

"You mean that you bought him from somebody that raises them up in the mountains?" Virg seemed impressed. "He sure raises some good ones."

The crowd was listening intently to the conversation. They had expected an angry exchange as Averill had been pretty upset the last time in town. Everybody seemed to know about Virg's involvement in it. Most thought he had been the cause of it.

Averill was more than willing to talk about his horse. "I didn't buy him."

"You didn't steal him did you?" Virg asked in a surprised voice. "That's against the law."

"Certainly not. I caught and broke him myself. Nobody has ever ridden him but me."

"Surely he belonged to somebody. You don't see horses just running around loose."

"In the country where I came from there are things called wild horses, kid. They don't belong to anyone, Of course you couldn't be expected to know about that I guess."

"Guess not." Virg scratched his head. "And you just caught him and he was yours. Is that right? That's all there is to it?"

"That's right. I caught him and he was mine. I broke him myself. He's never belonged to anybody but me. I plan to keep him."

"If someone took him away from you, I mean steal him, what would happen?"

"They would hang him for being a horse thief."

"You said he never belonged to anybody. Why does he belong to you more than anyone else?"

"I caught him. He's in my possession. He's my property. Steal him and they'd hang."

"You'd do it by going to the law I guess."

"That's right. You better not get any ideas or you'll have real trouble. I might enjoy seeing you hang. Might be worth a good horse."

"Oh, I wouldn't take him. I have a better horse than that already. Thanks for the advice anyway." Virg turned and went toward Newt's house.

156

"That kid has a lot of questions. He may turn into a lawyer." Mr. Higgins looked at Averill. "He's a pretty good thinker. Comes up with some pretty good ideas once in a while."

Averill watched Virg walk away. He had been surprised to see him. Sutton was supposed to take care of him but his horse had come in by itself. None of the hands had seen anything of the rifleman since he had ridden away from the headquarters.

"I wonder if something happened to him." Averill pondered. "Not much loss if it did. Maybe Mitch can enjoy himself a little after all."

"Did you say something?" Mr. Higgins asked.

Averill glared at him. "Nothing you would be interested in." He growled. This old man irritated him. He began to wonder why he had bothered to stop and talk to these people. He mounted his prize mustang and rode out of town.

"I just don't know if we can do anything. We scramble around and come up empty handed." Newt was clearly exasperated. "Things are sure to blow up if Dan Hale is convicted."

"We can't give up now. I'm just as frustrated as you are." Virg replied. "Maybe I've been depending to much on John Billy. He did such a good job on that deal over at Prague that I keep hoping he'll come up with something now."

"Maybe the rain will settle things down a bit. It sure looks like we are going to get some." Newt pointed to the northwest where a bank of dark clouds were piling up higher by the minute.

"A fellow told me yesterday that it was going to."

"He told you yesterday that it was going to rain today?" Newt asked. "Did you believe him?"

"Didn't have any reason not to. He's a pretty sharp fellow."

"What are we going to do?"

"Stay in out of the rain. Maw says that most people have enough sense to come in out of the rain. She also says

157

she sometimes wonders about me. Don't know why. I have come home wet a few times though."

"In that case I'm on my way to the house. Why not put Buck in that shed and join me. We'll get busy when the rain is over." Newt headed for his house. Virg followed him in after putting Buck away.

"We might get a bright idea if we eat a bite and then forget our problems for a while. You never know what's going to pop into a rested mind." Virg said as the relaxed in the house. "Doesn't look good though."

"Molly will expect to see me in church tomorrow." Newt said. "Maybe you'd like to come."

"It sure won't hurt anything. We need all the help we can get."

It had rained for a good portion of the night. With the morning came a clear sky with only a few scattered white puffy clouds in the southeast.

Virg and Newt went to the church and listened to the sermon along with most everybody else in town. Molly joined them as they left church. Newt made sure that she saw him there.

The preacher was one that grabbed your attention and held it. His readings from the Bible stuck with the theme of his sermon. He kept repeating the statement, 'The Lord will provide', over and over and read passages to illustrate this idea.

"He sure inspires a person to depend on the Lord." Virg said as they headed back to Newt's for a bite to eat.

"That's right. He sure does a good job of making his point." Newt replied. "If you don't get the wrong idea about what you are supposed to do."

"I believe you two are serious for a change. Makes a girl have hope. I better hurry along and help mom with dinner." Molly told them.

They walked on, each deep in his own thoughts. Those thoughts weren't very hopeful most of the time.

"If the Lord provides he'll do more than we have so far." Virg offered. "Maw says to trust him though."

"That's what I've always been told." Newt answered.

158

"He said, 'The Lord will provide', then went on to show that someone took action with what was provided." Virg said as much to himself as to Newt. "There's a lesson in that for us too, I believe."

"Well let's eat what is provided then we can look around to see what other provision is made." Newt added as he began to dig the food out.

It wasn't long until they were finished and were headed back to town.

"There's still a lot of people in town, Newt. I thought they would head for home after church." Virg observed. He exchanged greetings with several people.

"The crowd looks like it is getting bigger all the time. There are your folks over there." Newt told him.

"You're right. I better report or Maw'll be hunting for me. I've found it's better to not dally around when she expects to see me."

Virg headed for the wagon where Maw and Ab were preparing to climb down.

"Hi there. I didn't expect to see you here in town." Virg greeted them.

Maw grabbed Virg and hugged him. "We figured we could spare a couple of days. Good chance to visit with a lot of folks. Everybody'll be here."

"Maw, you'll have everybody in town laughing at me. They think I'm a big bad man and you treat me like a kid."

"You're still my baby boy no matter what people think." She reminded him.

Virg decided he better get the discussion on safer ground. He didn't want people overhearing her talk about him. "You mean you plan to stay?"

"When is the trial going to be?" Ab wanted to know. "I'd like to sit in on it."

"The judge hasn't made it back yet. He said the trial would be tomorrow but he'll have to be here." Virg told them. "The marshal may know more about it. I see him over by his office."

They continued to visit for a short time.

159

"I see some people I want to speak to. I'll be around."
Maw hurried off. "I think I see some of the Freeze family
over there.

"Think I'll check with the marshal." Ab said and then
headed in that direction. "He's usually pretty good at
giving me information."

"I meant to ask them about Jim and Mary." Virg
mused as he watched them move away. "They didn't say
anything about seeing John Billy either."

Newt walked up to where Virg was standing. They
both stood there for sometime watching the crowd of people.
Each was busy with his own thoughts.

"Let's mill around through the folks for a while. We
might find out something by just visiting with them."
Newt suggested. "Never know when someone will give out
something without realizing it."

"Okay with me. Do we go together or not?" Virg
asked. "You seem to be doing the best thinking right
now."

"Let's separate and meet back here in a couple of
hours." Newt suggested. "I'll go down this way."

Virg walked over and visited with one of the families for
a while and then moved on. He heard someone talking in a
loud voice. He turned to look and a woman was staring
straight at him as she talked.

"It's a shame, I say. Young people walking around
with pistols on their hips." The woman's voice carried
clearly to his ears. "Some of them aren't much more than
boys."

"Were you speaking to me, mam?" Virg asked. "I
thought I heard you say something."

"No I wasn't speaking to you. I was speaking about
you and the others like you carrying those guns everywhere
you go." The woman was a large person with a severe look
on her face.

"Mam, I'd be happy if it were so that I didn't have to
carry this thing."

"You don't have to. You could let the law take care of
the problems that come up."

"I guess you are right. If some one robbed me or shot

me down the law could punish them. I just don't much want the law to have to punish someone for killing me."

"It's better for the law to handle them in those cases." The woman gave him a stern look. "We can't take the law into our own hands. There's to many around here willing to do that now."

"It may be but I don't see how that would help me if I were dead. I'm sorry, mam, but until the law is strong enough to keep someone from shooting me I plan to try to watch out for myself as best I can."

"I still think it would be better if we didn't have so many guns being carried around."

"I agree with you lady. Hopefully someday it'll be safe enough for a person to go unarmed. That would be nice." Virg smiled at her. "Hope you folks have a good visit here in town."

He continued his way stopping to visit, talking about conditions, the rain and about the upcoming trial when the chance arose. He didn't come up with much information that sounded useful. He overheard several more remarks about kids carrying pistols.

He made his way back to the spot where Newt was supposed to meet him. There was no sign of him. Virg decided to walk over to the crowd under the tree. Mr. Higgins was sure to be holding court.

The bunch seemed to be having a pretty heated discussion about whatever the topic was. There was little doubt that the trial would be high on the agenda.

"I tell you that there is going to be trouble if that young man is found guilty. The Hales are not going to stand still and let anything happen to that boy." Mr. Higgins was expressing his thoughts on the upcoming trial. "He never stole anything in his life."

"You can't say that for sure. If he's guilty he ought to be punished." Someone in the crowd answered. There were some nods in agreement. Most of those present gave no indication of their thoughts.

"I don't care what anybody says, he's not guilty. I know him to well." Was a reply from another man. "I'll join the Hales if they have to do anything drastic. I can

161

still shoot a little if I have to."

"No outlaw talk now. We have to have some law."

"Who's law? Cattlemen's law?"

"We may have some things for the judge to decide when he gets back besides about Dan Hale." Mr. Higgins dropped the new idea into the discussion.

This immediately got the crowds attention. They began to fire questions. It calmed things for the time being.

Virg decided he didn't want to get involved in the discussion so went back to look for Newt. He hoped Mr. Higgins didn't reveal to much. He was fairly confident that wouldn't happen.

It was some time before Newt showed up. Virg was moving about nervously when he spotted him coming.

"I was afraid you had decided to go visit Molly and leave me at loose ends." Virg called out to Newt as he walked up. "Find out anything?"

"Nothing except that all these folks plan to stay right here until this trial is over. Some are saying we have to let the law handle things but quite a few are willing to join the Hales and bust Dan out if he's found guilty. Things could get hot."

"If a bunch tried to stop that we could have a real war on our hands with Averills bunch just sitting back and watching." Virg shook his head. "I wonder who would be best served by that."

"You know the answer to that. I'm worried about our ability to stop it. A couple of men almost got into a fist fight. I don't think it would take much to create a real split. It could start a real war. Then we'd all be losers."

"The grazers wouldn't be. Time's about to run out and all we have is a couple of things to poke fun at Averill's crowd. If he wins the big one the little ones won't matter." Virg thought for a moment. "Maybe they'll get to ambitious and slip up someway."

"The Lord will provide', don't forget the message. I guess our faith is being tested. Question is, can we pass the test?" Newt looked at Virg. "Your mother advised you to always have hope didn't she?"

"Yes she did. She's usually right about things but

they don't look very good right now."

"I can sure agree with you there." Newt was obviously discouraged. "What more can we do?"

"Don't know but we have to keep trying."

John Billy was pleased when the rain began to fall. I would make a difference in his efforts if anything happened.

"Better get Sam and Isaac busy." He said as he rode to the top of a hill and wig-wagged with a long pole with a feather fastened to the end of it. Then he returned to a position where he could watch for any movement of cattle.

He laughed as he recalled the discussion about predicting the rain in this part of the country.

"That Cherokee needs to listen to his Creek brother. He might learn something that he could use. Maybe he'll be ready when I see him."

"Boss, the whole town is full. It looks like every nester in the country is there." The man reported to Averill. "Lots of loud talk making the rounds."

"Let them talk. Were the Hales there?"

"Didn't see any of them."

"Did you hear anything else?"

"Seems the whole bunch plan to stay for the trial. Most said they were anyway. At least the ones I heard say anything. Plenty of argument going on."

"Good report, Dade. Tell Mitch and Bart to come up here." Averill went into the house.

Mitch and Bart soon joined him. They waited for him to speak.

"Looks like the nesters have given us our chance. I want you to move the two bunches east of here into place tonight."

"What about the ones south of town?" Mitch asked.

"You can take care of that Monday night after the trial starts. You can send one of the boys down there to tell them to be ready to move."

"Now?" Bart asked. "You want me to send him now?"

163

"No." Averill answered. "Wait until you're through tonight. Head into town, let people see you and then send your man on down."

"I hope that loud mouth half breed kid's in town. I'll fix him." Mitch growled. "Might add to the excitement of the trial."

"Mitch!" Averill stopped him. "You let your personal pleasure get in front of my plan and I'll deal with you myself. You wait until I tell you."

"Okay, boss. I'll wait. Let's go Bart." He stomped out of the house with Bart on his heels. "Waiting for things means fouling them up most of the time." He growled under his breath. "We need to quit waiting."

"That black thief thought this was a chance for him to grab a bunch of our cattle. I think him and Jim Cooper must of been in cahoots. Wouldn't be surprised if that mouthy Virg wasn't involved too. He's been pretty friendly to Vaughn." Dade had ridden into town under orders from Averill. "The boss wants you to round them up so they can get what's coming to them while the judge is here. Maybe we can stop this cattle rustling before it gets out of hand."

Marshal Simmons studied for a minute. He rubbed his chin while thinking it over. He shoved his hat back on his head.

"Come on, Marshal, quit stalling. The boss wants you to get out there and do your job. He says if you don't he's going to start hanging every rustler he catches. He's pretty hot about the stalling in the case of this Dan Hale thing."

"The judge is back so he better think twice about taking the law into his own hands." Simmons growled. "He might wind up on trial."

"No matter. He wants you to get popping and head out there."

"Now you listen here. I'm running this office. I'll get Saul Artman to go out there with you. He helps me out now and then. I need to stay in town and keep the lid on. Some of the arguments are getting pretty hot." Marshal Simmons didn't like it when someone tried to push him.

"Okay, but we better get a move on before they get rid

164

of the cattle somehow. Some have just disappeared into thin air We couldn't find hide nor hair of them."

The marshal soon had Saul Artman headed out of town with Dade.

"That Averill must think he can order me around like one of his hands." Marshal Simmons had a grim look on his face as he picked up his sawed- off double barrel ten guage, checked the loads, grabbed a handful of extra shells and stepped out in the street.

"Good morning marshal. Is everything going to be ready for the trial.?" Judge Harvey looked much better than he had before. At least he was sober.

"Good morning Judge. Everything should go as planned. The Hales will be here in time."

"I don't want any interruptions this time. I won't have my courtroom turn into a house of jesters. It's your job to back my orders." He glanced up and down the street. "Looks like plenty of folks will be here."

"There'll be a crowd all right. Say, Judge, we may have some more cases to try. There have been some more complaints signed."

The judge rubbed his hands together. "That's my job. The more the merrier, er, I mean better. We'll start with the least important ones first. Kind of a warm up for the real thing."

"You mean that Dan Hale will be one of the last ones tried?"

"Yes, that way folks will get used to what can be said and what is not relevant. See you in my court, marshal." Judge Harvey walked away. There was no stumbling in his stride this time.

As Marshal Simmons made his way down the street he was still fuming about Averill ordering him to come out and check on his cattle. He saw Newt and Virg coming up the street. In front of the local drinking establishment were three horses with the A-A brand.

Mitch and Bart walked out on the front walk near their horses. They started to mount then stopped.

Bart poked Mitch and nodded his head indicating Virg. They both turned that way. This put Simmons behind them. Evidently they hadn't noticed him.

"You two put your hands over your heads and keep
them there." Simmons ordered. "I've got a sawed off lined
on you. If it goes off we'll have to carry you off in four
pieces."

Mitch acted as if he planned to ignore the command and
put up a fight.

"Hold it Mitch. He's telling the truth." Bart warned
his partner. He could see the double barrel shotgun leveled
at them. "He ain't joking and I'm not ready to die yet.
Remember what the boss said."

"What are you holding a gun on us for?" Mitch
growled. "We haven't done anything."

"I have a warrant for your arrest and I'm taking you to
jail." Simmons told them. "Newt step up there and get
their pistols."

"Will do, Marshal." Newt had a grin on his face.

Marshal Simmons marched his prisoners off to jail.
They were busy protesting their innocence at every step.

All the marshal had to say was something about who
was running the office.

Newt was questioning Virg as they walked on down the
street. The answers only provoked more questions.

The Averill hand, that had ridden the third horse, came
out in time to see the marshal march Mitch and Bart off to
jail.

"I'm supposed to go on down south and give the word
to the men there but I better let the boss in on this ."
Taking his horse he headed toward the northwest.

"It's time we got a move on. We have a little chore to
do on our way into town." Dad Hale told his men. "Mr.
Slater, you two fellows just come along with us. We'll all
go into town together."

"I had planned to go on in not do chores on the way."
Toad informed him. "My job here is over."

"I insist that we all go in together. Zach there will go
in with us too." When Toad started to protest Dad Hale cut
him off. "I won't take no for an answer. You heard me
boys. We'll all go in together."

"Right Dad. We don't want Mr. Averill to think we just let his men wander off. We'll deliver them back to him safe and sound like good neighbors should."

"Well, let's get going then. We don't want to keep the folks waiting. It'll be interesting if they try to hang one of us. There's never been a Hale hung that I know of and I don't think I'm ready for it to happen yet."

"What do you mean, they're in jail? What did they do to stir things up? I'll take the hide off them if they mess up my plans." The more Averill talked the madder he got. "Well, give me an answer."

"They didn't do anything that I know of. The marshal just walked up and arrested them."

"Just walked up and arrested them. Did he say what for? Blast him anyway."

"Just that a complaint had been signed. I don't know who did it or what it's all about."

"Somebody will pay for this when Mitch gets out." Averill still wondered about it. Surely it wasn't over some old something out west. He decided he'd better get into town. "I'll have them out as soon as I get there. Such help a man has. Come give a report and don't know anything to fill me in. Blasted marshal."

"Now Vi, hold your temper. We need to keep our heads about this." Ab was trying to keep her calm. He knew what could happen when her temper got the best of her. "Just take it easy."

"Hold my temper nothing. The very idea of accusing Jim of stealing cattle or anything else." Maw's eyes fairly blazed with indignation. "None of my boys will steal. They ought to be after the ones that want to steal our land."

"You're right but we don't want to do anything to make it tougher on Jim."

"Well, we'll wait and see what develops before we declare war. We may need to join the Hales if it comes to that."

Saul Artman had ridden back in with Jim and Mary from their place. The news had spread quickly about the

167

arrest of Jim Cooper for stealing cattle.

"Maybe there is something to this deal about cattle being rustled." One man offered. He was standing with several others watching the deputy.

"You shut your mouth." Another snapped at him.

"Try and make me." The man looked like he was ready to go to 'fist city'.

"Lay off the wild talk. We'll get to the bottom of things. Meantime stop the arguing. It'll only lead to trouble and it looks like we have enough of that already." Newt shouted from the back of a wagon.

This appeared to settle the crowd a bit.

"Newt's right. We start fighting among ourselves and we're lost." Ab added. "Let the law do its duty. We know Saul well enough. He just did what he had to. We can't blame him for that."

"Come on Mary. Don't you worry about Jim. We'll find a way to get to the bottom of this." Ab urged.

Mary was visibly upset. "They better not try to do anything to Jim. I'll go on the warpath myself. I can handle a gun when I need to."

Virg walked up about this time. "I heard about Jim. Court will be in session in about an hour. We'll see then. Doesn't look very promising though."

"Virg we're counting on something to bring the truth of this matter out. If you know anything to make us feel better let's hear it." Maw was plainly worried.

"Maw, we've been working on this for some time now. Maybe we'll have some luck yet. The preacher said Sunday that, 'The Lord will provide.' I have John, Isaac and Sam doing their best. I better get to a place so I can see one of them if he gives me a signal." Virg hurried off.

"I'm worried about placing our fate in the hands of three Indian boys." Maw said as she led Mary away.

Chap 22

Averill rode up to the jail at a gallop. His horse came to a sliding halt at the hitch rack. Dismounting he

168

stormed into the jail.

Marshal Simmons rose to meet him.

"Come in, Mr. Averill."

"What do you mean putting my men in jail?" Averill demanded. "What did they do?"

"A complaint was signed against three of your men. I have two of them. I'll get the other one when I see him."

"Turn them loose. I'll vouch for them."

"Can't do that with the judge here. He's in charge of releasing prisoners."

"I'll go see him then. Won't be long until they're free. Mitch will be after anybody that had a hand in this. You're sure to be one of them, Simmons. I won't forget it either." Averill angrily left in search of Judge Harvey.

He found him with a drink of water in his hand.

"Put that stuff down and go turn my men loose." Averill ordered. "I don't want my men in jail."

"Harumph! Mr. Averill, you better give that another bit of thinking over. What's going to be the mood of the settlers if you walk in here and get your men loose? That fellow Hale had to put up valuable property to get out."

"I didn't come in here to discuss this with you. I want them out and now." Averill glared at Judge Harvey. "Just turn them loose."

The judge considered for a minute then spoke. "Mr. Averill, I would like to accommodate you on this but the mood of the people is not good. If they figure you have me in your pocket any decision I render against them will not be received very well. Those men won't be there long and it will show you to be willing to trust the court. Do you see what I'm driving at?"

Averill was beginning to recover his thinking ability. The old fool was right about it.

"If you'll put their case first I guess I could let it slide for now."

"That will be easy. They're first. Thank you sir, for being understanding."

Averill stalked out of the room. The very idea of this old sot giving him advice. He had brought him out here to follow orders not to help run things.

Judge Harvey was not entirely pleased either. He had entered the law profession with high ideals. To fall to a level of having cattlemen giving him orders was a little demeaning. It was near time for court to open.

"It's getting close to time for court and no sign of the Hales." Marshal Simmons was thinking to himself. "I sure hope they haven't decided to turn outlaw. They'd be a tough bunch to round up. I wouldn't want the job."

"I sure wish John would show up. I'd go look for him but it's to close to court time." Virg cast a worried look toward the tree where John had appeared before.

"If we have to go in there now we don't have anything to use." Newt said. "If the Lord is going to provide, he better do it pretty soon."

Virg considered. "The people in the Bible didn't give up." He told Newt. "They kept the faith. He has his own timetable."

"Well, my faith is getting pretty shaky right now."

Everybody seemed to be out in the open. It was time for Dan Hale to put in an appearance. It was difficult to avoid staring down the road to the south.

A boy had climbed up a tree so as to get a better view.

"Hey Tod, do you see a big bunch of horsemen coming?"

"Nope. All I can see is a bunch of cattle with some men driving them."

"Cattle? Who'd be driving cattle today?" Marshal Simmons wanted to know.

"Don't ask me. It's not any of my men for sure." Averill answered. It looked like Simmons was staring directly at him.

The small herd of cattle soon made it's way down the main street.

"It's the Hales." Tod shouted. "They're bringing that bunch of cattle in."

Dad Hale rode up to the marshal. "Well, I'm glad to see you here, Mr. Averill. Seeing you've been bothered by cow thieves I'm sure you'll be happy that we caught a couple of them for you."

170

"Wh-what do you mean?" Averill was clearly at a loss for words. "I'm not sure I catch your meaning."

"These are your cows I believe. We caught these two fellows with them way down west of where we live. Your two men were with us when we caught them. Of course, the cattle being yours, you'll have to sign the complaint. You said anyone stole your cattle they had to answer to the law for it. Right?"

"Y-Yeah, sure, that will be my affair." Averill replied. "I'll take care of my business."

"Won't stand for you prosecuting my boy and letting others go free." Dad Hale had a stern look.

"He's right, Averill." A bystander chipped in. "Treat everybody the same."

Averill cast a look at Rance and Trip. He placed his finger across his lips as if to say 'shh--', then finished by rubbing his chin in thought. "I'll do what I have to do. I know what I said."

"Lanny, put the cows in the town lot. Mr. Averill can pick them up when he wants. Marshal, you can have the thieves." With that Dad Hale dismounted. "When do we start the trial?"

Virg and Newt were enjoying the return of the cattle along with Mr. Higgins and others.

"Did you see the signal?" Virg asked. "Mr. Averill has a small problem. Watch him squirm. He's been shouting pretty loud about punishing cow thieves. Now we have a bunch of them, including Jim and Dan."

"This is getting complicated. If he pushes the case against them what is he going to do about his own men?" Newt was indeed puzzled.

"I sure would like to hear from John Billy." Virg scanned the surrounding country. "Hey! See that smoke? There it goes again. Newt you're going to have to go out there and talk to John Billy. Find out what he has if anything."

"How will I find him? You tell me he's hard to find."

"Ride Buck out there. John will recognize him. Don't worry. He'll find you."

"I better move. They're calling for court to open now.

171

I sure hate to miss it."

"I'll tell Molly to keep track of everything then you'll have the pleasure of listening to her while she tells it to you."

"Might have to have her tell it over and over before I could catch on." Newt shouted as he hurried off. The thought pleased him.

Virg headed for the courthouse. He was intercepted by his mother.

"Virg, they've arrested Zach. Saul Artman came over and took him to jail."

"I wonder what for. He just now rode in with the Hales. Are Mandy and the kids here?"

"You say Zach came in with the Hales? Mandy came to town because she said Zach hadn't been home for several days. That's sure not like him."

"You take care of Mandy. I'll see what I can find out about Zach. We still have Jim to worry about too."

"Seems like problems every way we turn." Maw said. "Virg, you be careful. Don't do anything rash."

"We sure need to do something, rash or not."

He headed for the courthouse again.

Stepping inside he glanced around to locate different people. He walked over to Molly and gave her the message about the note keeping.

"I'll be glad to do it." Molly assured him.

Alex Averill had a seat on the front row. He was flanked by two of his men. He had a smug look on his face.

Mr. Higgins was seated in the row behind Averill. All he needed was a chance and he'd slip in a barb or two.

Marshal Simmons was seated in one of two chairs at the table to be used by the judge.

"Marshal, where's Zach Vaughn?" Virg asked.

"He's in jail. Saul is keeping an eye on the prisoners."

"He has to be given a fair chance. We can't let people's prejudices lead them to do something wrong." Virg was emphatic.

"Virg, you stay close to the front here because Mitch and Bart will be the first tried."

"Okay."

"Everybody stand up." Marshal Simmons voice rang out loud and clear. Everybody stood. "The Honorable Judge Harvey." He announced.

Judge Harvey entered the room. His appearance was much improved over the one last week. Evidently the rigors of the trip had been good for him. It seemed to have also improved his disposition for he smiled as he viewed the crowd. Almost like a different man.

Bang! Bang! The gavel fell.

He struck the table with a real gavel. It felt good in his hand. And he had been introduced by Marshal Simmons as, 'The Honorable Judge Harvey'. It had a good sound to it. It made him remember the past.

"Court is now in session. Please be seated." He busily arranged some papers. Then he took another look at the crowd. He remembered his earlier appearance in Paden.

"Anybody want to see my credentials or question the men that rode to Okmulgee with me?"

There was no response.

"If not we'll call the first case. Marshal, bring in the prisoners."

Marshal Simmons stepped out of the room and returned with Mitch and Bart.

"What is the charge?" Judge Harvey asked.

"Armed robbery." The marshal answered. I have the signed paper.

"Who made the charge?" The judge looked up. "Is he present in the courtroom?"

"I did, your honor." Virg stood up and stepped forward. "I signed the complaint."

Puzzled looks were exchanged in several locations. No one had heard of him being robbed.

"What would he have that anyone would want? He's as poor as the rest of us."

The judge studied some papers for a minute.

"These two held you up and robbed you?"

"There were three of them. I see Toad Slater back there. He's the other one."

"Don't you call me Toad, smart mouth." Toad growled. I'm Tom Slater Junior."

173

"Marshal Simmons, bring Toad, er- Tom Slater Jr. forward." Judge Harvey instructed.

Toad was soon with his two friends.

"Now young man, tell your story. Try to keep it as short as you can. We need to move along."

Virg began telling about riding along minding his own business when these three pulled a pistol on him and relieved him of his critters.

"I understand it's against the law to take peoples property away from them by using a gun."

Mitch could hold it in no longer. He blurted out. "Bart and me didn't take nothin away from him. That fool Toad grabbed this sack out of his hand and-." He caught himself.

"Don't call me Toad, I told you. My name's Tom Slater Junior." Toad shouted.

Silence returned to the courtroom.

"Tom, hmm, that's what you call a turkey. He don't look like no turkey to me." Someone in the crowd said in a hushed voice. Maybe Mr. Higgins.

It carried to every corner as there was a continuation of the sudden spell of silence.

"I agree. Toad's a more fittin name for him as you can see." This too carried around the room.

There was a burst of laughter. The crowd was beginning to enjoy this trial.

Bang! Bang! The gavel fell. "Order! Order! You men quit badgering the witness, er defendant." The judge had a hard time keeping a straight face.

"He don't, well, he might look kinda like a badger."

"Order! Order! I said." The judge yelled. "Go on with your story, Mr. Slater."

Toad beamed at being called, Mr. Slater. He was still mad about the effort to lay the blame on him. Danged if he was going to take the whole thing.

"He just had this sack with a couple of snakes in it. These two were with me."

The judge was beginning to see an interesting case developing.

"And you grabbed it from him?"

174

"Yeah. er yezzir."

"Then what happened."

"I stuck my hand down in the sack after shakin it around a little."

"You stuck your hand down in a sack with snakes in it?" Judge Harvey exclaimed. "Why?"

"Yessir, but I didn't know that it had snakes in it at the time."

Grins began to spread across the faces in the room. A few chuckles could be heard.

Bang! The gavel fell. "Order, order. Go on."

"One of the darned things bit my finger. I jerked my hand out but it wouldn't let go."

"How did you get rid of it?"

"I gave it a sling and it flew off of my finger."

"You better keep your stupid mouth shut." Mitch warned Toad. "That's far enough with that palaver."

Judge Harvey gave Mitch a dirty look. "I'll decide who is to keep his mouth shut. Go on Toad, er, Mr. Slater, what happened to it?"

Toad glared about the use of the name but decided to keep still about it. The judge had corrected it.

"It flew through the air and wrapped around Mitch's neck. He dropped his gun and grabbed it with both han-."

He was interrupted again. This time by a roar of laughter.

It took a while to restore order.

"Go on." Judge Harvey was having trouble keeping his judicial manner.

"He grabbed it with both hands and started pulling to get it off."

"Did he succeed?"

"No, it was wrapped clean around his neck and the harder he pulled the tighter it got. He'd of strangled himself if I hadn't made him turn it loose."

"That thing bit a chunk out of Mitch's ear." Bart offered.

"Shut your mouth." Mitch snarled.

"Is that the whole story?" The judge asked.

"No sir." Toad had concluded that by telling the whole

175

story he might get off. "Bart almost shot me when he took a shot at the other snake. Hadn't been for my saddle horn he would've gut shot me. Then his horse stampeded."

"How did Mitch get rid of his snake?"

"Bart was fairly busy with his horse so I got Mitch's snake off of him. He had all this stuff on his neck and shirt. It looked like snake sh-"

"I told you to keep your fool mouth shut." Mitch interrupted at the top of his lungs. He jumped to his feet and glared around the room. "It warent my snake either."

The judge didn't even try to restore order for some time. He had to closely examine some papers that hid his face. They were shaking a good bit.

Finally things settled down a little. Averill hadn't found the story all that funny as it reflected badly on some of his men. He'd warned them about that.

"Harumph." Bang! Bang! The gavel fell. "Order, order. Then what happened?"

"The horses settled down and we went back to the ranch. Smart mouth there had disappeared."

The judge shuffled his papers. He appeared to be in deep thought. His body shook.

"The question is whether these critters as this young fellow calls them constitute property. They are just wild animals of a sort. Can you claim wild things are your property, young man?"

"They don't belong to anybody at all." Mitch volunteered. "I never saw one that did."

"Sounds like you were pretty close with one of them." Someone said. It sounded as if it came from Mr. Higgins. "Did you see it?"

Laughter erupted again. It continued for a while.

Bang! Bang! The gavel fell. "Order, order in the court. Order I say." Judge Harvey looked at Virg.

"Young man, do you have anyone here to vouch for the fact that a wild animal can be property?"

"Yes sir, I sure do." Virg said. He's right here in the courtroom and he's one of our leading citizens. I'm sure people will believe him."

"Have him say so then." Judge ordered. "I don't have

176

any precedent to go by."

"Mr. Averill can vouch for that, sir. He's an expert on catching wild animals and making them his very own."

Eyes turned toward Averill. Grins spread again.

"Are you depending on Mr. Averill to back your story?"

"That's right, your honor. Virg grinned. "Why just a while back he told me how he did just that."

The Judge peered at Averill. "Is that right, Mr. Averill?"

"I never heard of anybody taming a snake." Averill was furious. He glanced at Mitch and gave a slight nod.

"The question was about wild animals." Virg spoke out. "He told a bunch of us about catching wild animals and selling them. Surely he wouldn't want to deny that in a court of law."

" Hey, That's right."

"He sure did for a fact."

"You bet. I heard him."

"Me too."

These were some of the many statements from the crowd, backing Virg.

Averill ground his teeth. When the judge looked at him he nodded his head. He didn't appear to be eager to use words at the present time. He did have a mean look and he shot it in Virg's direction. Good thing it wasn't a bullet.

"In view of the evidence I find the parties guilty and fine each of them twenty dollars. Half will go to the court and half to the young man for his-er- uh-wild critters."

The people had another round of fun.

Someone was heard to say. "I better start rounding up some of the critters out my way. These fellows may want to buy them if they can't get away with stealing them."

Bang! The gavel fell. "Court will recess for five minutes." The judge was shaking as he headed for the back room.

Judge Harvey walked into the back room and sat down on a chair. Removing his hat he lowered his head and placed both hands on it. "What has happened to me?" He moaned in a low voice. "I used to be a reputable judge who could walk about with my head held high. Now I'm checking with someone to see if what I do is all right."

He moaned and moved his hands about, massaging his scalp. "Then this kid makes a fool of the man."

"How low can a man sink?" He asked. "There are some things better than a pat on the back and a hand holding a bottle."

He suddenly had a grin on his face. "Like helping a kid collect for some stolen snakes." He sat up a lot straighter.

"You'll get what's coming to you." Averill snarled at Virg in a low voice. "Just wait until we convict your brother. We'll hang him along with that black friend of yours. Side by side, two of a kind, both thieves." He stomped out of the room.

"Thank you, sir. I knew you would be eager to help." Virg answered in a loud voice. "You've already done your duty in the case just ended. I expect you to do as much in the next one."

"Tell us again about the snake rustlers, Virg." One townsman called out. "We may have to pass a bunch of laws to protect things like that."

"Do you have any more critters?" Another cut in. "I might be in the market for a couple."

"Not me. I'm gonna watch myself. I caught one of those things in my hen house eating my eggs and I killed it." A third voice was added to the fun.

"You better be careful about admitting that." Mr. Higgins advised. "It'd be fun to have another trial like this one. Let's have him arrested, Virg."

"Yeah, you could lay claim to all of them critters in these parts. All you have to do is catch them."

Every statement was followed by a round of laughter.

The folks were still enjoying the trial of the three Averill hands.

Virg laughed with them then tried to break away. He wondered what had become of Newt. Also he had a desire to talk to Zach if it was possible.

The call came for court to convene again.

No sign of Newt.

No chance to talk to Zach.

Didn't look good for the accused.

"Well, Maw taught me to never give up as long as there was any hope at all." Virg headed for the courthouse. "I'll just have to take things as they come. We need something to put a little dent in Averill's plans. If I could just get to talk to Zach. He may have something. I sure hope Newt gets some news from John Billy."

When court reconvened Zach was brought in. He appeared to be very discouraged. His eyes lit up a bit when he spotted Virg. He had at least one friend present.

Bang! The gavel fell.

"The next case involves Zach Vaughn." Judge Harvey stated. He gave the gavel a fond look. "What's the charge against this man?"

"Stealing cattle." Marshal Simmons stated.

"Who filed the complaint?" Judge Harvey was going through the procedure.

"I did." Averill stated. "Of course some of my men found the cattle. They will testify to that."

"That's fine." The judge turned to Zach. "Do you want to tell your part or do you have someone else to represent you?"

"Do you mean I can get someone else to do my talking for me, sir?"

"That's right. You can tell him your story and he will tell the court."

"Then I want Virg to speak for me. I know he's young but I have confidence in him. He's always treated me and mine nice. He's fairly sharp too, Your Honor."

"It's a little unusual to have a youngster do that but you make the decision. I can believe the part about him being pretty sharp." Judge Harvey turned back to the marshal. "Call the witnesses."

Two of Averills men told of following the trail of some cattle where they had been driven. They found them in a small pasture on Zach's place. Their stories were the same.

Dade came after the Marshal while the other hand had reported to Averill.

Saul Artman then told how he had accompanied Dade out to the Vaughn place. "The cattle were there but he was no where in sight. Then we went on over to Jim-"

Bang! The gavel fell. "Stick to the case at hand."

"That's about all. I arrested him here in town."

"Do you want to ask any of these men any questions?" Judge Harvey asked.

"No sir. I don't believe so. Thank you." Virg had been conferring with Zach.

"Looks like all has been said that needs to." Averill stated as he cast a look at the judge. A buzz went through the room.

Judge Harvey was not about to let Averill or anybody else run his courtroom. He'd attend to that. The gavel seemed to give him new purpose in life. Besides the young man was polite.

Bang! Bang! The gavel fell. "Order in the court. Does the defense have a case to present?"

"Yes sir, your honor."

"You have witnesses?"

"Yes sir, your honor."

"Call the first one."

"Toad, er, Tom Slater Junior, sir."

"Toad get up here." Judge Harvey spoke sharply as Toad started to shake his head. He had made no move to come forward. At the sharp command he got up and ambled forward.

"I don't like to be called Toad." He growled.

"Very well. We'll try to remember that."

Toad appeared to be a little confused as he was sworn in. He became nervous when the Bible was brought out and he was asked to place his hand on it and swear to tell the truth, the whole truth and nothing but the truth.

"Do I have to answer his questions?" Toad asked the judge. "I don't like him and he don't like me."

"Yes, unless you want to go to jail. Doesn't matter if you like him or not. I'm running things here." Was the response. "Go on, ask your questions."

180

Virg walked up to Toad and stood there studying him.

Toad began to squirm in his seat.

Finally Virg asked a question.

"You know what happens to people that swear by the Bible and then break that oath?"

Toad licked his lips. "No." He croaked.

"That's bad. Hate to see that happen to someone that doesn't know about it." Virg shook his head from side to side. He pursed his lips and gave a slow whistle.

Toad looked more uncomfortable than before.

"Next question." Virg hesitated. He turned to the Judge. "Could I speak with you, Sir?"

"Yes, come on up. Mr. Averill you may come up to hear what we say if you want to."

"I don't need to hear any of his smart lip." Averill snapped. "I've heard enough already."

Virg went over to the judge. "It's important to our evidence that the two men that have already testified don't hear what Toad says. Can you have them taken outside while he finishes? The time of the theft has not been established. If they hear what he says they can match their story to his."

"It has been done. They're by the back door so if you know someone we can send out with them I'll do it." Judge Harvey marveled at this move. "Clever."

"Ab Rankin and Mr. Higgins would be fine."

Judge Harvey called Marshal Simmons over and explained things to him. He walked to the back of the room taking Ab and Mr. Higgins with him. He then escorted Dade and his companion out.

"Proceed with your questions." Judge Harvey told Virg when Marshal Simmons returned.

"Mr. Slater, you are employed by Alex Averill are you not?"

"I work for him if that's what you mean."

"That's what I mean. Do you try to do a good job?"

"I shore do. I earn my pay."

"What have you been doing the last few days?"

"I've been over to the Hales."

"Mr. Averill sent you over there to help the Hales?"

181

"He sent me over there to see that none of them left to keep the judge from making it back."

"And you did not earn your money. You didn't do your job."

"I did to. Nobody left that place while we were over there."

"Nobody. Are you sure? It's hard to watch a bunch of people."

"I said nobody and I mean nobody."

"They tell me Zach Vaughn is pretty strong and a tough fighter." Virg suddenly sneered. " You couldn't keep him there because you were afraid he would beat the tar out of you. That's why you let him come and go as he wanted to isn't it?"

Toad raised up out of his chair. "That's what you think. I could whup him any day. Ask the whole bunch. He never left the place after he got there. To make sure I locked him in the smoke house at night. I know how to handle these blackies." He glared at Virg. "Just ask the Hales, smart mouth."

"Well, I don't know what to say. Maybe you're more of a man than I thought. I better not ask you any more questions. You might get mad at me."

Averill was squirming. He needed to get to Dade. He got up and made a move to leave.

"Mr. Averill, it's not finished yet. You need to stay here." Judge Harvey advised.

"Toad, you are dismissed."

"Don't call me Toad, I tell you."

"I'm sorry, Tom junior. We're through with you."

"You mean I can go?"

"Yes, that's what I mean. Just sit back down where you were in case you're needed again."

"Do you have any more questions?" Judge Harvey asked Virg. He had been talking quietly with Zach again.

"I would like to ask Dade a couple of questions now."

"Marshal, bring Dade in."

Marshal Simmons walked back up the aisle with Dade in front of him

Averill stepped in front of Dade in what appeared to

182

be an attempt to talk to him.

Virg slid in between the two. "Excuse me but you're not supposed to badger the witness."

Marshal Simmons pushed Dade forward to the witness chair. "That's right. The judge said so."

Averill glared at Virg but returned to his seat.

Virg gave Averill the benefit of a smile. Then he turned to Dade.

"You don't have to worry, Dade. I'm not going to try to trick you. Just a simple answer. When were the cattle stolen."

Dade began to think. All he had to do was tell the truth. If he lied he would get crossed up. This was a simple question. He tried to look at Averill but Virg blocked his view.

"We just want to know when they were stolen."

"Night before last."

"How do you know?"

"When we checked on them that day they were there. The next day they were gone. We followed their tracks."

"You mean it rained before they were stolen?"

"That's right, they left a clear trail."

"Thanks, Dade. It's good to meet an honest man. I don't have any more questions." Virg turned to Zach and punched him on the shoulder. They could not keep the smiles off their faces.

"Anybody have anything else. Mr. Averill, you have anything?" The judge asked.

"No, not in this case. I'm ready to go to the next one." Averill looked mockingly at Virg. He knew that Jim's trial was next. "Let the little smart mouth pull a fast one in this one." He muttered.

"Case against Zach Vaughn dismissed. He's not guilty." Bang! The gavel fell.

"A one hour recess is declared." Bang! The gavel fell. There was rush for the door.

Virg hurried outside. "I sure hope Newt and John show up. I don't have anything to help Jim or Dan." He cast a worried look up and down the street.

183

"I'm proud of the job you did for Zach." Ab followed him out of the courthouse. "No one else would have done that for him."

"Some day Zach will get the same chance everybody else has. He needs friends until that happens. We won't go wrong with him as a friend." Virg told him. He glanced around again hoping to catch site of Newt.

Mitch and Bart stepped off the walk across the street and started in his direction. They appeared to be ready for trouble. Mitch lifted his pistol and let it fall back into his holster.

"You fellows keep it peaceful." Marshal Simmons had come out of the courtroom with his double-barrel. He leaned against the wall as he watched the pair.

"I just wanted to tell him that it would be my pleasure to see him again sometime." Mitch replied. "He won't be able to have you around all the time. I can wait. I'll have a present for him."

"Thank you, kind sir. I like presents." Virg told Mitch. "I hope your ear gets better. Be a shame to go through life with a sore ear."

Mitch stopped, started to turn but then moved on down the street with a mean look on his face. "Just a little more and Averill won't be able to stop me."

"Boy, what a relief it is to see you." Virg said as Newt rode up. "We need something in a hurry or Jim and Dan are goners."

"John Billy didn't want to take a chance on me at first. I had to ride around back and forth for sometime before he came out. He wanted to talk to you." Newt told him.

"I've told him you could be trusted." Virg was puzzled about John's action.

"I guess he has some information that is really important. He wasn't going to let just anybody in on it." Newt replied. "The wrong party could destroy it he said."

"We'll need him here but we need Bill and Joe Nolan also. People may not pay attention to John unless he's backed by someone they trust."

"He's in town now with somebody. Is that a call for

court to start?"

Virg nodded his head. "Let's get over there. Newt, you do the talking. I think they're tired of listening to me."

They moved into the court room. The crowd was rapidly filling all available space.

"Hey Virg, you have any more tricks up your sleeve?" Someone called out. "Or maybe in a sack."

This caused a round of laughter.

Soon Averill and his crew were in their seats at the front of the room. Mitch and Bart were missing however. Toad was still casting angry glances at Virg. He didn't seem to enjoy the reference to the sack.

Marshal Simmons entered. "All rise." Evidently the judge had given some instructions.

Judge Harvey entered.

Bang! Bang! The gavel fell.

"Be seated. Court is now in session."

Virg and Newt had been busy discussing something.

"It's worth a try." Virg said.

Newt stood up. "Your Honor."

"Yes, what is it?"

"Could we talk to you for a minute?"

"I suppose. Come on up here."

Newt and Virg moved up to the table.

"Is he with you?" The question was directed at Virg.

"Yes sir."

"Start talking."

"In regard to the Zach Vaughn case. We think we could furnish you with information that would help you solve it. You could bring the real thieves to justice."

"It sure would boost your reputation." Virg added. "A judge is a powerful man. People respect judges."

"Harumph. We always want to catch the ones that break the law. What do you have in mind?"

They quickly outlined their plan.

"I'll do it. You two sit back down there."

Bang! Bang! "The court is interested in catching cow thieves and punishing them. Mr. Averill, you stated that you wanted this bunch of rustlers found out and punished. Is that right?"

"That's what we're here for. We've already caught some of them. I'm sure there are a bunch more out there." Averill wondered what the old fool was referring to.

"In that case I'm reopening the inquiry about the cattle at the Vaughn place." Judge Harvey indicated Newt who was in conversation with Virg. "This young man may have some further information about that."

"What the devil is going on?" Averill protested. "Let's deal with the thieves we have then you can go chasing after others."

"The court has already stated it's position. We'll continue with the inquiry. Present your evidence young man."

"I will furnish plenty of evidence but first I have to find out some things. If Toad will come forward."

"Don't call me Toad." Toad protested angrily in a loud voice. "I've already told all I know."

"That wasn't very much." Cackled Mr. Higgins.

"You shut your old mouth before I shut it for you." Toad glared at Higgins. "I ain't answering any more stupid questions cause they'll all laugh at me."

"Never mind the laughing. You get up here right now." Judge Harvey ordered. "You'll answer or else go to jail."

Averill jumped to his feet. "I object to this. It's not right to get some feeble minded dummy up there and start tricking him into saying things."

Toad glared at Averill. "I ain't no feeble minded dummy. I can read and write with the best of them."

Bang! "Order. All he has to do is tell the truth. Do you object to that, Mr. Averill?" The judge waited.

Averill sat down without comment.

Newt approached Toad. "Remember you swore on the Bible."

Toad nodded his head. "Yeah, I remember."

"We don't have any tricks. Just straight forward questions. They tell me you read a lot so you're plenty smart I'm sure."

"I'm as smart as most I guess." Toad grinned. "Maybe smarter than some around here." He glared in the

186

direction of Virg then shifted his eyes toward Averill. "You oughta hear some of his hands talk."

"Can you answer me this? Every time I see you men from the grazers you are always riding the same horse. Why is that?"

"Everybody has his own horse. You better not take anybody's horse if you know what's good for you."

"Do you always ride the same horse?"

"We have a bunch that we get one out of if we want to let our favorite one rest."

"Then someone could ride your horse when you left it in the herd?"

"It's called a remuda, dummy. They wouldn't do that or there would be the devil to pay. Nobody rides anybody else's horse I tell you." Toad looked around the room. "A man's horse is his most prized thing. He don't want anybody fooling with it. Ain't that right, boss?"

Averill nodded his head. He couldn't see where these stupid questions amounted to anything. Every cowhand knew that others didn't bother a fellows string of horses. Of course these farmers weren't to smart. Just another bunch of sodbusters.

Newt turned to the Judge. "That's all he can tell us, your honor."

"Anybody else?" The judge asked. "If so get them in here so we can move this along."

Newt looked at Virg who mouthed, 'Mitch'.

"I'd like to ask Mitch some questions."

"Marshal Simmons go out and bring Mitch in here."

The marshal soon returned with a very unhappy Mitch.

"I don't plan to answer any questions." He growled. "I've already said all I know."

"You didn't say very much." Mr. Higgins volunteered. "Guess that explains it."

Mitch cast a threatening look at him and then around the room as laughter moved across the crowd. They were used to Higgin's sharp tongue.

"Bang! "Order." Judge Harvey called. "You'll answer or face the consequences of your actions. You won't like them. Ask your questions."

Newt stepped forward.

"What's wrong? Is your smart half breed friend afraid to ask me? I thought he was the one with all the questions." Mitch shot a glance at Virg.

Newt ignored the question. "Mitch, there's been some talk about some of you fellows trying to get fresh with Mrs. Vaughn. When were you over there last?"

"I ain't never set foot on the place. I don't mess with that kind."

"Glad to clear that up. I didn't think you were that kind." Newt went on to give a short talk about how people had to respect themselves and expect others to respect property and such.

"Are you going to make speeches or ask questions? If you have any more stupid questions ask them. I'm tired of this. I guess your friend let's you ask them cause he's afraid to." Mitch looked at Newt. "Well, are both of you to scared to ask me something?"

"I doubt that." Newt responded. "Mitch, what would happen if I told you that Dade had been riding your horse?"

"I'd say you were a liar. Dade knows better than that. Nobody rides my horse but me. Nobody ever rides my horse but me. Is that clear?"

"Yes, I'd say it was fairly clear. Why not?"

"First thing I'd shoot him. Next, my bronk won't let anybody else ride him. He'd buck him off."

"Thanks Mitch, that's all I guess."

"You roust me in here just to ask two stupid questions?"

"That's all we wanted to know." Newt turned to the judge. "I'm through with him, sir."

"You may think you're through with me but don't count on it." Mitch snapped at Newt. "You and your little half breed friend, especially him."

"You may go." Judge Harvey told Mitch.

Mitch got up and swaggered out of the room. Averill went out behind him.

"We haven't done anything unless we get John Billy in here." Virg said to Newt in a low voice. "Did you say that Sam went after Bill and Joe Nolan?"

188

"We can get John anytime. It's a question if anyone will believe him. Sam went after Bill. I don't have any idea why they haven't come in. I'll try to stall a little."

Virg went over to whisper to Marshal Simmons. They turned to the judge and held a short conversation with him and then left the building.

"Court will recess for ten minutes." Bang, the gavel fell. Judge Harvey went into the back room.

Virg walked outside with the marshal. They spotted Averill holding a discussion with Mitch and Bart. It looked like he was giving them an ear full.

They soon found John Billy leaning against a wall. He didn't give any indication that he knew them until Virg spoke. "John, we've been wondering where you were. We're counting on you to clear things up for us. You're all we have."

"I find out plenty." John sometimes reverted to broken English when he was with people that might expect it.

"Come into court and tell it. You can help a bunch of people." Simmons assured him.

"That right, Virg?" John asked.

"Yep. Newt told me you had found some tracks. Come in and tell the folks about them."

"Okay." John Billy followed them into the room.

When they entered the courtroom there was quite a stir.

Newt was busy talking.

Averill was back in his seat.

"So you see folks we can show you." Newt said after he had talked a while.

"You have talked long enough." Judge Harvey told Newt. "If you have any more information present it otherwise say so and sit down."

"Yes sir. I ask you to bring John Billy, full blood Creek Indian, forward."

Simmons escorted John to the front. He started to swear him in.

"I object to this." Averill stood up. "He can't give evidence."

189

"Why not?"

"He's an Indian. What does the Bible mean to him? What does he know about the truth?" Averill turned to the crowd. "I wouldn't trust one to tell the truth at all."

A good number of the crowd appeared to side with him. Some looked at Newt to check his reaction. Then they shifted their attention to the judge.

There was no outward change in expression from John. He waited. Evidently this didn't surprise him at all. Same as always.

Virg gave him a small friendly wave and smiled at him.

Judge Harvey hesitated. He had to be careful here. "I must do the right thing," He said in a low voice.

"This is a little unusual. Will anyone vouch for him?" He asked. "If so come forward."

No one moved so Virg moved to the front.

"I will. I know him. You can depend on him to tell the truth better than most. It's a matter of pride. " Virg stated. "Most Indians have been truthful with me."

"Sure, he's the one that brought him in. He's part Indian too, Isn't he? I say, we can't use his word for it." Averill could see he was having an effect on the crowd. "Get some one else to vouch for him or forget about it."

There was a minute of silence.

Judge Harvey cleared his throat. "I don't know about this. It is unusual. The court will have to rule on whether to admit his testimony. This young man is involved in the cases all right. Mr. Averill has a point."

Two men had stepped into the back of the room and stood listening to the discussion. They hadn't been noticed due to the intensity of the discussion.

"Your Honor." One of them spoke up.

"Yes, who are you? Do you have anything to say about this?" Judge Harvey asked.

"I'm Bill Smith, from Prague, and this is Marshal Joe Nolan. Several of these people remember me, and yes I have something to say about this. I'll vouch for John Billy and so will Joe."

"Come up here and say your piece then." Harvey replied. "We need to get on with things."

"Boy, are we glad to see you guys." Virg told Bill as he walked by.

"We don't need strangers mixing in our business." Averill complained. "I don't know them."

"Won't hurt to hear them. We can decide if it has any bearing on things." Harvey informed him.

Bill faced the crowd. "It's good to have an honest and fair judge. Sometimes that's not the case."

Judge Harvey sat up straight and squared his shoulders. This had a good sound to it.

Bill continued. "Some of you remember the trouble all the settlers had a while back. John Billy was the main reason we solved the problems we had. He has some special skills that you would find hard to believe. And besides, I would accept anything he told me as the gospel truth."

"Are you going to tell us what these special skills are?" The judge asked.

"If I have to. I'm sure you'll find out about them if he wants you to. I'll wait and see. Now let Joe say his piece if you want him to."

"We don't need any word from any small town two-bit marshal. They don't usually know their way out of town." Averill fumed. He could see the problems that were headed his way.

"My name is Joe Nolan. As to being a small town two-bit marshal I guess that might fit me pretty good." He smiled at the crowd. "I have just been appointed United States Deputy Marshal for this area."

There was a ripple of talk running across the crowd. Then everybody was quiet. He had their attention.

"John has worked with me often. He can track and read sign with the best. If he tells you something you better listen because he knows what he's talking about. Telling the truth is a matter of pride with him."

Judge Harvey cleared his throat. He looked over the crowd then at Averill. He was trying to regain his respect. Might be good to have people look up to him again. An honest judge. Had a certain ring to it.

Bang! Bang! The gavel fell.

"We'll listen to what he has to say." He stated.

191

"Then we can decide the validity of it."

Newt indicated the chair to John.

"I talk to Virg." John said.

Newt turned to Virg and shrugged his shoulders.

Virg stood up and smiled at John. He winked at Newt.

"Newt, thanks for your work. John and I kinda talk the same language. He meant no offense."

"None taken. The Lord will provide, remember."

Virg turned back to John. "I'm going to ask you some questions that you may be puzzled about. You know that I know the answers but the folks here don't. That's why I ask them. See what I mean?"

"Yes, you want them to know about what I do. You ask. I answer."

"That's it. Now, do all horse tracks look alike?"

"No."

"Everybody knows that horses have different sizes of hooves." Averill called out.

"That's right." Came an agreement.

"What's new about that?"

"We need an Indian to tell us that?"

These came from Averill's crew. Virg turned to look at them.

"I don't remember asking you fellows any questions." Virg said. He looked at the judge.

Bang! The gavel fell.

"Order. Don't interrupt the witness." Judge Harvey said sternly. He did not look at Averill.

Virg grinned as he turned back to John.

"Are there differences in horses hooves that are the same size?" He asked.

"Yes, almost always."

"Can you explain what you mean?"

"Yes." John said no more.

"Will you do that?"

"Yes."

"Go on and do it for me then.?"

"Yes." John hesitated. There was some laughter. "Some horses have broken places in hoof. Some people don't take care and hoof grow out. Make big round track.

192

That why part break off. Have gaps in track."

"What about when the owner takes good care of hoof?"

"Hoof of one horse not shaped like hoof of another."

"Any other way you tell the difference?"

"Sure, check all four hoof. Two horses might have one hoof look alike but not four."

"John, can you tell which horse has made tracks that you find?"

"Yes."

"How?"

"Look at track or look at hoof."

"Is there any way you can show the people here?"

"Show them tracks. Show them horse." John smiled slightly. "Horse always leave tracks."

Averill stood up. "How long--Your honor, excuse me. How long do we have to listen to this?"

Judge Harvey looked at Averill. He started to rap the table with his gavel but did not. "I find this discussion interesting. We may find out why the Indians are such good trackers. It never hurts to learn a few things."

Turning back to John he said. "Go on."

"Horses always leave tracks." Averill snarled. "We're sure learning a lot. Any fool knows that horses leave tracks. Indian secrets, ha."

Judge Harvey gave Averill another long look.

"John, you say show them the tracks and show them the horse. Do you have any other way?"

"Sure, show picture."

"This is ridiculous, Judge. Does he have a picture taker riding around with him? " Averill stormed. "We have thieves locked up and instead of trying them we waste time listening to an Indian tell how he can tell one horse track from another one. I say let's get on with the business at hand. We can go to school some other time."

Bang! The gavel fell.

"Mr. Averill, I've warned you. I'm in charge of these proceedings." Judge Harvey's face was getting a bit red.

"Well get on with it then. I'm tired of these delays. I may remember who my friends are." Averill voiced a veiled threat.

Bang! The gavel fell. "Order! Go on with the testimony. I'll fine the next one that interrupts. Then if he doesn't stop I'll have the marshal lock him up."

Judge Harvey glanced at Virg. "Make it short if you can, young man."

"Yes sir, I will. John you said you would show a picture. Do you have one?"

John reached in his shirt and drew out a piece of brown paper and handed it to Virg. "Here it is." He said.

"Your honor, take a look at this." Virg went over to the judge and spread the paper on the table. It had three separate drawings of hoof prints.

Marshal Simmons joined them.

"This is amazing." Judge Harvey exclaimed. "John, come over here. Did you draw these?"

"Yes sir."

"Marshal Nolan, come up here." Judge Harvey instructed. "I want you to see this too."

When they were gathered around, the judge asked John to tell them about the pictures.

"That left front." John pointed to a drawing. He continued. "Right front. Right back."

The judge held the drawing up for the people to see.

There were exclamations of appreciation all over the room.

"Doesn't prove a thing. It's just a pretty picture. Now that we have had our show let's get on with the cow thieves." Averill shouted. "This is a waste of time. If you want to look at pictures go over and take a peek at the one over the bar."

This brought a laugh as everybody knew about the picture of the pretty lady on the wall there.

Bang! Bang! The gavel fell. "Order, order." The judge turned back to Virg and John. "What about what he says?"

"Well John." Virg looked at his friend. "Can you prove that it does mean something?"

"Yes, I show tracks. Have covered up. I find horse. Show you."

"What does he mean?" Judge Harvey asked.

"We'll need to go to the place where the tracks are your honor."

"We are not going to run all over the country looking at horse tracks are we?" Averill demanded. "I never heard of such a thing."

Judge Harvey was getting tired of Averill's effort to interfere.

"We sure are." He snapped. "Folks, we will go out there and look. I'll pick a delegation. Bill Smith, you, and of course Marshal Nolan will be in it." He soon had his people named. "The rest of you stay here. We don't want a whole crowd stomping all over the place."

Chap. 25

Judge Harvey in his buggy was accompanied by Mr. Higgins. Virg and John Billy led the way, followed by Bill and Joe Nolan. Marshal Simmons rode along visiting with Joe. Alex Averill, Toad and Dade formed another line with Dad Hale and Lem bringing up the rear.

"Just a wild goose chase I tell you. I'm for ending all this stalling and getting on with the trials. We hang a couple of these nesters and it'll put an end to the stealing." Averill growled in a loud voice.

"That's right, boss."

"Maybe we can start with the two I brought in." Dad Hale offered. "Then turn all the innocent ones loose."

"Like that thieving son of yours I suppose." Averill snapped.

"I'll just jerk you off that horse and--." Dad Hale moved toward Averill.

"Stop the argument, right now." Joe Nolan had dropped back. "We didn't come out here to fight. Mr. Hale, move on back and Mr. Averill, it will help if you keep your thoughts to yourself."

"Okay, but I still think we're wasting time."

"I thought you were interested in catching the thieves." Joe Nolan reminded him. "Are you? I wonder."

They rode on. Soon John Billy held up his hand

195

stopping the cavalcade.

"We walk now. Place right up there." He said.

They all dismounted and followed him into a small clearing.

"Tracks right there." John stepped forward and moved a good sized flat rock. Clearly outlined was the track of a horse. Two other flat rocks were nearby. All of them were propped up with smaller rocks on the edges.

"No you don't." Virg said as he stepped in front of Dade and pushed him back. "You hold it right there too, Toad."

"Don't call me Toad." Slater growled. "I'll see you later. I'll fix you."

"Hope you're not on the end of a rope at the time you see me."

"Take a pretty stout rope for him." Mr Higgins laughed as he shot a stream of tobacco juice aside.

Toad turned a bit pale and moved back to join Averill.

They moved toward the other flat rocks.

"Everybody keep back until John calls us forward." Joe Nolan stated. "Wouldn't that be right, Judge?"

"Yes Marshal, that way no one will accidentally mess up the tracks." The judge agreed. "Here is this drawing. John you take charge. Show them to us."

John took the drawing and pointed out the tracks as represented. He had uncovered the other two. He indicated every unusual feature of each track and how it matched his drawing.

"By golly, I never saw the like." Mr. Higgins exclaimed. "The fellow might as well of left a note with his name on it."

"All I see is some horse tracks." Averill stated with a sneer. "Don't prove a thing."

"Then there must be something wrong with your eyes." Bill Smith informed him. "You'd have to be half blind not to see they fit his drawing."

"So he's good at drawing pictures."

"John, how about looking at the horses here and see if any of them match those tracks." Joe Nolan suggested.

"He better stay away from our horses." Averill bristled

at the suggestion.

"No need to." John answered. "Virg and me already checked."

Judge Harvey had been quiet until now. "You have checked them. When? I didn't see you checking. You said you and Virg had checked."

John Billy grinned at Virg. "He read tracks good like me. He not draw pictures very good. When we walked around the horses we look at tracks. I show you. Bring me horse." He proceeded to point out the distinct features of each hoof of the horse.

"Anywhere he leave tracks I know him. Virg can do it as good as I can." John had forgotten to use his broken English.

"I have another set of tracks over there." He said. "A different horse."

"Can you make a drawing of them?" Judge Harvey asked.

"Already have one." John answered. "You want to see tracks?"

"We'll go by them but you've convinced me. What about the rest of you?" Judge Harvey asked.

Everybody agreed except Averill and his crew. They just sat in sullen silence.

"By crackey, that was mighty clever the way he propped those flat rocks up off of the tracks. Using little rocks to keep the one on top up in the air away from them. Mighty clever indeed." Mr. Higgins chuckled as he said this. "And some say that Indians are dumb. This one's smarter than the one that left them tracks."

"What does a track out in this clearing have to do with stolen cattle?" Averill asked.

"Even a dumb farmer like me can see that these horses were with those cows that made the tracks right over there." Dad Hale answered him. "Maybe cattlemen have a hard time seeing things they don't want to see."

"More tracks at the gate where cows put in pen." John told them. "We go see."

"This is Zach's place. His house is right over that rise there." Virg informed them. "We proved he didn't put them there. I'd bet on who did."

Several pairs of eyes turned his way.

"I'd say it was enough evidence to arrest a man on if we can find the horse that fits the tracks." Marshal Simmons stated. "Wouldn't you, Joe?"

"Make a mighty strong case." Joe responded. "I think we'll be able to find them."

"Could have been that nester, Cooper." Averill suggested. "He stole some cows too."

"Same tracks over there." John said.

"That proves it then." Averill crowed. "Let's get back in and hold his trial. This Indian will be our star witness. We'll hang one cow thief anyway." He cast a smiling look at Virg.

"Don't get your rope out until you hear the whole story." Virg cautioned. "Be a shame to see a fellow hung with his own rope."

Averill glared at him. "Wise mouthed young snot." He muttered in a voice that wasn't really low.

"I guess we have seen enough. Time to get back to town. Leave the covered tracks like they were." Judge Harvey instructed after they had looked over the other set of covered tracks and those at the gate. "No use going by Jim Cooper's place. I believe we can depend on John's statement."

"You can do that for a fact." Joe Nolan assured him.

They were soon mounted and headed back to Paden.

One of Averill's men broke off from the slow moving column and started off in the direction of his headquarters at a lope.

Buck soon overtook him. "The judge wants all of us to ride in together." Virg informed him.

"Averill told me to head for home and take care of some things."

"I believe you better go with us, Lem."

Lem started to protest. "The boss-."

"Judge Harvey is the boss of this trip so move on back and join up. Weren't planning to spread the news to your crew were you?"

Marshal Nolan had joined them by this time.

"I was just telling him we didn't want to miss out on his company." Virg told the marshal.

"We would like for him to go back in with us all right. He's now a witness about the tracks. He can ride off if he insists, but if he warns anyone that is guilty of a crime that makes him an accessory."

"Can he be hung for that?"

"I've known it to happen. When a bunch get in a hanging mood they take most everybody."

"Okay, Lem, you can go your way but I think I'll just ride along with you for a spell. I wouldn't want you to lose your way. A fellow might get turned around and wind up in Paden."

"Guess I might as well ride along with the bunch. Averill will be mad as the devil about you two stopping me from carrying out his orders."

"We're not stopping you. I plan to ride along with you so lead off. The marshal can go on back." Virg informed him. "Lead the way."

Lem just growled something and headed back to join the procession headed for town.

"I tell you I'm going to blast that nester brat. Him and his smart mouth. I'll put a slug right in the middle of it." Mitch was still fuming about the laughter resulting from the snake rustling charges.

"Yeah and they turned that black bird, Vaughn, loose too." Bart added. "That stupid Toad cleared him. He doesn't know enough to keep his mouth shut. I wish he'd walk in here and say he didn't like to be called Toad. You notice I didn't say anything."

"I might run a slug between his teeth too." Mitch growled. "If Averill had done things my way all our problems would be over by now. Instead he rode out with them to look at something."

"Look at all these nesters snickering at us behind our back." Bart snarled as some men came in to get a drink. "Watch this."

Boom! Pow! He whipped out his pistol and put two bullets over the heads of the men at the bar.

The men dropped to the floor and cast nervous glances at the pair at the table in the back.

"I'm getting out of here."

"Me too. They're crazy drunk."

They scrambled to their feet and made for the door.

"Watch the sheep run." Pow! Mitch put a shot into the floor behind the last of the departing settlers.

The place was soon empty. No one wanted to stay and chance getting a bullet in them.

"Ha ha, sheep is the right name for them." Bart agreed. "Watch this one."

Pow! He put a bullet through the door.

"Let's go see if that fast gun is back in town." Mitch said as he lurched to his feet. "I hope Gomez is in town. I want him to watch a real gun slinger."

"Yeah, that'll be fun. Then let Averill tell us to go easy. He set there and let them laugh us out of court. Didn't raise a hand."

They replaced the fired shells and stalked out after returning their pistols to their holsters.

The cavalcade had ridden back into Paden a few minutes before the shots came from the saloon.

"We will resume court in fifteen minutes." Judge Harvey informed them. "That ought to give everybody time enough to get ready."

John Billy dropped off his horse and motioned for Virg to join him. After a short conference they separated. They started walking down the street in opposite directions stopping at each horse and studying the ground.

"Marshal we're going to check some tracks while we have a little time." Virg then moved on down the main street checking tracks. In some cases it took very little time to eliminate the horse. He spotted a group of horses in a lot behind a building a short distance from the main street.

"Simmons, you and I better keep an eye on them." Joe Nolan said.

"Okay, I'll tag along after Virg."

"I better take a look over there. I think I know where the checking needs to be done but better not pass anything

200

up to make sure." Virg muttered to himself.

Marshal Simmons followed at a distance. He hesitated when he heard the muffled shots from down the street. He glanced back that way. Sounded like they came from inside a building.

"This is going to take more time than I have to do a thorough job." Virg said as he spent some more time checking. He started back toward the court room. "I don't think any of that bunch are the ones."

Bam! Bam!-Bam! There was a short delay then----Boom! another short delay --------Crack!---Crack!

The shots rang out from back down the Main street. These weren't inside for sure.

Marshall Simmons started running in that direction. He pulled his pistol as he charged into the middle of the street.

By this time Virg was right on his heels.

There were two groups of people gathered about a hundred feet past the drinking establishment. There was the sound of hoof beats moving away to the northwest.

"What happened?" Marshal Simmons asked as he dashed up to the first group.

"That Mitch and Bart shot this fellow and that Indian." Someone volunteered. "One fellow let loose at them with a shotgun and another took a couple of quick pops with a rifle but they didn't hit anything I don't believe."

Virg pushed into the first group of people. It was difficult to see who was on the ground.

"Don't believe he's hit too bad." Dad Hale said as he knelt over the man. "Has someone gone after the doctor?"

"He probably heard the shots. He'll be here in a hurry."

Virg could now see that this was Joe Nolan. He forced his way out of the crowd and hurried to the other group.

"Let me through. Let me through." He shoved people aside in order to make his way to the figure lying stretched out face down in the dirt. There was a pool of blood near his head.

"John, John, old boy it's me, Virg. Can you hear me? Hang on boy. Let me see where you're hit." He was kneeling by his friend's side.

201

Virg quickly felt for a pulse and checked for any evidence of breathing.

"Somebody give me a rag. I've got to stop this bleeding." He could see that John had a wound on the side of his head. He had not been able to detect much of a pulse but thought that he was still breathing.

"Virg, let me help. Here's a clean bandage. The doctor better hurry over here and see how bad this is." Molly was there beside the prostrate figure pressing the bandage against the side of his head.

"Here, help me pick him up. We'll lay him on his back in that wagon. Then we can examine the wound better." Virg grabbed John by one shoulder, Newt got the other one and someone picked up his feet. Molly held his head so that it didn't sag.

"O-ah-n-n." The sound came from John. His eyelids fluttered.

"Isn't that beautiful." Virg yelped. "What do you think, Doc?"

"I'll have to examine him first. Give me time. Molly, I see you're already here so you can help."

Doctor Dovell stooped over John and felt of the side of his head. Then he ran his hand all over the rest of it. "The bullet is either inside his head or it bounced off. Hard to tell without a probe."

John opened his eyes. He made an effort to raise his hand up to the side of his head.

"Did you see that, Doc?" Virg practically shouted the words. "He's still alive."

The doctor smiled at him. "I did."

"What does it mean?"

"Probably means his head is as hard as yours and the bullet bounced off."

"Thanks, Doc, that's the nicest thing I've heard in a long time." Virg told him. He grabbed Johns hand and squeezed it. "How's the marshal?"

"He has a hole through the front of his shoulder but he'll be okay. He hit his head on the sidewalk when he fell. Put a lump on his head."

"What about John?"

202

"He may have a dandy of a headache but he should recover. He'll probably head for his own people for a cure. May need to lay around in the shade a few days."

Chap 26

John Billy was beginning to stir. When he tried to sit up he fell sideways and Virg caught him just in time to keep his head from hitting the side of the wagon.

"Your head is so hard it would likely bust the boards." Virg told him. "Seems it's harder than a bullet anyway."

All John could do was give him a weak smile.

"Bring John and Marshal Nolan over to my office and I'll do a proper job of fixing them up. Molly you come along and help." The doctor lead the way while his orders were carried out..

"Our first order of business is to get a clear understanding of what happened in the shooting out there." Judge Harvey called the court to order. "It will be sometime before the marshal can tell us and the Indian might not be ready any sooner. Did anybody see it."

Two or three held up their hands.

"I want the man that can give us the best account of the affair." Judge Harvey said as he eyed the three men.

"I guess Higgins was the closest to the action." One of the men offered. The other man nodded in agreement.

"I can tell you what happened and I can also tell you what was said." Mr. Higgins volunteered. "I heard the whole thing."

"Seems you were right in the middle of things." Judge Harvey observed. "Tell your story."

"I was right there close. They might of shot me too if that shotgun hadn't gone off."

"Well, give us a complete account of it then. Don't skip anything at all. This has legal aspects to it. It's not just a story to tell." Judge Harvey instructed him. "And don't anybody interrupt. If you have something different to say or something to add you can do it when he's finished."

"The Indian was going down the street looking at horses and tracks. The marshal was trailing along behind a bit. I was kinda trailing along also. Wanted to hear if anything was said." Higgins paused. "I like to know what's going on."

"I can believe that. Go on."

"John, the Indian, stopped and studied these two horses longer than he had been looking at the others. Then he pointed to the tracks and then to the horses. The marshal asked him. 'What do you say, John?'. He said. 'These are the horses'." Higgins stopped again.

"Don't stop, finish the account."

"Okay Judge, Marshal Nolan asked. 'You mean the ones that made the tracks you showed us out yonder?' John nodded his head and answered. "These horses made tracks out at Vaughn place and at Jim Cooper's. They drive cattle."

Higgins glanced around the room and his eyes settled on Alex Averill.

"Then the marshal said. 'When we find the owners of these horses we will have our cow thieves.' John just said 'right'. About that time some shots rang out and some people ran out of the saloon. Marshal Nolan asked if anybody had been shot. Some fellow said no that it was just a couple of toughs with to much liquor showing off." Higgins stopped again for air.

"The marshal turned to go toward the horses and these two guys came out of the saloon. One of them yelled, 'What are you doing to my horse.' John had made to pick up one of it's front feet. He jumped away from it."

"Who came out of the saloon?" Marshal Simmons asked.

Judge Harvey frowned at him.

"Mitch and Bart, two of Averill's men. You know, the snake thieves. Marshal Nolan told them, 'Hold it, you're under arrest for stealing cattle'. He started to pull out his gun but those guys had theirs out and in action almost before he touched his. They are really fast with a pistol. One of them shot the marshal and the other one got the Indian."

"You said you figured they were going to shoot you."

"One of the gunnies fired again in my direction but I didn't just stand still to be shot. I ducked. Then this shotgun went off up the street. They jumped their horses and took off. They dodged around a building and I got out of there. A couple of rifle shots were fired and it was all over."

"You are sure it was Mitch and Bart, the men we tried earlier?"

"As sure as I'm sitting here. I don't think I want to get that close to that pair again. They're to fast with those pistols for me." Higgins cleared his throat. "That's about it. Looks like we located Mr. Averill's cow thieves for him. Some of his own crew."

"Wouldn't be the first time for an employee to steal from his boss." Judge Harvey said. "I suppose he'll sign complaints against them."

"What about it Averill? You said you wanted to hang all the cow thieves. We've caught two of your hands with cattle and now two more have enough evidence against them. You better sign them papers." Dad Hale bellowed. "You were quick enough to sign against my boy."

Several shouts from the crowd echoed these sentiments.

Averill took a nervous look around the crowd. He had talked tough about the way they should deal with cow thieves all right.

"Looks like I'll have to back my words up." He conceded. "I can't let the whole thing blow up in my face." This last was said under his breath.

"Bring in the pair that Mr. Hale brought in and let's try them now." Some one shouted. There were a chorus of agreement.

"We'll clean up the rustlers now while Mr. Averill is here. He's in favor of that. Then he can go back to raising cows as soon as we catch the other two and hang them."

"We'll hang these two first just to show we mean business."

This brought thunderous approval.

Bang! Bang! The gavel fell.

"Order. order" Yelled Judge Harvey. "Bring in the

205

two prisoners." He was concerned with the mood of the crowd. Maybe he could get a new start. Running a courtroom properly was something he had always been proud of. "I'll decide the sentences."

Averill started to protest then thought better. He was trapped. He decided to keep in the clear. This pair didn't know anything anyway. Better to let the crowd have them. He'd better be ready to come up with something before he was dragged into the center of this whole mess.

Rance and Trip were ushered into the court by Saul Artman.

It was apparent to all present that they were a pair of scared cow hands.

Bang! Judge Harvey struck the table with his gavel. "You men have been charged with stealng cattle. You were caught with cattle in your possession according to the witnesses. What do you have to say? Guilty or not guilty."

The two looked at each other. Rance cleared his throat. "I'm not taking the blame for stealing cattle. We were told to drive them down there and hold them. We had help from some of the other hands. We didn't steal them."

"What were you doing with them then?" Judge Harvey had a stern look on his face.

"We were just holding them there."

"You expect us to believe you drove some of Mr. Averill's cattle ten miles from home just to hold them?" Marshal Simmons had decided to join the questioning.

"That's right. That's what we were told to do."

"Who told you? Did Averill tell you to?"

"Yeah, he-"

"That's a lie. I did no such thing." Averill was on his feet yelling. "I don't steal my own cattle. Any fool ought to know better than that."

"Sit down, Mr. Averill." Judge Harvey ordered. "Proceed, Marshal."

"You started to say when I asked you if Averill told you."

"I said yeah."

"He told you?"

"He knew about it. Mitch told us that."

Averill was on his feet again. "He's lying. I didn't know a thing about it."

Bang! Bang! The Gavel fell.

"Mr. Averill I told you to sit down." Judge Harvey roared. "And keep quiet."

Averill sat down with a shocked look on his face. It seemed he had lost a backer.

The judge turned back to Rance. "Mr., you tell us what you know. We have evidence that Mitch is a cow thief. If you helped him, you are one too. So if you want to save your hide you better speak up."

"We were supposed to hold them until all the nesters came in to the trial and then we were to put some cattle on as many of their places as we could. Then we would find them and have the marshal arrest them. I was just following orders."

"Averill knew about it?"

There was silence as the crowd waited for the answer.

Rance hesitated as he glanced around the room. He cleared his throat then looked toward Averill before dropping his eyes.

"I thought he did. Mitch said-" Rance stopped. He looked at the judge.

Averill stood up but did not speak. He had to do something in a hurry or he was going to be in a lot of trouble. The mood of the crowd was bad. As far as he could tell there weren't any friendly faces present. If he worked it right maybe the judge could help him.

Judge Harvey started to bring his gavel down but stopped. "Mr. Averill."

"It looks like Mitch has been working his own deal. I don't quite know what yet. I'm willing to help get to the bottom of it." Averill spoke in an even voice. "These men have been taken in by him I believe. I'll file my charges against him." He looked around to weigh the effect on the crowd.

"I'm ready to agree with you I think." Judge Harvey held up his hand as several angry voices were raised. "Folks there is no evidence yet that Mr. Averill is guilty of

207

this. It will be hard to get that evidence. My advice is to take him up on signing those complaints."

"This should put an end to the cattle stealing problems." Simmons added. "What about this pair?"

"We wouldn't want to hang two men because their boss told them to do something and they did it." Judge Harvey told them. "Hold on to them right now and we'll decide in a little while." He wanted to give the crowd time to cool off a bit.

"Judge, er, Your Honor."

"Yes Virg. Do you have something to say?"

"Yes sir. Dan and Jim are still in jail charged with stealing cattle. I think we have proof that Jim had nothing to do with that but what about Dan?" Virg asked and then turned to Rance. "Which of you put those cows on Dan Hale's place."

"Lem and Dade helped Bart. Mitch told them to. Mitch and Bart were to run the ones to Jim Cooper's and that black man's place. I think Lem helped there too." Rance was now more than eager to talk. Trip often nodded his head.

Judge Harvey saw that the crowd was in a much better mood. He decided to do something while that mood prevailed.

"I think we've heard enough. The charges against Jim Cooper and Dan Hale are dismissed. These other two could be held but I think it would be better to turn them loose. If they are seen in this country again I doubt if anybody would be prosecuted for shooting them."

"Good idea. Let 'em go. Starting tomorrow if they're seen we start shooting." Someone yelled. This brought a cheer.

"I'm getting my old muzzle loader out tonight, by dang."

Bang! The gavel fell. "Court dismissed. Bang! The gavel fell.

The crowd was indeed in a festive mood. They were enjoying themselves.

"Newt, what was it that preacher said?" Virg elbowed him in the ribs.

"If I remember right it was, 'the Lord will provide.'"
Newt chuckled as he finished. "I don't believe Mr. Averill
is going to join the party." He was referring to Alex Averill
and his men as they rode out of town.

"Why he ought to be happy." Virg said as he waved
to the departing riders. "He came out of this clean as a
whistle."

There weren't any smiles on the faces of the cattlemen
as they left town.

Averill didn't have a smile on his face but he sure had a
feeling of relief in his innards. That bunch of dumb nesters
had almost introduced him to a noose. Them and that smart
mouthed kid and his Indian friends.

"Mitch, I'm telling you, you two better head for New
Mexico." Averill told the angry gunman. "I had no choice
and they'll be hunting for you in bunches as soon as the
marshal is back on his feet. Shooting a United States
Marshal is bad business."

"I'm not leaving til I've finished that half breed. He
tried to make a fool out of me. Nobody does that and gets
away with it." Mitch glared at the rest of the crew. "I better
not hear any noise from you either."

"I'm with Mitch." Bart stated. "We'll head out as
soon as we finish him. I don't think you did us right either,
Averill." He brushed his gun butt.

Averill placed a pearl handled pistol on the desk in
front of him. His hand rested lightly on the weapon. He
leveled his gaze on Bart.

"Don't get any wrong ideas. Mitch can tell you that I
know how to use this." Averill waited. "I've said my
piece, now get out."

Mitch and Bart walked outside and headed for the cabin
they shared. It didn't take them long to pack their gear.
They walked outside and stopped.

"What do you want, Gomez?" Mitch demanded when
he spotted him coming around the corner of the cabin.

"I come to tell you. You be smart to take off for New
Mexico. Forget the kid."

"What do you mean, forget the kid? You've been
209

telling us how fast he is. Are you trying to say that he might beat me?" Mitch laughed. "You've probably never seen a real hand work with a pistol."

"Let's take him along with us so he'll really have something to tell." Bart suggested. "Get your horse and come along, Gomez."

"That's a good idea. We'll give you a show you won't forget. We're headed for Paden."

"You go on. I need to get my things and go away also." Gomez had a note of fear in his voice. "You won't want me along."

"You're going to get your horse and go with us. So don't argue." Mitch agreed with Bart. "You wouldn't want to miss out on something to tell your grandchildren. You talked about having some day. They'll want to hear about the big gunfight."

They soon rode off. Gomez was trying to explain that he only wanted to do them a favor. They only laughed and informed him that he was going with them anyway because they didn't want him to miss the show.

"Maw, I need to go to that meeting. I'll be home pretty soon, if you can't wait on me." Virg told his mother. "It shouldn't take very long."

"I came back into town to get some things. Everything was so up in the air the other day we forgot them." She replied. "I'm in no hurry though. It'll be so good to have you home I just might wait."

"I'll try to get through as fast as I can."

Chap 27

Judge Harvey had asked several of the people involved in the cattle rustling cases to meet with him. The judge had completely turned his loyalties toward the settlers. He had been heard to say, "It feels good to be a real judge again."

Virg, Newt, Dad Hale and Marshal Nolan were present. Marshal Simmons had taken a large posse and gone out looking for Mitch and Bart.

210

"I doubt if he'll find anything." Marshal Nolan said. "Without any trackers it would be hard." He was still to weak to ride. "John Billy is still out of action."

Judge Harvey cleared his throat. "The purpose of this meeting is to determine if we have good enough evidence to go after Averill." He looked at the others.

"We still have Sutton staked out where we can get him." Virg told them. "I'm pretty sure he'll talk. He doesn't like living with Indians and sure won't if they decide he should tell his story."

The others had nothing to offer.

"The problem is that we have no evidence that will stand up in court." Judge Harvey said. He went over the different things. "Everything has been laid to Mitch and Bart. We know better but can it be proved. I say no. It would come down to his word against Sutton's."

"But he shot at Virg." Newt protested. "He was on Averill's payroll."

"That's right. People will remember that." Virg added. "At least I think they will."

"Everybody knows Sutton was mad at you, Virg, and that he lies. Now they'll think he's just saying things to save his own hide or to keep you from going after him by doing what you want."

"He wouldn't make a very reliable witness for sure. Don't seem right but that's the way it is I guess." Dad Hale voiced his opinion. "At least Averill's scheme didn't work. We haven't been hurt any by it."

"I'll check with the committee about his lease being canceled. If I can get that done it'll hurt him as much as anything." Joe Nolan told them. "We've had to much trouble from that place."

Bam! Bam! Two shots rang out.

"What the devil is that?" Newt exclaimed. He rushed to the door and looked out. "We've got trouble."

"What trouble?" The judge asked. He crowded in behind Newt. Dad Hale was right on his heels.

"It's those two gun slingers, Mitch and Bart. They have an old fellow out there with a gun to his head." Newt informed them. "There's another Averill man off to the

211

side a little ways."

The street was clear. Everybody had ducked for cover.

"Hey! Get out here. I've come after that smart half breed kid. I want him out here where he can't sneak off." Mitch yelled. "Hurry it up or Bart'll blow this old sod buster's brains out."

"Yeah my trigger finger is getting shaky." Bart laughed. "I can't hold off long."

"Hey kid, Gomez here says you're fast on the draw. Come out and prove it unless you want to see this old bum's head blown off."

Joe Nolan had pushed his way through the jam at the door and looked out. "You men let him go and toss your guns down. You're already wanted by the law."

"Ha. Ha." Bam! Splinters flew off the door near the marshal's head. He ducked back inside. "Want to stick it out again? My aim might improve." Mitch laughed. "I need to finish what I started the other day anyway. Come on, stick your head back out."

"What are we going to do?" Newt asked. "We can't just stand here and let them shoot that old man. I'm sure they'll do it too. By the way where did Virg go? He was right here."

"I don't know. Marshal, you better take charge here." Judge Harvey offered. "I'm not much good in cases like this."

"Virg ducked out the back door."

"It's not like him to run."

"The marshal's not in any shape to do anything about that pair." Dad Hale stated. "I'd go out but they would only shoot me and that wouldn't change things. Same for Newt. Why you don't even have a gun."

"Didn't think I'd need one."

Another shout came from outside.

"Don't try anything or this old coot gets it. Send that heathen kid out. That's all we want. Send him out and we'll take care of him then be on our way. Maybe he's to yellow to show his face. Not going to give you more than a minute more, and I have a fast clock." Mitch was clearly enjoying the situation.

The farmer had a pleading look on his face which was white with fright. He was unable to talk for one reason or other.

"Yeah send that smart mouth kid out. He can't sneak around in the woods out here. Time's about up." Bart turned to see if he had the pistol in the right position.

"We can't send him out. He's not here." Newt yelled.

"We saw him go in there so send him out." Mitch snarled. "We'll shoot this old geezer and then go after anyone we can find."

"I figured all along that he was yellow." Bart added. "Never saw a breed that wasn't."

"You fellows looking for me?" Virg spoke from behind them. He had ducked out the back door, raced along behind the buildings until he was some distance from where Mitch and Bart stood facing the court house.

Then he crossed the street and approached them by going back up the street behind the buildings there. He was sure Gomez had seen him but hadn't made any move to alert the others. He then stepped out from between the two buildings.

Mitch and Bart both whirled to face him. This freed their captive who scuttled across the street and dived past the corner of the court house.

Virg had not drawn his pistol because of the captive and he still hoped this might end without any killing.

"If they turn and see me with a gun ready they'll shoot the old fellow and start firing at anything in sight." He reasoned . "This is pretty risky but so is that way."

"Don't shoot, Bart. I want to see how fast he is. And I want that Gomez bird to get a chance to watch a real gun hand at work." Mitch holstered his weapon. "Keep your gun handy in case anyone makes a false move. You can plug him."

"Don't anyone do anything." Virg called out. "Give them a chance to surrender peacefully."

"We're going to walk down to where Gomez is and then I'm going to make my play." Mitch said. "I don't plan to have this bunch over here at my back when I start."

"Dad gum, I planned to down one of them the instant they made a move." Dad Hale exclaimed. "Now they'll be way down the street."

"I planned to try for one of them too." Joe Nolan said. "Doubt if I could hit anything though, as weak as I am."

"Maybe someone will hit them from down there." Judge Harvey offered.

"Doubt if there's an able bodied man left in town. Where did Newt go?"

Newt now realized how Virg had left the place and decided to follow his lead. "If I can only make it to the house and get my rifle. I could get one from the store but Amos locked up and went with the posse."

Mitch and Bart were almost to Gomez. That would put them about fifty or sixty feet from Virg. Bart was a mite closer and he still held his pistol steady.

Virg had turned to keep facing them as they moved past. Suddenly he caught sight of someone approaching the opening between the buildings.

"My Gosh! It's Maw. I can't let her get out here into this." She was striding right along but was getting close.

Maw was indeed moving right along. She had heard the shooting and was hunting for Virg. It was time they headed for home and she planned to have them started in that direction as soon as she located him.

"I think I saw him go between those two buldings Hope the shooting didn't involve him." She looked worried. "I think the shots were before he went in there."

"You two snake thieves can make your move any time you are ready." He called. He wanted them to hurry before Maw walked out into the middle of things.

"Why I'll teach you." Mitch snarled. "You hear me, you sneakin half breed.?"

"What did you say, gotch ear. I'm still only about a quarter Cherokee, more or less. Anyway I know enough not to choke myself with a snake."

This proved to be to much. Mitch went for his gun.

When Virg had made his first statement Bart had holstered his weapon also. He wanted to be a part of the action when it started.

It wouldn't do to be seen as a gunman that cheated. That would tarnish his big bad reputation.

"Let's see who gets the first slug in him." He yelled as he snatched at his pistol.

Both men had been standing in something of a crouch with arms bent and tense waiting to draw.

Watching Virg you would have thought he was standing and watching something interesting. He appeared to be absolutely relaxed. His mind had been racing at a very fast pace however.

"Can't let Maw get out here. She might get hurt."

"Mitch talks a lot but is probably able to make it good."

"Bart doesn't say much. Quiet ones are usually the most dangerous. Which one first. I better guess right. What am I thinking? I may not get either one. They may both beat me. Stop that. Negative thinking won't get the job done."

"Concentrate on who's first and then go to the second one. My mind's made up, time for action." This all raced through his mind at the same time his hand was in motion. "The natural recoil of the pistol will move it toward the second one if I get the first one." Bart would be first.

Mitch's hand slapped his gun butt. Bart's hit his. It looked like a tie. Fingers gripped and muscles started the exertion to lift. There was no doubt left about how fast they were. They were quick as lightening as the saying goes.

One pistol cleared leather.

Two others were close behind. It would probably depend on which was the most accurate.

Bam, Ba-Bam!--! It sounded like two shots unless examined closely. There had been three.

Silence descended and held for an eternity.

Virg was down on the walk. His pistol fell out of his hand. He attempted to raise his head to peer in the direction of the other two. He realized he no longer held his pistol so made an attempt to find it. His hand made feeble moves from side to side. No luck. Blackness began to descend. "Darn that hurts." Virg groaned as some sense returned. Reaching over he felt of his left side. It felt a little

215

numb but it still hurt like the dickens. Things were a bit dark. Where was Maw?

The noise of doors being opened traveled up and down the street. People were shouting something. They sounded far away.

Virg seemed to have trouble concentrating on what he wanted to do. "They must have won I guess." His hands still felt around for his pistol. "Can't give up now. Maw might get hurt."

Mitch was sitting in the dust staring straight ahead. His eyes didn't appear to be looking at anything in particular. He wondered where Bart was. The kid wasn't in sight. They must have got him.

Mitch's pistol was behind him. The third shot had come from it. He'd almost shot himself in the foot when it went off.

Virg made another effort to get to his feet. It did not succeed. Had to keep Maw from getting out here. He could feel blackness returning. Had to fight it off.

Where was Bart? The question raced through Virg's mind. Must find him before Maw gets out here.

Bart lay flat of his back staring straight up into the sky. Not a muscle moved. His weapon was not completely clear of the holster.

"Virg, what happened? Are you all right? Why are you laying on the walk? Who are those two men? Did you shoot them? Well, are you going to answer me?" Maw was kneeling by Virg with her arms around him. She had tears in her eyes.

Virg's eyes blinked and his mind suddenly came back into focus. "Which one do you want me to answer first?" He asked as he gave her a weak grin.

"You're okay for sure. Now if you ask for something to eat I'll know for doggoned sure nothing is wrong." Maw laughed but her eyes still had tears in them. "Thank you, Lord." She said and began humming a hymn as she rocked him back and forth.

Newt came charging up followed by Dad Hale and the judge. Several people had gathered by this time.

"Some of you folks help me and I'll take charge of this

216

pair. This one isn't dead. I don't know about the other one. He sure looks it. Let's get them over to the doctor and find out." Dad Hale took charge of that part. "Hate to see them miss a hanging."

"Are you hit, Virg?" Newt wanted to know. "You fell over on that walk. I thought you were a goner."

"I tripped on the walk when I dodged to the side. I sure took a dive. Don't think I was hit though except by that awning post." He had regained his feet with his mother's help. She wouldn't turn him loose.

"What about this one?" Dad Hale asked as he pushed Gomez forward. "He didn't take part in it I don't think. He just keeps saying he tried to warn them."

"Please, I did nothing. They forced me to come. I tried to warn them. They think they are fast. I tried to warn them not to try him. I did not help them. I'm not crazy enough to try to shoot that one." Gomez still had big eyes as he pointed at Virg. "I see him before. I'm just a cow herder. Please let me go."

"Let him go. He's been around for some time but as far as I know he's never hurt anyone." Virg told them. "But you need to find someone else to work for, Mr. Gomez."

"I head for New Mexico or Texas." Gomez promised. He sure was a happy prospective New Mexican when he rode off muttering. "I try to tell Mitch they crazy. They sorry they no listen I bet."

The crowd still milled around. They were still buzzing over the rapid nature of what had happened.

"Let me through, Let me through. I've got to get to that boy's side." A large woman pushed her way through the crowd.

Suddenly someone grabbed Virg's hand and pumped it up and down. "Thank you, son. You saved my Job's life. That terrible man was going to shoot him down like a dog. We'll never be able to thank you enough."

"You don't have to thank me for doing what any other person would have done." Virg stared at her, then at the man. It was the hostage. Where had he seen this woman before?

217

It suddenly dawned on him. Yes, that's right. She was the one that scolded him for carrying his pistol.

"I want to say thank you just the same."

"Glad he's okay, mam. I've heard, like the preacher said, 'The Lord will provide'. Reckon it's a good thing I had my pistol handy."

The woman looked a little sheepish as she returned to her husband. She could be heard muttering. "Just think, I scolded him for carrying that pistol and then it saved your life, honey."

"It sure did but I believe he had a bit of a hand in the matter." He reminded her.

"Virg, can we go home now?" Maw was tugging on his sleeve. "I'll fix a batch of cornbread to go with that pot of beans I have on the stove."

"Nothing would please me more, Maw. I'll get Buck and be right back. Maybe Ab can get you to fix some of 'Vi's fried pies."

"You can count on it."

They were soon headed out of town sitting side by side on the wagon seat. They weren't talking much. Virg was busy reading a book and his mother had thoughts of her baby boy to keep her occupied. She had a gleam in her eyes. Might call it pride.

She started to hum her favorite hymn and soon started putting it into words.

Virg looked up from his book. This was beautiful music to his ears.

Even Buck, trotting along behind, appeared to think it was a good day.

About the author

Virgil R. Cooper was born March 19, 1923 in rural Okfuskee County, Oklahoma which was a part of the original Creek Indian Nation. The record low temperature for March 19 in Oklahoma was also reached that same day.

The site of his birth, about three miles from where his mother was born in Indian Territory, was a small house made up of one room constructed of logs with a side room made of rough lumber. He still lives within 35 miles of this spot but in a more adequate dwelling.

Cooper spent three years in the army during WWII with two of these in Europe. On his return home he finished his college work and spent the next 34 years teaching school in Okfuskee and Creek counties, both of which are a part of the old Creek Nation.

Never having run for office of any kind, in 1994 he decided to run for Congress in the 2nd District of Oklahoma because he didn't agree with the ideas of the man in the office. His opponent was a highly regarded 8 term incumbent who some people said was unbeatable.

Cooper came in second in the primary election then beat the incumbent in a runoff only to lose to a well financed Republican in the general election. He was outspent about $30 to $1.

He now lives in Drumright, Oklahoma with his wife of 56 years. They have 3 children and 6 very wonderful grandchildren.

He does volunteer work for his church, delivers Mobile Meals, provides rides for people in need of transportation and writes in his spare time. He hopes to finish several more books before the final roundup occurs.

OTHER BOOKS BY COOPER

According to Maw, Virg seems to have a knack for getting involved.

VIRG-1 PROMISED LAND- The family migrates to Indian Territory to claim land offered by the Cherokee's. Getting it is easy. Holding it isn't. A boy grows to manhood on the move out and while fighting to retain their precious land.

VIRG-2 A HELPING HAND Seems that trouble will not go away. Attacks on settlers and close family members calls for others to lend a hand. This can lead to trouble but Virg is prepared to do his part.

VIRG-4 PETTIQUAH CROSSING Some very hard hombres decide to put a toll booth at the only good crossing on the Pettiquah. The settlers have promised to keep it open for Texas trail herds. Trouble ahead for drovers and settlers. Virg and his black buddy, Zach, attempt to solve the problem.

VIRG-5 KEOKUK KILLERS. A nest of outlaws are operating from a place where all they have to do is jump across the line if any lawmen show up. Virg joins lawmen from three Indian tribes to smoke them out

VIRG-6 KID CURRY A good friend goes bad. He becomes moody and unpredictable. This brings on problems for Virg, a girl he likes, and others in and around Prague.

VIRG-7 TEXAS ROUNDUP Virg and some of his friends go to Texas to help round up a herd. A family of tough brothers decide to take over the area. A beautiful sister complicates love and war.

VIRG-8 DRIVE FOR GOLD. Driving a large herd through hostile Indians, rustlers, floods and stampedes is tough. The Sharps and Zach's pointing finger help solve things.